Hero's Song

"Perhaps it is time I told you more," the wizard said. "I hope you will never see it, but it is well for Eirrenians to be prepared." He drew a breath.

"In form, the Firewurme is much like the earth-worms you find in your garden, only it is the size of a dun. Its body is supple and wrinkled, and it gleams pale white. It has no teeth, nor does it breathe fire. But in the Firewurme's white skin there is death, for it secretes an oozing, colorless guam, and this guam burns without flame. It is said to strip flesh from bone in a matter of minutes."

Collun shivered at the wizard's words.

"It has a long black tongue," continued Crann, "which is also coated with the deadly guam, and the tongue moves with lightning speed. The Firewurme can-not be harmed through its skin. It is many layers deep and, like its earthworm cousins, can regenerate itself. It is rumored that its only vulnerable point is the eye, but the creature's eyelids are as hard as stone." Crann sighed deeply. "Yes, I am troubled by the Firewurme. And frightened. All the armies of the land will amount to naught if the Firewurme comes to Eirren."

Hero's Song

Hero's Song

EDITH PATTOU

The First Song of Eirren

MAGIC CARPET BOOKS

HARCOURT BRACE & COMPANY

San Diego   New York   London

Chapter One from *Fire Arrow* copyright © 1998 by Edith Pattou

First Magic Carpet Books edition 1998
First published 1991

Magic Carpet Books is a registered trademark of
Harcourt Brace & Company.

Library of Congress Cataloging-in-Publication Data
Pattou, Edith.
Hero's song: the first song of Eirren/by Edith Pattou.—
1st Magic Carpet Books ed.
p.   cm.—(The songs of Eirren)
"Magic Carpet Books."
Summary: On a quest to rescue his kidnapped sister, Collun discovers that he is a key figure in the struggle to save the kingdom of Eirren from conquest by Medb, the Queen of Ghosts.
ISBN 0-15-201636-8
[1. Fantasy.]   I. Title.   II. Series: Pattou, Edith. Songs of Eirren.
PZ7.P278325Hg   1998
[Fic]—dc21   97-30181

Text set in Granjon
Designed by Kaelin Chappell

A C E F D B

Printed in the United States of America

For my grandmother, Hollis,
who planted the garden,
and for Charles

I am a salmon in wisdom's fountain

—from *The Song of Amergin*
Irish poet, ca. 1270 B.C.
(translation by A. P. Graves)

CRANN'S MAP

Hero's Song

ONE

The Kesil

Collun was on his knees, working in the flower beds, when he spotted the kesil coming up the road. He leaned back on his heels, watching the tall figure approach. Pinching off the dead head of a cornflower, he wondered why the ragged forest man was back so soon.

Ordinarily the kesil only came through Inkberrow twice a year, begging for food and muttering strange words under his breath. He had visited their farmhold, Aonarach, just a month ago. Collun's mother had given him food as she always did.

But here he was back again, and, even more odd, instead of heading around to the back door to beg for scraps, he walked right up to Collun.

"Good evening," Collun said, his voice uneasy.

The kesil mumbled words that Collun could not understand. He kept running his hands up and down his knotted gray beard.

"Are you hungry? May I bring you bread? Or a drink from our well?"

The wild man shook his head.

"It won't be long before the first frost," Collun said awkwardly, to fill the silence. The kesil's hands continued moving on his beard, and Collun turned back to his work. He concentrated on uprooting a weed with his trine. A feeling of dread made his hands shake and he cut the weed off short, its jagged edge white against the soil. Collun stared at it. Why did the kesil not go away?

Abruptly the old man reached out his dirt-encrusted hand and firmly grasped Collun's arm. Almost against his will, Collun looked up into his face. The kesil's eyes were focused and alert, not wandering and dull as they had always been before. The last rays of the sun caught them. They were an incandescent shade of silver-blue. Collun slowly rose to his feet, his breath coming fast.

The kesil spoke. "You know what you must do. Delay no longer." The words were spoken softly, yet each one was clear and direct.

"Do not travel on the high road. It is not safe." He loosed his grip from Collun's arm but held the boy's gaze a moment longer, his eyes glittering. Then abruptly the kesil turned away. He shuffled to the gate, opened it, and slowly moved down the road.

Collun watched the kesil go. His heart thudded unevenly. Was this man perhaps *not* a kesil? For a moment his eyes had been so clear, hardly those of a madman.

Did the kesil know about Nessa? And of the fear that wrapped around Collun like a dank smell? Collun shook his head in confusion and returned to his work, bent on thrusting away all reminders of his cowardice. There was much to be done in the garden.

And yet the moon rose, dinnertime came and went, and still Collun sat crouched in his garden. The trine had long since been laid aside, along with the watering can and the spade. All he had been trying to forget came flooding back.

Collun's lips moved silently as he counted the days since the news had first arrived.

A week and a day.

A week and a day since the messenger from Temair had come up the dusty road to Aonarach. A week and a day since Collun had learned that his sister, Nessa, had disappeared.

Collun leaned over one of the neatly planted beds of flowers and broke off a spray of alyssum. He held it up and in the moonlight could see a fire ant climbing the purple-black stem. He spun the alyssum between his thumb and forefinger, but the fire ant climbed on, making its way steadily through the honey-sweet blossoms.

Collun wished that he could trade places with the fire ant. The insect's path was clear. There was food to collect, shelter to build, danger to avoid. Collun's hand trembled. The ant paused a moment, then resumed its climb. When it came to a fork in the alyssum stem, the ant did not hesitate. It knew which way to go.

Collun did not.

Since that day when the messenger came to Aonarach, Collun had gone about his daily routine on the farm and at his father's smithy, but his body felt slack, his muscles weary. He watched his hands pound nails into hooves and stake drooping tomato vines, but he was unable to find sense in what he did.

Less than a year apart in age, Collun and Nessa had always been close. When Nessa had left the farmhold for Temair, Collun felt as if everything had dimmed—the colors of the flowers, the light of the sun. If something had happened to her . . . He could not bear even the thought of it.

Collun remembered how his younger sister had looked the day she departed for Temair. Her plentiful dark hair had been tied up in a dozen trailing ribbons. Too many, their mother, Emer, had said, removing a yellow, a blue, and a pink one.

Nessa had been up at dawn that morning, unable to sit still long enough to eat breakfast. Their father, Goban, had grumbled at her fidgeting, but Nessa kept running to the door every few moments to see if Aunt Fial's curricle was coming down the road. She fretted each time she came back to the table. What if they had the day wrong? Or worse, what if Aunt Fial had changed her mind?

But Aunt Fial's curricle had arrived on schedule, driven by a small, wiry man named Quince with heavy brows and a sword buckled at his hip. Nessa's eyes had widened at the sight of the sword. Quince explained that the road between Inkberrow and Temair had its dangers, especially of late. He had had no trouble coming and expected none on the way back, but it was well to be prepared.

Quince had placed Nessa's single case in the back of

the curricle while she said her good-byes. Nessa hugged her mother and father, but when she came to Collun, tears blurred her dark eyes.

"I wish you were coming with me," she had said, a catch in her voice.

"I shall miss you, Nessa."

"I made this for you," she whispered, pressing a small square object into his hand. A book.

Nessa gave Collun a last fierce hug and then jumped up next to Quince on the driver's seat. As he cracked the whip, Nessa raised her hand in farewell, tears still wet on her cheeks.

They stood and watched the curricle bump along the dusty road. Then Collun's father turned away, growling, "The day's half gone. There's work to do."

"I hope Fial will take good care of her," Emer said softly.

"Aye," replied Goban, but his tone held doubt.

Emer looked worried. "Have we done wrong, letting her go to Temair?"

"Right or wrong, it's too late now," Goban grunted. "Leastways 'twas nothing else to be done, once Nessa set her mind on it."

And Goban spoke the truth, Collun thought. There was no one as stubborn as Nessa.

Emer twisted her hands in her apron. "I hope Fial watches out for her," she said again.

Goban did not respond. Collun knew his father had little use for the widow of Emer's elder brother; he thought her vain and foolish. Fial, for her part, was ill at ease with the remote blacksmith and always seemed relieved to end her visits and return to Temair.

Fial was all that remained of Emer's family, though she was not blood kin. Emer's father, mother, and two brothers were all dead. She never spoke of them, nor did she visit Fial in Temair. Their interaction was limited to short visits by Fial to Inkberrow once every five years.

During her most recent visit, Aunt Fial had been delighted with Nessa, who had blossomed since she had last seen her. But none of them had been prepared for the long letter that arrived on Nessa's birthday, inviting her to come live in Temair for a year. Temair was the seat of the king and queen and as such was a powerful stronghold and the largest city in Eirren. Fial offered to present Nessa at court and give her all the advantages of life in the royal dun. For her part, Nessa would provide welcome companionship to a lonely widow.

Emer had been distressed by Fial's offer and at first had refused to even consider it. But Nessa had been so determined to go that at last she wore Emer down.

Emer wrote and told Fial of their decision. Arrangements were made for the curricle to come for Nessa in a fortnight.

The time had gone quickly. And as Collun watched the dust on the road settle, the curricle lost to sight, he felt numb. Goban had returned to his forge, Emer to her kitchen. Slowly Collun made his way to his favorite shade tree, a white willow at the edge of the east meadow. He settled himself under it and opened the book Nessa had given him. At once he saw she had made it herself.

Nessa had loved books for as long as Collun could

remember. They had but few at the farmhold Aonarach, and of late Nessa had been experimenting with making her own.

It had taken her a long time to master the art of crafting paper thin enough to bind between two covers. Collun smiled, remembering the smelly messes she had created in the process. Most recently she had been trying her hand at dyes, and her fingers were often stained by the different berries and barks she used.

The cover of the book was leather, and a simple design had been etched into it. What followed was a short tale about a seabird. Every other page was decorated with a picture of the varied places the seabird flew.

Collun drew in his breath. He had not known his sister had such a delicate and true hand at drawing. He came to the end of the book reluctantly. Then he stood, carefully stowing the book in an inside pocket of his jersey.

He kept it there in the weeks that followed, and when he found himself missing her the most, he would take it out and read it through again.

They had received a short message from Aunt Fial not long after Nessa left, saying she had arrived safely and was settling comfortably into her new life. That was all, until the middle of a hot day two months later when the messenger from Temair had arrived.

Collun had been in his garden spreading mulch. The messenger's raiment was travel-stained, his horse flecked with foam. He was a young man, barely out of his teens, and he looked hot and ill-tempered. He seemed particularly cross about a black bird he claimed to have spotted several times since leaving Temair.

"Bad omen," he muttered. "Like as not it means I'm about to be sent up north to the border country where all the trouble is," he said sourly, giving Collun a dark look as though it were his fault.

Collun quickly called his parents, and the messenger handed over the letter with Fial's seal on it.

Goban wordlessly passed the letter to Emer while he went to tend to the messenger's overheated horse.

Emer entered the house, and Collun followed. He peered over her shoulder at the ink-filled pages as she read them. But Emer moved away so he could not see the letter.

When she had finished, Emer looked up at her son and made a small gesture, like a bird with a broken wing.

"Nessa's gone," she said, her voice dim.

"What?" Collun felt a chill spread through him. He instinctively reached for Fial's letter, but Emer held it from him.

"What do you mean, 'gone'?" Collun demanded, his tone harsher than he intended.

"Disappeared. During the feast to celebrate her coming-of-age ceremony. Fial says an important noble-man named Bricriu hosted the feast, and the court had gathered at his dun, a half day's journey from Temair..." Emer trailed off.

"Yes?"

"Halfway through Bricriu's feast Nessa disappeared, leaving not a trace behind." Emer paused, taking in a deep breath. "A search party was organized, even the king's three sons took part, but..."

"How could this happen?" Collun said, his body rigid, hands clamped onto the top rung of a wooden chair.

"Fial wants to know if we have heard from Nessa, if she might have been homesick and come back to Inkberrow."

"Was she unhappy in Temair?"

Emer shook her head. "According to Fial, Nessa loved her life in Temair. The queen herself had taken a liking to her."

Emer's voice died out. Her face was still and white as milkstone. Slowly she turned and glided out of the room. Collun's hands tightened on the chair. Nessa gone. He felt numb, unbelieving. He released the chair rung and went to find Emer. She was lying on her bed, her face turned to the wall. The letter was still clutched in her hands.

Dinner that night was eaten in silence. Emer had not moved from the bed. Collun had prepared the meal, and father and son ate quickly.

Collun knew it was his duty as the only son to go in search of his sister. But the thought of leaving Aonarach, of leaving his garden and fields, made his breath come thin and fast in his chest. His muscles shook with fear. He cursed himself for a coward and went sleepless as each night went by.

He felt his father watching him as the days passed. They had never been close. Goban's life centered around the smithy. He had a reputation for sound, careful work. Collun had disappointed Goban early on by showing no skill at the forge. He was clumsy and slow, and he hated the stink of the burning keratin in the horses' hooves, and the black metal dust that stung the inside of his nose, and the ear-numbing sound of the pounding of iron. He had tried, over and over, but his heart was not in it, and the misshapen lumps he pulled from the water-filled trough after tempering were greeted with silence from Goban.

Collun's talent lay in giving life to green growing things, in bringing vegetables to the table, grain to the oven, and flowers to the windowsill. He seemed to have been born with an innate knowledge of seeds, soil, and weather. At an early age, he had miraculously brought life to a field that had lain desolate for years. When the corn Collun planted that first year grew to the height of Goban's shoulders and the squash came up in great, ungainly shapes, the blacksmith's only response had been a nod of grudging respect.

Collun was never as happy as when he was kneeling in a patch of rich, dark earth, his trine in hand, winnowing the weeds from the plants, with the sun on his back or rain in his hair.

Because of Collun's skill, the few acres around the smithy that had previously been used for nothing but grazing were now flourishing with crops of fat vegetables. There was always more than enough for both eating and selling at the market in Inkberrow. The garden by the house was usually ablaze with one type of flower or another, depending on the season. There were herbs, too, for cooking and healing, and Collun had developed a small reputation for herb craft. He had begun carrying the most useful of his herbs in a leather wallet he wore slung across his chest. When he went into town he was called on to minister to minor injuries and sicknesses. A few villagers had even begun to make their way out to the lonely farmhold to seek his advice.

At home, Nessa had been the only one who could ease the strain between father and son. Emer would try to bring them together, but her careful efforts always seemed to make things worse. But then Nessa would come along with her latest attempt at bookmaking and soon even Goban's face would crease into a smile. Nessa brought warmth and light into the house. When she left for Temair, Aonarach seemed to go dark.

Collun knew his father would have gone in search of Nessa himself, but his left leg had been lamed in an accident at the forge some years back, and he walked with a limp. If he was on his feet for too long, his mouth went white at the corners with pain. There was also the smithy to run, and Collun did not have the ability to stand in for his father.

But still Collun put off leaving. He kept hoping another messenger from Temair would come up the dusty road with a letter explaining that it had all been a great mistake, that Nessa had been found in some overlooked corner, lost in a book. But no messenger came. The silence between father and son deepened. Mealtimes grew unbearable for Collun, and he began to avoid them, taking food with him out to the fields. Before leaving in the morning, though, he would go to his mother's room.

Each day, she grew thinner, barely leaving her bed, never speaking, her hands cold as ice. Filled with foreboding, Collun tried to cure his mother with hot broth made of healing herbs from his garden. But even as he ladled the liquid into her mouth, he knew her illness was not of the body but of the spirit. She loved Nessa deeply, Collun knew, but something else ate at her. He wondered if she blamed herself for letting Nessa leave the farmhold.

Emer had always been protective of both daughter and son. Aonarach was some distance from Inkberrow, and neither Emer nor Goban made the trip often. The blacksmith was a dour, solitary man, and Emer, too, showed no interest in mingling with the people of Inkberrow; her family was enough for her, she had always said. Emer fretted when Nessa or Collun was out of her sight for too long. Staying home did not bother Collun overmuch. He had one friend, Talisen, an aspiring bard who lived in Inkberrow, and had no desire for more. But Nessa chafed at her mother's restrictions, and it was partly these that had made her so determined to go to Temair.

Collun worked in the fields or in his garden each day from dawn until long past nightfall, but he found it more and more difficult to concentrate. His trine, the two-pronged tool he always carried that served him for weeding, tilling, and sowing, felt clumsy and heavy in his hand. The ground seemed harder, the weeds tougher and more plentiful.

And then the kesil had come.

All that night after his encounter with the old man, Collun remained in the garden, his thoughts full of Nessa, the kesil's burning eyes, and Emer's white face turned to the wall. When dawn's light filtered through the branches of the small hazel tree beside him, the spray of alyssum was still clutched in his fingers, the fire ant long gone.

Emer had told Collun long ago that this hazel was his birth tree, planted when he was born. Goban's tree was a large copper beech out beside the west field, and Nessa's was the whitethorn that grew at the other end of the garden. Emer's birth tree was the silver fir, but it had been planted somewhere near Temair.

Collun rose stiffly, his joints cold. He went and stood for a moment by the whitethorn tree. Collun told himself he did not believe in the superstition of the birth tree—that it reflected the health of the person for whom it was planted. Even so, it comforted him to see that the tree looked as it always did, its leaves shiny and deep green.

Collun entered the house and walked into the kitchen, where his father already sat at the worn wooden table, eating a bowl of oats and sugared maple. Father and son acknowledged each other with their eyes but did not speak. Collun heated a pan of chicory tea and poured it into a mug. Wrapping his fingers around the bowl of the cup, grateful for the warmth, he sat down at the table facing his father.

"I leave tomorrow for Temair."

There was a momentary glimmer of surprise in the older man's eyes. Collun's face flushed. He felt a hot bud of anger in his throat. He swallowed hard, and the anger was replaced by the familiar ache of knowing that, no matter what he did, his father would feel no pride in him. Then the moment passed and Goban simply nodded.

"I cannot spare Febo, you know. He is having trouble with his back leg, anyway."

"I had intended to walk."

"It is a long journey to Temair. Two weeks or more by horse," observed Goban.

"Yes," replied Collun, and he closed his eyes and drank down the chicory, savoring the hot burn as it filled his mouth.

TWO

Dagger

ollun spent the rest of the morning working in the fields. He labored hard, with a sense of urgency. The first frost was not far off, and he did not know if he would be back in time for the spring planting.

The fields done, Collun moved to the garden by the house, where he weeded and finished planting the bulbs. He cut most of the remaining late summer flowers and put them in an earthenware pitcher. He took them in to his mother. She turned her face toward him, but she did not notice the brightly colored blooms.

"Goban told me," Emer said, and she looked frightened.

"I must go. I should have gone earlier."

"You cannot. I will not lose both my son and my daughter."

"I will find Nessa and bring her back," Collun replied with a confidence that rang as false in the small room as it did inside him. "Perhaps we will even return to you by the month of Ruis, and we can all celebrate the Feast of Tuilioc together."

"No!" Emer cried out. "You must not go."

Collun stared at his mother's stretched, pale face. "Why do you not want me to go?"

Emer's eyes slid away from his. "You must not," she repeated dully.

❧

Late in the afternoon, as Collun was tamping down the earth over the last of his bulbs, his father approached.

"What will you use as a weapon?" Goban asked.

"I do not know...I hadn't thought."

"You will need a weapon. The road to Temair is not safe. Especially on foot."

He held out his hand. Collun looked at him, puzzled.

"Your trine. Give it to me."

"What?"

"I will make it useful."

Collun hesitated. He had carried the trine with him for many years. It fit his hand exactly, its handle smooth and worn.

Embedded in the handle at the top of the trine was a dull blue-gray stone. His mother had given it to him when he was a small boy.

It was on a spring morning, he remembered, and he had been out riding the then young farm horse, Febo.

The animal had suddenly shied at a field mouse that darted across his path, and Collun had been thrown. He could not breathe, the wind knocked out of him. Emer had come, hearing his strangled cry. She held him, soothing the panic in him until his breath came back. Later that day she had handed Collun the stone. She smiled and told him it would bring him luck, and even if he should fall off Febo again and lose his breath, he had only to touch the lucky stone and he would know his breath would come back.

It had been Collun's own idea to set the stone into the handle of his trine. Thereafter it seemed to him that the trine with its lucky stone could till the soil like no other. The plants seemed to grow faster, the flowers bigger and brighter.

His father made a sound of impatience. "You cannot defend yourself with a trine. Give it to me."

And so Collun reluctantly handed over his trine. Later that evening, Goban returned from the smithy, his face red from the heat of the forge, and gave it back to Collun. Only it was no longer a trine but rather a shining, sharp-bladed dagger. Its handle was the same, the lucky stone still embedded at the top, but in place of the two graceful prongs which slid into hard ground like knives into warm butter, there was a thin and deadly looking blade.

The smith's eyes shone with pride.

"Test it," he said.

Collun ran his finger over the blade. A few drops of blood sprang up suddenly, and he almost dropped the knife in surprise.

"It is ... very sharp. Thank you, Father."

Goban then silently handed Collun a leather sheath for holding the dagger on his belt. Collun took it, again thanking him.

He was relieved when his father limped off, leaving him alone with his new weapon. Collun looked down blankly at the knife that had been a trine. He had a sudden overwhelming urge to throw it as far away as he could. It was as if some evil thing had come and taken away a beloved friend and left a changeling in its place.

And yet his father was right. He had made his choice, and it would be foolish to set off with the wrong tools. A gardener knew this as well as a blacksmith. There would be no use for a trine on the road that lay ahead.

Collun slept through the night for the first time since the messenger's arrival. His decision had been made, and yet when he woke in the morning he did not feel any comforting sense of certainty. He feared his choice, and he realized suddenly it had been Nessa who, unknowingly, had first shown Collun that he was a coward.

He had not been more than seven years old when it happened. He had been in the garden as usual. Nessa had just finished her chores and was sitting on a fence watching the chickens. She was eating a peach, her short legs dangling. Suddenly he heard her give a strangled cough and a gasp. He turned and saw to his horror that her face, shiny around the mouth with peach juice, was turning a mottled shade of red, her dark eyes wide and frightened. Her hand clutched at her throat. The peach pit had lodged there. She was choking.

Collun dropped the rake he had been using and his knees suddenly turned to water. He staggered and nearly fell forward. Panic filled him. He must help Nessa. She might die. But he could not get his legs to move.

Then he felt his mother's skirts brush past him, heard her soothing words as she struck Nessa sharply on the back and the peach pit shot out of her throat. Nessa croaked painfully and gasped for breath, tears running down her face, arms wrapped tightly around Emer's neck.

Collun had crept away then, sunk deep in shame. He was sure if Emer had not come when she did, Nessa would have died and it would have been his fault. He was a coward.

He had turned more and more to his gardening. When he went into Inkberrow to sell vegetables, he kept to himself. He made no friends among the villagers. Except Talisen.

That morning Collun packed the few belongings he had decided to take with him into a worn leather bag with straps for carrying on his back. It smelled of earth and seed, for he used it to carry his farming gear out to the fields. He then took stock of the herbs in his leather wallet, replenished several that were running low, and strapped it over his chest.

When he went into the kitchen he saw that his father had set out a loaf of bread, a block of cheese, and some salted meat. Collun thanked him and added the food to his bag.

"Father, I would ask a favor of you. If Talisen should come here, asking for me, tell him I have gone and there was not time to say good-bye."

Goban nodded, then said with a frown, "Where is the blade I forged for you?"

"In my pack."

His father snorted. "It will do you little good there." He turned and left the kitchen. Collun could hear him putting on his long boots and leather apron in preparation for the day's work.

Collun sat at the table finishing his chicory. He thought about Talisen and smiled slightly. It was ironic that he should be the one leaving Inkberrow when it was Talisen who constantly talked about leaving to seek his fortune.

He couldn't remember how they first met, but it seemed to Collun that he and Talisen had always been friends. They were an unlikely pair; Talisen was a charmer with a quick grin and a way with words, while Collun tended to keep more to himself.

Collun thought of stopping by the Whicklow farmhold where Talisen made his home to say good-bye, but it was in the opposite direction, and he felt the press of time already lost.

Leaving his pack on a kitchen chair, Collun went to his mother's room.

"Collun?" she said, pulling herself into a sitting position as he entered the room.

"I am ready to go, Mother."

Collun stood by the side of the bed and looked down into Emer's pain-darkened eyes. Even as a child Collun had been aware of a remoteness in his mother. For all that she loved her children, he had always felt there was a private sadness in Emer no one could ever touch or know.

"You are going then?" Emer asked, her voice muted.

"Yes."

"There is nothing I can say that would persuade you to stay?"

"No."

"Very well." Her tone was resigned. Then she reached out and took Collun's brown, rough hand in hers and said, "Protect yourself well, son. There may be those who would harm you, as they would harm Nessa."

Collun was startled. "Why?"

Her eyes shifted away. "I cannot explain. I made a pledge to Eira long ago, and I must not break it, even now." Collun knew Emer's feelings for the goddess Eira ran deep. Every morning at dawn and every evening at twilight, even during this illness, Emer sat by the fireplace, her eyes closed and her lips moving silently as she prayed to Eira.

"But, Collun," Emer said, "if you should hear of my death . . ." He let out a sound of protest, but Emer continued, "Find Crann. He will help you, if you are in need."

"Who is Crann?"

"I cannot explain," she repeated. "One thing more, son. It is important. Do not speak of me on your journey or say my name. Especially when you arrive in Temair. Will you promise?"

"Your name? Why?"

"Promise me."

Collun was puzzled, but he agreed to do as she asked. Emer looked relieved. "Have you food for your journey?"

"Yes. Father gave me food."

She smiled sadly. "He is a good man, Goban. He has done his best."

"Mother . . ."

"Go now, with my love. And tell Nessa—"

"You will tell her yourself when we return." Collun made his voice loud.

"Yes."

He stood, looking down at her white face. He suddenly felt he would not see it again. Holding back the tears, he leaned over and kissed his mother's brow. Then he left the room, his heart beating painfully.

He returned to the kitchen and checked his gear once more, feeling in his jersey pocket for the book Nessa had given him. Then he hoisted his pack onto his back and went out the door.

He paused at the wooden gate at the bottom of the path and heard the clang of iron against iron coming from the smithy. He could see his father's set and sweating face as his powerful shoulders heaved the large hammer. Emer called him a good man, and perhaps he was, but for father and son there were no more words to be said.

He set off.

THREE

Talisen

It was a fine morning. The air was cool, but the sun warmed Collun's face. Had this been a short walk into Inkberrow for seed and bulbs, his spirits would have been high.

Uneasily he remembered the sword buckled at the hip of Fial's man, Quince. There was a time, he had heard, when the high road between Inkberrow and Temair had been safe. But that was before Medb had named herself queen of Scath, a country that lay to the north of Eirren.

Long ago Scath had been part of Eirren, consisting mostly of the country's sparsely populated northern reaches. It was an area with a harsh climate and rocky

soil, and it stretched with many fingers into the northern sea.

Collun had learned of Scath from the coulin, the old songs of Eirren. The songs told of a dark lord named Cruachan, who, skilled at wizardry, had spread his power like a black shadow over the desolate north. He rose up against Amergin, the bard who ruled Eirren, and calling the land Scath, Cruachan named himself its ruler. To strengthen his power and ensure his claim, he allied himself with morgs, evil creatures who dwelled in the northern island kingdoms of Usna and Uneach.

When the morgs had fulfilled their bargain with the dark lord and established him in his kingdom, most returned to their own lands, preferring the perpetual night and cold temperatures of Usna and Uneach. But some stayed. And those Eirrenians who had chosen to remain in Scath, and who were loyal to Cruachan, now called themselves Scathians.

Medb, the present queen of Scath, was a descendant of Cruachan. It was rumored that morg blood also ran in her veins. She was called bhannion annam, Queen of Ghosts.

The border between Scath and Eirren had from the beginning been an uneasy one, but never more so than when Medb named herself queen. She demanded of the young king and queen of Eirren that the border be opened and that unrestricted travel be allowed between the two countries. The king and queen had agreed to Medb's demands. But the Northerners who came into Eirren roamed in bands with strange weapons and brutal faces, and they preyed on those who traveled Eirren's roads. The rulers of Eirren swiftly placed reasonable and just restrictions on those entering Eirren from the north.

Medb responded by invading Eirren.

The invasion was hastily mounted, but its savage and unexpected force wreaked devastation on northern Eirren. Forests burned, homes were laid waste, and countless Eirrenians lost their lives.

Led by young King Gwynn of the long shoulders and burning dark eyes and a handful of brave, fierce men, the army of Eirren set forth to meet Medb's deadly host.

The Eamh War, named for the plain on which the tide of battle finally turned, lasted for two years. Eirren ultimately triumphed, and the men who had stood at the head of her army were named heroes. Chief among them was a young man called Cuillean, whose bravery became legend in Eirren. Many songs were composed lauding his mighty deeds. It was said that on the Eamh Plain alone, Cuillean had single-handedly killed more than a hundred Scathians.

A truce was forged, and for fifteen years it was upheld. In response to overtures by a seemingly repentant Medb, the king and queen of Eirren even reopened the border, allowing restricted travel between Eirren and Scath. But in recent years the roads had gradually become unsafe again, and there were many who feared another war between Scath and Eirren. Talisen had learned this from the traveling bards, although few in Inkberrow were much concerned with the news.

Collun suddenly thought of the kesil. "Do not travel on the high road. It is not safe." Those had been his words. The small winding road that Collun now walked joined with the high road to Temair several leagues ahead.

Did the kesil speak of Scathians when he said the

road was not safe? Or was there something else, something that he, Collun, had reason to fear? His mother had said as much. "Those who would harm you." But why? Who was he but a gardener and farmer, the son of a blacksmith? Who could possibly wish to harm him? Or his sister? And yet Nessa had disappeared. Collun's hand shook slightly as he wiped away the sweat on his upper lip.

It was late afternoon by the time the road from Inkberrow joined with the main road. Collun was beginning to feel hungry, so he stopped and settled himself under an ancient yew tree. So far he had seen only one group of travelers, all on horseback. They were Eirrenians and had greeted him pleasantly enough, but they looked at him curiously, as though surprised to see a lone boy on the road.

As he fished in his pack for food, Collun suddenly felt someone was watching him. He looked sharply up and down the empty road. There was nobody in sight. Then he heard a sound from above. He gazed up and saw a large black bird in the branches over his head. It was opening and closing its wings slowly, as though readying itself for flight. Yet it remained in the tree.

At first he thought it was a raven, but it was slightly smaller and its black feathers had a bluish gleam to them. A scald-crow, he guessed. He had never seen one before, but he knew of them. They were not common in the south of Eirren.

Collun quickly finished his meal and repacked his bag. He stood, and as he moved away from the tree, so did the scald-crow. It slowly mounted into the sky and, making a graceful curl in the air, headed down the road toward Temair.

Collun gave a fleeting thought to the ill-tempered messenger from Temair who had been convinced black birds were omens of ill fortune. Reminding himself that he did not believe in foolish superstitions, he shrugged his pack into a more comfortable position on his back and followed in the same direction as the scald-crow.

His thoughts drifted back to Talisen, who was always one to believe in bad omens or good-luck charms. If Collun so much as scratched his nose, Talisen would immediately claim, "You're about to meet a stranger." Or kiss a fool, or walk into danger, depending on Talisen's whim of the moment.

When the sun went down, the air grew cold. Collun breathed in the crisp air, wondering when the first frost would come. He started to think about the work that needed to be done at Aonarach, but then remembered he was on the road, away from Inkberrow and his garden and fields.

As twilight deepened Collun began to look for a spot to make camp for the night. The moon was new, a bright crescent shining in the night, and Collun could see the faint outline of the full moon behind it. The old moon in the arms of the new, as Talisen would say, calling it a lucky omen. Abruptly Collun caught the sound of footsteps behind him. He stopped and listened. Nothing. But as he began walking, he heard the sound again. He stopped again. And the footsteps stopped as well. Collun peered back over his shoulder and thought he could see a muffled, dark shape behind him. Fear made his mouth go dry. He wet his lips and thought of the dagger that had been a trine, buried deep within his pack. "Little good it will do you there," Goban had said.

Collun kept walking, faster and faster, while he reached behind him and fumbled at the opening of his pack. It was no use. In order to get at its contents he would first have to take the bag off his back and then unloose the thongs that held it closed.

He was almost running now. Quickly he swung the bag off his shoulder, but even as he tugged desperately at the thongs, an arm wrapped around his shoulders. He swung his head around to face his attacker, but instead of a Scathian, he was looking into the laughing face of Talisen.

"What's in the bag that's so precious?" Talisen said, brushing his black hair out of eyes that were narrowed in mock greed.

"Talisen!" Collun cried, caught between relief and anger.

"Sorry, Collun, I couldn't help myself. But you deserve it for running off without me, without even saying good-bye. Is that any way to treat your old friend?"

"I am sorry, but there was no time."

"I will forgive you for that, perhaps, but never for keeping the news about Nessa from me." Talisen's face, for once, was grave. "I wondered why I had not seen you for some days. I would have come out to you, but Farmer Whicklow was working me from dawn to dark, paying him back for his missing pig, which of course had nothing to do with me. But is it true? Has Nessa really disappeared from Temair?"

"Yes. I am going there to find her, if I can." While he spoke, Collun rummaged in his pack for the dagger his father had forged. When he found it, he resolutely fastened the sheath to his belt.

"That's the stone that was in the handle of your trine," Talisen said, eyebrows raised. "Is your trine now a dagger?"

Collun nodded.

"You expect danger?"

"Yes."

"Then I am glad I have come prepared." Talisen drew a blade from the sheath at his own hip.

Collun shook his head. "No. You are not coming with me, Talisen."

"Of course I am."

"This is no tale out of one of your old songs. The danger is real."

"Then all the more reason. Besides, Collun, you will need a bard along to chronicle your adventures."

Talisen began to pull the harp from his back, but as he did so another bundle fell to the ground with a dull thud.

"What is that?" asked Collun, momentarily distracted.

"This? Why, it is Farmer Whicklow's biggest and fattest goose, of course."

Collun shook his head in dismay. "You will spend the rest of your days repaying your debt to Farmer Whicklow."

"Spend the rest of my days working for big-bellied, tightfisted Farmer Whicklow?" Talisen threw back his head and laughed. "You know this is what I have been waiting for, Collun: a reason to leave Inkberrow for good!"

They found a place to sleep under a stand of alder trees. Collun kindled a fire using the teine stone he always carried with him, while Talisen plucked and cleaned the goose. They built a makeshift spit and soon the fowl was giving off a delicious aroma as it sizzled over the fire.

Later, when their stomachs were full, Talisen let out a contented burp and reached for his harp.

"How shall we begin the tale?" Talisen mused. " 'The Lay of Collun and Talisen on the Road to Temair'? No, something more poetic. It will come to me. These are early days yet." His fingers began to weave a melody from the strings. Collun recognized it as one of his friend's favorites, about the bard Amergin and the gemstone called Cailceadon Lir that he used to save Eirren from the evil wizard Cruachan.

Talisen sang, and Collun listened sleepily to the familiar words, pulling his cloak close around him.

The haunting final note hung in the air for several moments, then was fractured by the harsh call of a bird. Collun shivered slightly, remembering the scald-crow. He looked over at Talisen, who had not noticed the sound. He was already beginning a new song, his fingers nimble on the harp strings despite the coolness of the night air. Collun was suddenly very glad Talisen had joined him.

FOUR

Scald-crow

Collun woke early, his body stiff from sleeping on the ground. He rekindled the fire. The sky was overcast and the air damp.

When Talisen awoke he gave a loud groan. "My feet hurt, my back hurts, my neck hurts, and I hardly slept a wink." He pulled off his boots and displayed three angry blisters for Collun's sympathy.

"It will only get worse," Collun said, rummaging in his wallet of herbs. He handed Talisen several beech leaves to press against the blisters. "We're at least four weeks from Temair, probably more if we meet bad weather, as I have no doubt we will."

Talisen gave a sudden grin and stuffed his feet back

into his boots. "You'll not be getting rid of me that easily. If I have to crawl on my stomach through the gates of Temair, I shall. Temair . . . Just think of it, Collun. We shall see the royal dun itself!" He paused, then added with a wink, "I shall no doubt be the queen's favorite bard in no time at all."

"No doubt," Collun replied with a smile. In Inkberrow Talisen was much admired for his musical skill. But Collun had heard that to be a true bard in Eirren one must have the skill for making songs as well as playing them. He knew Talisen had not yet been able to master the art of making songs. He acted as if it did not matter to him, but Collun knew it did.

"So," Talisen said, breaking into Collun's thoughts, "what delicacies have we for breakfast? A little goose flesh, perhaps?"

They supplemented the fowl with small pieces of cheese and bread, and, heating a panful of water from a nearby stream, Collun brewed some chicory tea to wash it all down. After they had eaten, they wrapped the rest of the goose in leaves.

Just as they were about to set out, Collun felt a rush of air on his face. A black shape swept by within inches of his nose. It circled once then settled on the ground a short distance away.

Another scald-crow. Or perhaps it was the one he had seen before. Collun wasn't sure. He could see its eyes this time; they were the color of fresh blood.

The bird appeared to be looking at him, its head cocked to one side. Then it began to move. It took a few steps to the side, flapped its wings, took a few more steps, and then flapped its wings again. It moved in a circle around them, performing a kind of hopping dance.

Talisen had not noticed the bird. Collun laid a hand on his shoulder and pointed, feeling he should not speak aloud.

"What is it?" Talisen's voice broke the eerie quiet. "What's that bird doing? Must be after our food... Shoo! Go away!" He waved his hands at the scald-crow.

Collun clutched Talisen's shoulder tightly. "Stop," he whispered. "Something is wrong."

"What? You mean it's injured?"

"No. There is...danger. I'm sure of it."

Talisen laughed. "You're in a state, aren't you? It's just a bird. Here, go away, nasty bird." He picked up a charred stick from the campfire and threw it at the scald-crow.

The crow stepped aside easily. Then it turned, trained its eyes on them, and began flapping its wings with a steadily increasing tempo. Suddenly it was airborne and heading straight for Talisen's face.

Collun's blood went cold, but he somehow managed to jerk his shoulders forward in a clumsy thrust, knocking Talisen off balance and toppling him to his knees. The crow sliced by, missing Talisen. But its feathers brushed Collun's forehead as it passed, leaving a line of bitter cold where they touched. Collun rubbed his forehead and watched, dazed and frightened, as the scald-crow sped off, heading north toward Temair.

Talisen heaved himself to his feet, grumbling and brushing himself off.

"Clumsy oaf. What's gotten into you?"

Collun did not reply. His fingers tried to rub some

heat back into the numb spot where the scald-crow's feathers had touched him.

"What's wrong? Did it scratch you? I don't see anything." Talisen peered at Collun's forehead.

"Its feathers. They've made my forehead numb."

"What? How could a bird's feathers do that? You're imagining things."

"No, Talisen." Collun's voice shook slightly. "There is something happening . . . something I do not understand."

"What are you talking about?"

And so Collun told Talisen about the kesil and about Emer's warning. When he finished, Collun dropped his hand from his forehead. The rubbing had not helped. It still ached with cold.

Talisen was silent for a moment. "Well, there's nothing I like better than a mystery. It's like a riddle, and you know how good I am at riddles," he said with enthusiasm. "If you wish, I will also be careful not to speak of Emer. I wonder why, though," he added with a speculative look.

Collun nodded absently, looking off across the land that lay to the north. "I have decided to go on that way, away from the high road"—he pointed in the direction he was gazing—"as the kesil suggested." Then he looked straight at Talisen, adding, "And I will go alone."

"Don't be an idiot," Talisen replied with a groan. "We have been over this before. I journey with you and let that be the end of it."

Collun shook his head, but he did not protest further. As they left the campsite, Collun thought he heard the harsh call of a bird again, but when he looked around, he saw no sign of one.

He unwrapped his harp from its protective leather covering and examined it with concern to make sure the damp had not harmed it. Satisfied, he touched the strings. A row of clear, true notes sounded, and Talisen's voice, vibrant and deep, filled the damp night.

After leaving the road, they traveled along gently sloping moorland overgrown with bracken, heather, and rushes. The perpetual drizzle did not abate, and by the fifth night their tempers had begun to fray. Collun was unable to kindle a fire. With a disgusted sound Talisen spat a mouthful of stale bread into the rain-soaked grass.

"We have precious little food to be wasting it like that," snapped Collun.

"Here, you can have it all," said Talisen, thrusting his portion of the hard bread toward Collun, who ignored him. Talisen lapsed into a sulky silence.

"I know what we need," Talisen said finally, breaking the silence.

"What's that?"

"A song," Talisen responded with a sudden grin.

He unwrapped his harp from its protective leather covering and examined it with concern to make sure the damp had not harmed it. Satisfied, he touched the strings. A row of clear, true notes sounded, and Talisen's voice, vibrant and deep, filled the damp night.

> *"Sing cuckoo, cuckoo-o,*
>   *The spring is coming-o.*
>   *The daffadowndilly, the quince,*
>   *and the rose,*
>   *Underneath the earth, the tiny*
>   *bud grows."*

Collun lay back, his wet clothing and cold limbs forgotten for the moment. As he watched the familiar expression of joy that transformed Talisen's face when he played, Collun felt his body relax.

Just as Collun was falling asleep, he thought he heard a bird call out. He remembered the scald-crow and its bloodred eyes. Idly he ran his finger over the line on his forehead where its feathers had touched him. The chill was less but the numbness remained.

He slept fitfully. Sometime in the middle of the night he came fully awake, body sweating and eyes wide open. He had been dreaming of Nessa. She was screaming in horror as a scald-crow pecked at her neck. It took Collun a long time to get back to sleep.

When he woke again at dawn he felt jittery and cold, and all that day he kept remembering the dream.

The drizzle that had plagued them for days gradually changed into a hard, wind-driven rain. The sky became so dark that Collun often lost sight of the sun entirely.

As the rain-soaked days began blending into each other, Collun couldn't shake the feeling that they were heading in the wrong direction. The moors became harder to navigate the wetter the ground got and offered no protection from the wind.

Early one evening Talisen came to an abrupt stop, swearing he could not move another step. Looking out over the bleak, rain-swept moor, Collun not very hopefully suggested they find a place to stop and finish the last of their food.

"Look!" exclaimed Talisen.

Collun peered through the gloom and saw what appeared to be a light.

"Come on," urged Talisen. "It must be a farm."

They trudged forward through the rain, every inch of them chilled through. As they drew closer they saw that the light emanated from a long, two-story building with several smaller buildings adjoining it. Just beyond the structures Collun could see a wide road.

With a sinking heart, he realized this was the Traveler's Rest, an inn that served those who journeyed on the high road to Temair. Somehow they had made their way back to the road.

Talisen let out a whoop of pleasure. "Traveler's Rest! I hear they have the finest ale this side of Temair. And warm beds and good food. I think I will survive after all."

Remembering the kesil's words, Collun was on the verge of protesting, but the temptation of hot food and a chance to dry off was too overwhelming to resist. Wearily he followed Talisen in the direction of the brightly lit inn.

FIVE

Mister Urlacan

The Traveler's Rest had been built of large blocks of stone, with mullioned windows that were now fogged from the warmth inside. The inn looked as if it had stood where it was for many hundreds of years, surviving the bleakness of its surroundings by sheer stubbornness.

Its sign blew crazily on creaking hinges. The semblance of a puff-cheeked man in a striped nightcap sleeping in a snug bed was faintly visible despite the peeling paint.

When Collun and Talisen opened the door, a warm blast of air blew into their faces. Closing the door behind them, they stood still for several moments, savoring the warmth.

A small boy, dressed in worn but clean clothing, ran into the entranceway. He skidded slightly in the pools of water that were forming as their soaked garments dripped onto the floor.

Talisen steadied the boy with a wink and a friendly hand, but the boy drew back and looked at them with wary, bright eyes.

"You be wanting a bed for the night?"

"Indeed we do. Your softest beds and your hottest water, and then as much good food and ale as your table can hold," Talisen said with gusto.

"And have you the gold to pay for it?" boomed a deep voice. A large stomach appeared around the corner, followed by its owner, a mountain of a man with a head that was large and round and completely bald. His eyes were not small, but they seemed so, lost as they were in the expanse of flesh that surrounded them. He wore a small gold hoop in one substantial earlobe. Like the boy, the large man's eyes held a guarded expression, as if he was used to encountering trouble.

"Are you the esteemed landlord of this legendary inn?" Talisen queried in his most engaging manner.

"That I am. Job Wall is my name, and I'm asking you again: Have you the means to pay for your lodging?"

Collun was about to ask the huge man the cost of his smallest room, thinking of the three silver pieces in his pocket, which was all the money he possessed in the world, but Talisen spoke first.

"Will this be adequate?" Pulling a leather pouch from his pocket, Talisen dropped a large gold coin into the landlord's hand. Collun stared.

The landlord peered at the coin, then put it between his yellow teeth and bit down. Satisfied, he nodded. "Aye. Have you horses to stable?"

They shook their heads. The landlord raised his eyebrows but made no comment. "Rince, show them to the top room on the end, with the two beds, and make sure they get hot water. Mind you hurry, boy. We've got a fair crowd in the main room tonight."

The boy called Rince showed them to a small room on the second floor. It was plain but cozy. Though the two swaybacked beds looked ancient, there were several blankets at the foot of each.

Rince said he would fetch the hot water. When the door closed behind him, Collun said sharply, "Where did you get the gold?"

"Oh, that. Just another parting gift from dear Farmer Whicklow," Talisen responded cheerfully, sitting on the edge of one rickety bed to take off his damp boots.

Collun shook his head in dismay. "Old Whicklow will have you thrown into prison the moment you return to Inkberrow."

"To begin with," said Talisen patiently, "I have no intention of returning to Inkberrow, but even if by some ill fortune I were to do so, the good farmer would not lift a finger against me. You see, he really did give me the money."

Collun gave a snort of disbelief.

"It's true," Talisen protested. "A token of his esteem and perhaps a small measure of appreciation for keeping to myself the fact that just before I left to join you, I saw four cows with Farmer Pilbeam's mark in the Whicklow barn."

"So it's blackmail. Talisen, you are as low as..."

"Farmer Whicklow." Talisen laughed. "But never mind. We need it more than he does. After all, we'd be of very little use to Nessa lying frozen and lifeless out there on the moor."

There was a light knock on the door. Collun opened it and in staggered Rince, carrying a large basin of steaming water. Talisen stepped forward in his stocking feet and helped the boy with his load. Rince looked up at Talisen with surprise, as though unused to such consideration.

"You're faster than a jackrabbit, I'm thinking," said Talisen as they set the basin on a low table. "That old Job Wall keeps you dancing, doesn't he?"

The boy nodded shyly, a glimmer of a smile appearing on his face.

"Treats you fairly, though, I hope."

"Oh, yes. He be good to me, all in all."

"Is the inn full tonight?"

"Only half, sir. Job Wall says how we don't get near as many travelers along the road as we used to. And many of 'em are Northerners these days. 'Those scurvy Scathians,' he calls 'em.'' Talisen and Collun laughed as the boy imitated his master, using a deep voice and sticking his stomach straight out.

"We have a big group of Scathians tonight in the main room," Rince continued, "getting sotted and making lots of noise. Job Wall don't like 'em."

"I'm looking forward to meeting my first Scathian," Talisen said cheerfully as he started to wash himself with the hot water. "We don't get many down in Inkberrow. I wonder what their songs are like."

The boy came alert at Talisen's words. "Did you say you was from Inkberrow?"

"Yes. Have you been there?"

"No." Rince paused and clasped his small hands together in a nervous gesture.

"What is it, Rince?"

"It's just that . . . the one traveling with the Scathians, the one calling himself Mister Urlacan, well, I heard him asking Job Wall if we'd had any folks traveling from the south. From Inkberrow, in particular."

"He said Inkberrow? Are you sure?" Collun asked, more sharply than he had intended.

Rince nodded, uneasy.

"Talisen . . . ," Collun began, his body tense.

"I know, I know, but let's not go jumping to conclusions," Talisen said.

"We should leave, right now." Collun reached for his pack.

"Hold on, Collun." Talisen laid a reassuring hand on Collun's arm. "More likely than not it has nothing to do with us. But, just to be safe, all we'll do is not let on we're from Inkberrow. We can say we're traveling south—that we're from north of Temair and have business in the south."

Collun shook his head.

"Come on, forewarned is forearmed, and there's no reason to deny ourselves a hot meal and a decent bed for the night on the basis of such flimsy evidence. What say you, Rince? Can you keep a secret?" Rince nodded eagerly. "And I promise, Collun, we'll leave at the first sign of trouble."

Against his better judgment, Collun allowed himself

to be convinced. They quickly washed up and headed down to the main room.

There was a large peat fire burning in a fireplace at the center of the room. A vast black pot bubbling with stew hung suspended over it. Assorted tables and benches were grouped around the fireplace, and roughly half of these were occupied, mostly by clusters of two or three. The exception was a large group of dark-bearded Scathians who had pushed several tables together and were sprawled drunkenly around them.

The Scathians were thick and muscular and wore rough, travel-stained clothing. They spoke in loud, slurred voices, punctuated by bursts of coarse laughter. For the most part they used the language of Eirren, though with the guttural accent of the Scathian dialect.

But there was one among them who did not speak at all. He wore a long cloak. Despite the warmth of the room, he had the hood pulled up over his head. It kept his face shadowed. He sat back in his chair, almost motionless. Now and again he lifted a long black cheroot to his shadowed mouth. Collun could see that his skin was gray, and he had only three fingers.

When they took their seats, the hooded face turned briefly in their direction. The gray hand holding the cheroot paused. Collun thought he caught a glitter of yellow eyes. He quickly looked away, wondering if this was the man who had been asking about travelers from Inkberrow.

Then Collun's eyes fell on a slim youth with brown hair who sat by himself at a table nearby. He was the only lone traveler in the room and was draining a large mug of ale.

Rince came over soon after with large earthenware bowls of steaming hot stew thick with meat, carrots, potatoes, and gravy. Collun couldn't remember a time when a meal had been so welcome or had tasted so good.

They emptied their bowls quickly. The boy came to refill them, bringing thick slices of crusty dark bread and two brimming mugs of ale.

"You are a most splendid and delightful fellow, my young jackrabbit," Talisen commented appreciatively.

The Scathians, including their silent, hooded companion, showed no interest in the two boys. They called loudly for more ale and commenced playing a game of cards. Collun slowly began to relax.

When he had finished his second bowl of stew, Collun leaned back in the wooden chair, his stomach comfortably full. He felt his eyelids droop. With a pint of ale by his hand and a warm fire at his feet, he forgot about the hardships of the past week and about the stranger who had been asking after travelers from Inkberrow. He opened his eyes with an effort and happened to glance toward the solitary youth he had noticed before. The boy seemed to be staring fixedly at him with an expression that was difficult to read. Collun blinked and looked again but realized it must have been a trick of the light, for now the boy was fast asleep in his chair. As Collun sleepily wondered if perhaps *this* was the one asking about Inkberrow travelers, his own lids fell shut again and he dozed.

He woke with a start and looked beside him. Talisen was not there. Then he spotted him sitting across the room at the Scathians' table, cards in his hand. Collun's stomach tightened in alarm.

The rest of the room was almost empty, save for Job Wall, Rince, and the dark youth Collun had noticed earlier. He was still sleeping, his chair tilted back against the wall.

"Back in Mallaig," Talisen was saying, "that's up north, a small village above Temair, where my friend and I live, we have a tradition that in the third hand all deuces are wild."

The Scathian dealer just grunted.

"Only a suggestion, my good man," Talisen said blithely.

A round of betting ensued and Collun groaned inwardly when he saw one of Talisen's gold pieces go into the pot. He tried unsuccessfully to catch his friend's eye, cursing Talisen's lack of caution.

"Ah, my turn, is it? Let's see ... Well, it's not much, but it looks like it beats your royal split." Talisen laid his cards down with a flourish and began to reach for the pot.

The Scathian he had bested slammed the table with one fist and pulled a knife with the other. He slashed the steel blade down within inches of Talisen's fingers, his small eyes narrow with anger. The boy quickly withdrew his hand, cleared his throat nervously, and said, "I must have read the cards wrong: an honest mistake ..."

The figure in the cloak suddenly leaned forward and deliberately stamped out his cheroot on the surface of the wooden table. "You were not mistaken." The voice was soft and sibilant. Collun suddenly remembered a long gray snake he had once surprised under a rotting tree. The hissing noise it made as its glittering eyes fastened on Collun was very like the voice of the man in the cloak. "Please, take the money. I am Mister Urlacan. Perhaps you and your companion will join me and my friends in a last round of ale?" The hood slowly swiveled in Collun's direction, and he again saw a glint of yellow from inside the shadowed depths.

Collun awkwardly got to his feet and licked his lips. "Uh, thank you, but we're, uh, heading south, early in the morning. We need to get to bed. Come on, Talisen."

Collun immediately realized he'd made a mistake when he saw Talisen roll his eyes. "Thought you said your name was Boregin," one of the Scathians said suspiciously to Talisen.

But Mister Urlacan ignored the interruption. "Ah, south, is it? Then perhaps you'll ride with us. We, too, journey south." The three-fingered hand lit up another cheroot.

"You are very kind, but we are in some haste; we leave well before dawn." Collun was afraid he would press him further, but to his relief, the hissing voice said only, "As you like. Pleasant dreams to you."

Talisen quickly scooped up his winnings and followed Collun out of the room, wishing the Scathians a cheerful good night.

Once they were in their room, Collun locked the door behind them. He turned to Talisen, his eyebrows drawn together and his eyes dark.

"Of all the foolish things you have done—"

"I know, I know." Talisen held up his hand to forestall Collun's angry words. "I was wrong. But all's well that ends well, especially when it's me who winds up with a bag full of gold."

"Talisen!"

The sound of a soft knock on the door interrupted them.

"Who's there?" Collun said apprehensively.

"Rince," came the whispered voice.

Collun let him in.

"Master says to come quick," Rince whispered urgently. "Says it's not safe, that they'll have found out your room by now."

"Who?" asked Talisen.

"That Mister Urlacan and the Scathians with him," replied the boy.

"But...," began Talisen.

"Hurry!" whispered Rince, fear in his eyes.

Collun and Talisen grabbed their belongings and followed him.

They made their way through the silent hall and down into the back entryway. Rince led them out into the darkness, where a soft drizzle furred their faces. As they followed Rince toward a barn some distance from the inn and stables, Collun heard a harsh "caw" from above. He craned his neck, trying to see if it was a scald-crow, but it was too dark to tell. Suppressing a shiver, he quickly followed Rince and Talisen into the barn. Collun could hear the rustling sound of a hen settling herself on her nest and the rhythmic grinding of a cow chewing its cud.

Job Wall entered the barn soon after, shutting the door behind him. His gold earring gleamed in the dim light.

"So, what's this all about?" Talisen said sleepily, making no effort to keep quiet. "Do those crooks want their money back after all?"

Job Wall reached out a massive hand and took Talisen by the collar of his jersey and said in a loud whisper, "Young fool. This has nothing to do with money. Keep your voice down." Slowly he released Talisen, and both boys could see that the man was pale and sweating.

"Those Scathians stayed in the main room after you left, and I overheard the one calling himself Urlacan saying there was no time to waste, that you two were the quarry they sought. I don't know how he found out you were from Inkberrow, unless it was your foolish prattling gave you away." Job Wall glared at Talisen, who looked a little sheepish.

"They'll be at your room by now," continued the landlord. "I saw them talking to Seb, the cook, who'll tell anything to anyone for a little gold."

"Did they say *why* they're looking for travelers from Inkberrow?" asked Collun anxiously.

"No, nothing about that. I only heard Mister Urlacan gloating that you'd walked right into his hands." The huge man looked down at the two boys. "So you don't know what it is they're after?"

"No, sir," responded Collun.

Job Wall exhaled noisily. "Wouldn't matter to me what it was. Not when it comes to Scathians and to—" He broke off. "You know what that Mister Urlacan is?" he said abruptly, mopping his perspiring brow with a large white handkerchief.

Both boys shook their heads.

"A morg, that's what." Job Wall looked at them sharply. "Don't you know what morgs are?"

"Yes," answered Talisen. "They were creatures from up north, from Usna and Uneach. They helped Cruachan conquer North Eirren."

"Aye. Demon creatures with a love for killing and a fear of nothing, except perhaps the bright light of day."

"But most of them went back to Usna and Uneach, right? And the ones that stayed died out a long time ago."

Job Wall shook his head. "That's what I've always heard, too, but I'd bet the Traveler's Rest itself that this Mister Urlacan, with his gray skin, three fingers, and eyes that could put a man off eating, is a morg."

Collun leaned back against a stall, his mind jumbled by fear.

"There's not much can get to me, but a morg..." Job Wall shook his head. "You'd better leave now. You can have the mare in the next stable."

Talisen took out his bag of gold. "What do we owe you?"

Job Wall frowned, waving Talisen away. "Nought. The gold you gave me before was payment enough." The landlord shook his head. "These are bad times in Eirren. Now, you stay here. I'll bring the horse." He left the barn after making sure the yard was still deserted.

Collun and Talisen waited, listening intently for the sound of the landlord's return. They heard the faint cry of a bird. Collun flinched, resisting the urge to stick his head out the barn door.

Finally they heard footsteps approaching and the sound of a bridle jingling. The barn door opened and their eyes were momentarily dazzled by the light from an oil lamp.

The figure holding the lamp was shrouded in a cloak. Collun could not see the face. Then his gaze fell on the hand holding the flickering light. It had only three fingers.

SIX

Breo-Saight

Two large Scathians stood behind the morg. One of them carried a horse's bridle, which he shook at the boys with a mocking smile. A third Scathian came up, pushing a bound and terrified Rince ahead of him.

The two boys backed away. Collun's hand sought the handle of his dagger.

The creature calling himself Mister Urlacan spoke in his soft, caressing voice. "We meet again. It seems our way does indeed lie together after all. Come..." His yellow eyes shone at Collun from under his hood.

"What is it you want from us?" Collun asked in a strangled voice.

"Oh, I have no personal interest in the matter. It is merely a commission."

"They killed the master!" Rince suddenly cried out, near tears.

The morg paid no attention to the boy's words. "Now, drop your little knife and come with us." The yellow eyes bored into Collun's. He backed farther away from the creature.

Mister Urlacan sighed impatiently. "If you do not, I will be obliged to kill the small one here." The morg nodded at the Scathian who held Rince, and the man put his knife to the boy's throat.

"Well?" said Mister Urlacan impatiently. He gestured to the Scathian. Collun could see the knife bite into the boy's skin. A line of red appeared on the thin white throat.

Collun dropped his dagger. It fell on its side in a clump of hay. The lucky stone glittered slightly in the light of the oil lamp. Collun took a deep breath, then deliberately walked across the barn to Mister Urlacan. A three-fingered hand closed over his wrist. Collun recoiled at the touch. The morg's grip was like iron.

"Kill the other first, then the small one," Mister Urlacan hissed softly to the two Scathians behind him. They began to move toward Talisen. The morg turned to leave the barn, pulling Collun with him.

Collun resisted, trying in vain to wrench himself free. "Ah, you prefer to stay and watch? As you like." The morg stopped but maintained his iron hold on Collun.

The two Scathians began to circle Talisen. Collun stood still; the damp hand encircling his wrist seemed to have paralyzed his whole body, radiating a cold lethargy through every limb. He could not budge his legs; they felt brittle, like icicles that would shatter if he moved them.

A cock crowed somewhere nearby. Mister Urlacan whipped his head around to look out into the yard. Dawn was just beginning to break, and the morg pulled the cowl of his hood lower to shield himself from the light.

"Hurry," he hissed.

Talisen had been darting nimbly from side to side, but the Scathians were closing on him. Collun watched in terror as his friend stumbled. One of the Scathians grabbed Talisen's arm and brutally wrenched it behind his back. A deadly looking knife had appeared in the man's hand.

Collun tightened his muscles, desperately battling against the freezing torpor that held him. He twisted his body and kicked out with a foot. The lantern jerked out of the morg's hand. It fell onto a patch of dirt and, though it sputtered, remained lit. In his surprise, the morg briefly loosened his grip and Collun broke free. He ran toward Talisen. The second Scathian pivoted and knocked Collun to the ground, planting a thick knee on his chest. The knife in the man's hand caught a beam of dawn light and dazzled Collun's eyes. He could smell the man's sour breath.

"No! Stop, fool! That one is not to be killed," came Mister Urlacan's voice. "Bring him. It grows late."

The Scathian reluctantly sheathed his knife and pulled Collun up by the front of his jersey. He began to drag him toward the morg.

Suddenly a voice called out, "Hold!"

In the hayloft above was a slim boy with a bow at

his shoulder and an arrow poised for flight. Collun immediately recognized him as the quiet stranger from the inn.

The Scathian hesitated. Mister Urlacan let out an impatient hiss and swiftly crossed to Collun, reaching out to grab him.

There was a rush of air and then, a split second later, another. The morg let out a grating, wheezing sound. His hand had been shot through by a quivering arrow. Black blood dripped onto the floor of the barn.

The Scathian holding Talisen gazed in astonishment at the arrow that protruded from his own shoulder. Talisen quickly squirmed away and grabbed a nearby pitchfork.

"My next two arrows will find your hearts, if you have any," called the youth.

"He speaks the truth." It was Job Wall's voice. The large man stood at the barn's entrance, holding a bloodstained cloth to his stomach. In the other hand he held a long knife.

"Master!" cried out Rince.

"The boy is called Breo-Saight, or Fire Arrow. It is said that he has yet to miss his mark," boomed Job Wall.

The Scathians hesitated and looked to Mister Urlacan. The morg seemed to have shrunk, and his breath was coming in noisy rasps. Collun watched in horror as Urlacan broke the tip off the arrow and pulled the shaft through his hand. Blood flowed freely. The morg darted another look back at the brightening sun, and a shudder went through his body. He snarled to the Scathians, "Come, fools."

Then the morg pivoted and made a strange little bow

to Collun, saying, "We will meet again." His yellow eyes flashed up at the boy in the hayloft, then back at Collun. Mister Urlacan pulled his hood down over his face, leaving only a thin crack to see through. Trailing black blood, he hurried out of the barn. The three Scathians followed behind.

Job Wall watched from the barn door. "They're gone," he said after a short silence.

Collun retrieved his dagger. The stone in the handle again seemed to glow in the dawn light. Breo-Saight nimbly descended from the hayloft, his bow slung over his shoulder. Collun's eye was caught by the design carved into the upper limb of the bow. It was the likeness of a large bear.

"We are in your debt, Breo-Saight," Collun said, extending his hand.

The youth shrugged, shaking the offered hand. "Like Job Wall, I do not like Scathians. Or morgs, though this is the first I've seen," he added.

When they were back in the inn, Collun tended to Job Wall's wound with his herbs. The landlord had protested that it was only a slight injury, but his face was pale from loss of blood.

As soon as Collun had finished with him, Job Wall sent off two of his men to discover, if they could, where Urlacan and his men had gone.

Rince served breakfast to the three boys. Talisen and Breo-Saight set to with a hearty appetite, but Collun barely touched his food. He stood, crossed to the window, and peered out anxiously.

"Come back here and eat," said Talisen. "The grannach is excellent."

Collun shook his head.

Talisen and Breo-Saight were on their second helping when Collun let out a sound. "Someone is coming." Job Wall joined him at the window.

"Ah, that is Ned. Let's see if he has anything to report." The large man left the kitchen.

He returned soon after. "Ned says that Farmer Olmveg saw some men on horseback out on the edge of his west field. There's an old shed out there. Could be the morg is sheltering there until nightfall. If you leave now, you may be able to get a jump on them." Job Wall paused, looking speculatively at Collun. "Where are you headed?"

"North," said Collun, "but not by the road."

"Have you a route in mind?" asked Breo-Saight.

Collun shook his head.

"Hardly," said Talisen, his mouth full.

"I know a way," said Breo-Saight, "and would offer myself to you as guide. I, too, am heading north, and like you, I have no wish to cross paths with the morg Urlacan."

Collun hesitated. Aside from Breo-Saight's skill with bow and arrow, they knew nothing of him.

"Better take him up on it," Job Wall put in matter-of-factly. "There's no one knows these lands better. Besides, that bow arm of his may come in handy."

"I don't suppose you sing, Breo-Saight?" Talisen asked, giving his bowl to Rince for a third helping of grannach. "We could use another voice by the fire at night. My friend Collun here has a tin ear."

"I sing a little," the youth replied, his eyes on Collun.

Collun suddenly came to a decision. "We would welcome your company."

Breo-Saight smiled. "In that case, please call me Brie. It is the name I go by among companions."

Job Wall provided them with a generous supply of food, water, and ale. Rince readied the mare as well as a pony the landlord had added at the last minute.

"There are three of you now," he said, refusing any additional payment. "Whatever your business is, if a morg is out to stop you, it must be something worth doing."

Collun thanked the large man and soon they were on their way, Brie and Collun on the mare, with Talisen following behind on the pony.

Brie guided the horse with a sure hand, moving across the moorland at a brisk pace. They traveled hard, then stopped at midday for food and rest since none had slept the night before. In the late afternoon, as the sky cleared and the sun shone, Talisen softly sang all twenty-four verses of the "Cuckoo Song" to keep their spirits up. There was no sign of Scathians or the morg.

Brie led them on an easterly route, veering at a wide angle from the high road.

"The land we will travel over is much like this," Brie said, gesturing at the undulating moors around them. "Until we come to the Forest of Eld."

Collun had heard of the Forest of Eld back in Inkberrow. There were tales of men who had lost their way for half a lifetime in the ancient and massive wood, as well as those who never returned at all.

"I know of only two ways through the Forest of Eld," said Brie. "One is the high road, which cuts through the western end. The other is a path that winds through Eld's very center. Not many know of it. The safest course would be the high road, at least in terms of the forest itself. It is well maintained and the wood is not so dense. But it is also the first place Urlacan will be watching."

"And the path?" asked Collun.

"I have traveled it once before and met no trouble. But it is overgrown in places and not always easy to follow." Brie paused. "I would cast my vote for the path, but it is up to you."

Collun hesitated. "There is no way around the forest?"

"Not unless you wish to add a month or more to the journey."

"The path it is, then," said Collun, trying to set aside his fear.

They made camp that night near a dense thicket of rowan trees. Brie left them for a time, and when he returned he reported, "I see no sign of Scathians or Urlacan. So far."

During Brie's absence Collun had made a stew using turnips and salted meat from Job Wall's kitchen. He had added acorns, rosemary, and small wild onions. In between bites, Brie complimented Collun on his culinary skill, then asked why he and Talisen were journeying to Temair.

"My sister," Collun said slowly, "was living in Temair. We received word that she is missing. I go there to aid in the search."

Brie shook his head. "These are dark times in Eirren. You said you live in Inkberrow?"

Collun nodded.

"Do you live with your mother and father?"

Collun nodded again. "My father runs the smithy in Inkberrow."

"What is his name?" Brie asked. "I traveled through Inkberrow once and had my horse shod by an able blacksmith."

"Goban," Collun replied, refilling Brie's bowl with stew. He glanced up briefly and thought he saw a curious expression in the boy's eyes.

But all Brie said was, "That was the name. I remember now."

"And you, Breo-Saight? Where are you from?" asked Talisen, handing his bowl to Collun for seconds.

"A small town northwest of Temair. You would not know it."

"And your mother and father?"

"My mother died when I was born. That is a handsome harp you carry, Talisen. What is the workmanship?"

"I do not know," answered Talisen. "Are you trying to change the subject, Brie?"

"Not at all. It is only that I fear my history would bore you. I suspect yours is much more intriguing. What is the story of your harp?"

Talisen paused but was clearly unable to resist the temptation to talk about himself. "I have had it since I was a babe."

Brie raised his eyebrows.

"They found me one day, the good people of Inkberrow, in the middle of town, wearing no more than a linen diaper and this harp strung across my back. I was barely able to walk, they tell me, and the harp was twice my size, but I was able to balance it with ease."

"It was strapped to your back?" Brie responded in disbelief.

"And the linen cloth of the diaper was soaked through with seawater, among other things," Talisen said with a grin.

"Inkberrow is nowhere near the shore," Brie pointed out.

"Exactly!" responded Talisen. "Is it not strange and mysterious?"

"It makes a good story, anyway," said Brie with a smile.

"The truth often does," Talisen retorted. "Now, how about some music?" He began one of the old songs, badgering Brie to join in while Collun washed their dinner utensils in a nearby stream.

Though Brie's voice was softer than Talisen's, it was true and clear, and the two harmonized well. Collun rejoined them by the fire and listened while they sang several more songs, until Talisen suggested a song about the hero Cuillean.

Brie rose and stretched, saying, "That's enough for me tonight."

"Do you not care for songs of Cuillean and the Eamh War?" asked Talisen.

Brie shook his head. "It is only that I am weary. And we need to be up early."

"Tell me," Talisen went on, ignoring Brie's pointed yawn, "is it true what we have heard in Inkberrow? That Cuillean has been missing for over a year?"

"As far as I know, it is true," replied Brie.

"Do you think he is dead?"

"Perhaps."

As Collun rose to stir the glowing embers of the fire, he felt Brie's eyes on him. Watching the small sparks that flew up, Collun said, "I am tired, too, Talisen. Stop pestering Breo-Saight with your questions and let us get some sleep."

&

The next day the weather stayed brisk and clear, and they made good progress. But in the late afternoon they came across a wide swath of knee-high burdock. Sticky burrs jabbed at the animals' legs and flanks and clung to the boys' clothing. The mare occasionally reared with an exasperated whinny, while the pony constantly shied and finally came to a complete halt, refusing to budge another inch.

After several minutes of futile cajoling and kicking, Talisen let out an ear-blistering curse and swung himself off the stubborn pony. "Damnable hurr-burrs," he muttered, peeling several off his clothing. "They're driving me mad."

"There are worse things than hurr-burrs," replied Brie, pulling up on the mare's reins.

"Perhaps, but that doesn't make their bite any less sharp," countered Talisen testily.

"I believe it does."

"Have you always been so stoic, Breo-Saight?"

"My father raised me so."

"Is that so? Tell me, are you your father's only son?"

"Yes," Brie answered shortly.

"I think not."

"I beg your pardon?"

With a sly grin, Talisen suddenly dipped into a low bow. He began to recite in a singsong voice, " 'A father's child, a mother's child, yet no one's son.' Am I not right... *m'lady?*"

Collun stared down at Talisen. "What brand of nonsense is this?"

Talisen laughed and said to Brie, whose face had turned a vivid shade of red, "You can't deceive a bard when it comes to the fair sex. We are a sensitive breed, you know."

Brie glared at Talisen, her eyes like lightning in a storm. "I am a warrior and a marksman, no matter what my sex, and I understand little of the sensitivities of a bard!"

"Temper, temper, my dear girl. I believe I will rename you Flame-girl. Much more apt than Fire Arrow, don't you think?"

Brie swung the horse around furiously, urging it forward.

"Is it true?" Collun asked, staring at the back of Brie's head.

At first she did not answer. Then, stopping the mare, she turned toward Collun. "Yes," she said simply.

Collun stared at her. "I do not understand. Why do you disguise yourself?"

Brie swung herself off the horse and Collun followed. "I am the daughter of a warrior who wanted a son," Brie began. "When I was a babe, my father laid the marksman's bow and arrow on my chest, even though I was a girl. My mother had died bearing me, and when my father realized there would be no son for him, he trained me as he would a boy. I learned quickly and he was pleased. When I first started traveling on my own, I was often mistaken for a boy. I decided it was easier and safer to maintain the charade."

"I never guessed." Collun examined her face closely, trying to picture her with longer hair and wearing feminine clothes. She was not beautiful—not, at least, the way Nessa or Emer was. Yet Brie's face had strength, with angles and shadows that drew his eyes. Her limbs were lithe, he realized now, in a way that most boys' were not.

He saw something else in her eyes, something unknowable, sadness perhaps, mixed with something darker.

"Of all people, it is extraordinary that *he*"—she gestured back toward Talisen, who was plucking hurr-burrs off the pony's coat as he muttered encouraging words to the stubborn animal—"should have seen through my disguise. There are only one or two others who know the truth."

"We shall not reveal what you do not wish revealed," Collun promised.

She turned and smiled at him. There was a radiance in her face when she smiled that made Collun stare. He dropped his gaze quickly.

Brie's smile dimmed as she cast a doubtful glance back toward Talisen.

"Do not worry," Collun said. "Talisen can keep a secret when he understands it is important to do so. I will tell him."

"Thank you."

The weather stayed fair and their progress the next day was even better than the two before. But just before twilight, as they came to the top of a rise high enough to command a view of much of the surrounding countryside, they spotted a band of riders coming up behind them. They were too far off to recognize, but the companions all had the same thought: Scathians.

Brie quickly led them down the other side of the rise and along the bottom of the moor. For the next several hours they traveled hard, moving at the fastest pace the pony could muster.

They finally came to a large stream. Brie urged the mare forward. After hesitating a few moments, the animal plunged into the water, which came up to her knees. The pony took a little more cajoling, but it, too, went in. Talisen let out a groan as the chilly water filled his boots.

"It will make it harder for the Scathians to track us," said Brie.

"If you don't mind fish swimming between your toes," Talisen grumbled.

They traveled along in the stream until dawn, when they ate and rested for several hours. Then they resumed the same urgent pace of the night before, zigzagging across the land and trying to keep away from the tops of the moors, where their pursuers might be able to spot them.

By late afternoon Brie felt confident they had shaken the Scathians, at least for the time being.

They made camp that night on the far side of a hill.

"The Forest of Eld is not far now," said Brie as they rubbed down the travel-weary animals. "And once we get through the forest, Temair is less than a week's journey beyond."

"How long will it take to get through Eld?" asked Collun.

Brie shrugged. "It is hard to say. At best nine or ten days."

While searching for kindling, Collun noticed a strange kind of ivy growing near their campsite. He had never seen its like before—thick black stems with broad leaves shot through with dull red veins. It grew along the ground in a dense mass, clinging mostly to the opposite side of the hill on which they were camped.

That night, as they ate the last of Job Wall's provisions, Collun became aware of a strange odor. It smelled like something dead that had been lying in the sun too long. Perhaps there was a skunk nearby, he thought.

Then Talisen drew out his harp and badgered Brie into teaching him several songs she knew. Collun found himself feeling envious when he heard how well Brie and Talisen harmonized.

"One more," Talisen urged as Brie began to yawn. But she suddenly let out a small cry. A tendril of green was shooting up her leg, winding round and round her calf, her knee, her thigh. The ivy Collun had noticed on the other side of the hill had crept into their campsite and was growing at an impossible rate.

Talisen dropped his harp and reached down to push away a tendril that had begun to encircle his ankles. Collun heard the pony let out a terrified bray. He looked over to see it and the mare kicking out at a mass of green that was clutching their legs. The pony went down, then the mare.

Suddenly Collun felt pressure on his ankle and looked down to see a green shoot climbing his own leg. When he put his hand down to fend it off, it changed course to wind around his hand and up his arm.

The plant was tough. When Collun tried to lift his arm, it wouldn't budge. It felt as if it had been bound by metal bands. Meanwhile, ivy swarmed up his other leg, and no matter how he struggled or tried to squirm away, the tendrils kept winding and cinching. Soon Collun could not move his legs at all.

By now Brie was almost completely encased. The ivy even concealed her face. A squirming, shouting Talisen was covered to his shoulders, arms bound to his sides.

Collun had managed to keep his other arm free by sticking it straight out to the side, and his hand found a knife they had been using to cut cheese and bread for their meal. It was not the dagger his father had made for him, but its edge was almost as sharp. He brought the blade down hard on the thick stem of the vine that imprisoned his right hand. Though his movements were clumsy, he made direct contact.

To his horror the knife didn't even score the surface of the thick stem. Even as he sawed, an ivy shoot spiraled up his left arm and back down, binding the arm awkwardly across his chest, the knife still in his hand.

The three travelers and their animals were now completely sheathed. The only sounds that could be heard were the crackling of the campfire and the pulsing, scratching noise the ivy made as it blanketed the hill.

Collun could see out of only one eye; the other was sealed shut by an ivy stem. His nostrils were only partially covered, so he was still able to breathe. The smell was not like that of any ordinary plant, and he realized this was the rotten odor he had noticed earlier. The stench made him gag.

The vine was still growing. Collun knew it was only a matter of time before his sight and his breath were cut off for good. He struggled against panic. He remembered, as if from a long time ago, Emer's voice as she pressed the lucky stone in his hand. "So you will know that even as you lose your breath, it will always come back." But the lucky stone was in the dagger that had been a trine, which was now buried at his waist under layers of ivy.

Then through his one open eye Collun suddenly spotted a figure stride up to the campsite. He blinked to make sure the flickering light of the fire was not playing tricks. No, someone was there. His head was cocked to one side, as if he was studying the scene that lay before him.

Moving quickly, the stranger crossed to their pile of kindling. He removed a long slender branch. He deftly stripped the branch of smaller offshoots, then, still crouching, placed his hand around one end. He stayed motionless in that position for several moments. Collun could swear he heard the faint sound of music through the blood roaring in his ears.

Collun could not feel his toes anymore. The ivy was pulling tighter and tighter around his legs. The pain made him dizzy. Then he felt a stinging sensation as though his skin were being pierced by hundreds of sharp needles.

The stranger abruptly rose and, still holding his hand over the end of the branch, crossed to the green bundle that was Talisen. He knelt beside the mound of ivy and slowly took his hand from the branch. A soft pink light glowed from its tip. In the faint light Collun could just see the stranger's face. He had fair hair and his lips were moving. Now Collun was sure that he was singing.

The figure took the glowing end of the branch and ran it along Talisen's body. Though his vision wavered, it looked to Collun as though the ivy was shriveling and falling away from Talisen's body. Then a green tendril snaked across Collun's open eye, forcing it shut, and he saw no more. Ivy pressed against his nostrils and the choking smell of decay filled his nose and mouth. It was harder and harder to breathe. His lungs were bursting.

Through the haze, he felt someone crouch beside him. He dimly heard Talisen's voice. It was as if he were in a deep hole and Talisen was calling to him from above. They were playing hide-me-and-find-me, back behind the smithy. That roaring noise must be the sound of his father's furnace. Why couldn't Talisen find him? What was taking him so long?

Suddenly he felt something wet and cool on his lips and someone blowing into his mouth. "Talisen, stop that," he protested. "It was a good hiding place. You couldn't find me..." He stopped short. What had happened? Why couldn't he move his legs? Then he saw Talisen's anxious face hovering over him and the dark eyes of Breo-Saight. Of course. The ivy. He took a deep breath of air, then another, and another.

The stranger with the golden hair was leaning over Collun's legs, holding the branch with the pink light at the end, which now seemed dimmer than before. He was running the pink light along the stem of the ivy around Collun's leg, and as he did so, the ivy withered and fell away. Talisen and Brie were pulling away the dead vine.

Soon Collun was able to sit up and help them draw the long tendrils away from his body. He took sidelong glances at their mysterious rescuer. The stranger's face was very pale and was covered with a fine film of moisture. He was small, a head shorter than Talisen, and wore simple clothing of white and blue. His golden hair was longer than theirs and curled down the back of his neck.

As he rose, before crossing to the mare and pony, he met Collun's gaze. The stranger's eyes were silver. The golden-haired figure was an Ellyl.

SEVEN

The Ellyl

When he had run his fading pink light down the last of the ivy covering the two animals, the Ellyl looked from one to the other of them. His eyelids flickered slightly with fatigue. Then he smiled gently, lay down on the ground, and was soon fast asleep.

Talisen bent over and picked up the branch the Ellyl had used to free them from the ivy. The end that had glowed with pink light now looked slightly charred.

"He is an Ellyl, isn't he?" Collun said, breaking the silence.

"Yes," replied Brie.

Collun stood, disentangling the last remnant of dead ivy from his ankle. He noticed there were tiny pink

marks on his bare skin and minuscule holes in his clothing. "I have never seen anything like it," he said. "It was as if the vine was alive."

"And wanted us dead," responded Talisen with a shudder. "Thank Amergin the Ellyl came along when he did."

Suddenly a knee-high white shape glided into the clearing. Talisen let out a shout and jumped back, as if at a ghost.

"What is it?" he whispered loudly.

At first Collun thought the animal was a cat. Its movements were lithe and feline. But it was larger than a cat, and its legs were longer. It had a thick tail, almost as long as its body.

The animal turned its head toward Collun at that moment. The white fur of the animal's forehead bore a star-shaped burst of gold, and its eyes were large and silver. Though the ears were pointed and alert, it was not the face of a cat.

"I think it is called a faol," said Brie, her eyes kindling with interest. "It is an Ellyl animal—part cat, part wolf." As the white creature approached, Brie knelt and put out her hand.

"Brie . . . ," Collun began in alarm. The faol did not look like a tame animal. There was a fierceness and arrogance in the face and in the way it moved.

But to Collun's surprise the faol arrested its movements and lifted its head to sniff Brie's fingers. The animal's silver eyes even closed halfway as it allowed Brie to lightly run the backs of her fingers along its spine. Then it opened its eyes, stared unblinking at Brie for several moments, and resumed its course. It came to a stop beside the Ellyl's golden head. With almost regal grace the faol lay down, resting its head on its paws. It looked prepared to keep a vigil over the Ellyl for some time.

"I always thought Ellylon were supposed to be small, with little wings for flying," Talisen said, taking a step closer to the Ellyl. But he jumped back when the faol narrowed its eyes and lifted its upper lip, revealing a row of sharp teeth.

"No, my father told me about Ellylon," said Brie. "He knew a man who had seen one once, and he said they were our size, only shorter, with silver eyes and fair hair. My father also told me that Ellylon are not to be trusted. They have an old hatred for Eirrenians."

Collun began clearing dead ivy from their camp. He thought back on what he knew about the Ellylon.

Before Amergin and his people came to Eirren, the land had belonged to the Ellylon, whom Amergin dubbed the Fair Folk for their bright hair and silver eyes. They had lived in the land since memory began.

There was no bloodshed when Amergin came to the land and renamed it Eirren. The Ellylon continued to call it by their own name, Tir a Ceol, and if they did not welcome the Eirrenians, at least they made room for them.

But soon after coming to the land, Amergin, with his winning ways and a streak of something very like Ellyl blood in his veins, won the heart of the beautiful daughter of the Ellyl king. The two were wed, forging a bond between the two races.

Despite the differences between them, Eirrenians and Ellylon lived together in peace. They even fought side by side when the land was threatened by the evil wizard Cruachan. It was only after Amergin died that the trouble began. A headstrong and distant young cousin of Amergin's seized control of the throne, banished his Ellyl wife, and tried to exert his power over the proud Ellylon. They resisted and war broke out between the two races. Scores of Ellylon and Eirrenians were slain in the conflict.

In disgust and horror, the Ellyl king made a swift and far-reaching decision. He removed his people and Tir a Ceol to the hidden places of the land, using old magic to obscure themselves from the Eirrenians they had come to despise. Since that time very few Ellylon had been seen by men. Indeed, many Eirrenians had come to believe that they did not exist at all and were merely the remnants of old superstition and legend.

"Yet this Ellyl saved our lives," Collun said to Brie, looking thoughtfully at the pale, exhausted face. "And at some cost to himself, it seems."

"I wonder how long he will sleep," said Talisen excitedly. "I have heard such tales of Ellylon and of their music. Think of the songs I could learn!"

Brie helped Collun clear away the rest of the vine from their camp. Collun had been worried it might grow again, but when he crossed to the other side of the hill, he found it lay dead and withered.

When they went to sleep that night, the Ellyl was deep in slumber, and when they awoke at dawn, he still had not stirred. His chest rose and fell in a gentle rhythm. The faol remained at his head, its white face alert and watchful.

"I hope he's not ill," Talisen said, looking down at the Ellyl's pale face with concern.

"We cannot stay here long," Brie said shortly. Soon after, she set off to scout for Scathians. While she was gone, Collun foraged for food.

When he returned, arms laden with ripe bilberries and hazelnuts, he found Talisen and the now-awake Ellyl laughing together as if they were old friends. The faol was calmly washing itself nearby.

Collun nervously approached the Ellyl. "Thank you," he said awkwardly, "for saving our lives."

The Ellyl nodded slightly, a half-smile on his face.

"He says it is called cro-olachan, or blood-drinker," broke in Talisen. "It climbs up your body, suffocating you, and pierces your flesh with thousands of tiny pointed thorns that are really roots. That's why we have those marks on our skin. It feeds on blood. It is very rare, he says, but he's been seeing more of it over the past year or so. His name is Silien. Silien, this is Collun." Collun extended his hand and the Ellyl took it.

Brie rode up shortly afterward and Talisen introduced her to the Ellyl as well. Silien examined her face intently. She grew uncomfortable under his gaze and spoke.

"We are in your debt, Ellyl. The animal with you, is it a faol?"

The Ellyl nodded. "She is Fara," he said. His voice was light and filled with music. "She told me she approves of you. But she wants to know why you disguise yourself as a boy."

Brie's cheeks flushed.

Talisen answered for Brie. "She says it's because her father treated her as a son. Her other name is

Breo-Saight because of her skill with bow and arrow, but I call her Flame-girl because of her temper. She was very angry when I saw through her disguise, so tread lightly. She does not want anyone to know."

Talisen turned to Collun. "I invited Silien to join us, and he said he would. He also said he may teach me Ellyl songs!" Talisen's enthusiasm was infectious.

"You are welcome," said Collun gravely, "but you should know that we are being pursued by Scathians and a morg."

"A morg?" Silien looked thoughtful. "Unusual. I have never seen a morg. In any case, I would like to join you, for a time."

Collun noticed from the corner of his eye that Brie's mouth grew tight. He sensed that she was not pleased.

When she spoke, though, her voice was neutral. "I saw no sign of the Scathians," she said. "But we should move on. We are still a day away from Eld."

As they set about breaking camp, taking care to obliterate all traces of their presence, Brie turned to the Ellyl. "What brings you into Eirren? It is not usual for Ellylon to travel among us."

"My father says I am unusual for an Ellyl."

"Really? Then do all the rest of you fly about on little gossamer wings, no bigger than the palm of my hand?" asked Talisen, kicking bracken over the sodden ashes of their campfire.

Silien laughed, shaking his head. "I am afraid we disappoint you."

"Not at all," he replied, "especially if you promise to teach me an Ellyl song."

"We shall see."

Later, when they had resumed their journey, the Ellyl on the pony with Talisen, Collun asked Brie why she had not wanted him to join them. Talisen and Silien had fallen some distance behind and were exchanging favorite riddles.

"It is what I said before. My father told me of Ellylon, of their hatred for us. And that they have their own reasons for the things they do. They are...changeable, he said. Like the direction of the wind on Eydon Heath."

"I see. And are Ellyl animals also not to be trusted?" He gazed pointedly down at the faol trotting along beside the mare.

"I have always liked animals," she replied stiffly. "I understand them better than I do people. Animals kill only to survive. Not like people." She leaned down and ran her hand along Fara's back. The faol's tail went up in pleasure.

They continued on in silence as Collun thought about what Brie had said. They were not so different, he and Breo-Saight. As she was drawn to animals, he was drawn to plants. Though people often surprised you, a green sprout always behaved the same. If you gave it sunlight, water, and fertilizer, it grew. It bore fruit or flower. When it died, there was a cause, be it drought, frost, scavenging animals, or disease. It did not turn away from you for no reason.

He was brought out of his reflections by the merry laughter of Talisen. He and the Ellyl had come up beside them.

"Riddle me this riddle," Talisen challenged with a grin.

"I come out of the earth,
I am sold in the market,
He who buys me cuts my tail,
Takes off my suit of silk,
And weeps beside me when I'm dead.

"So, what is it?" Talisen waited a flicker of a moment before bursting out, "Why, an *onion,* of course! I have never missed a riddle yet, have I, Collun?" Collun was on the verge of refreshing Talisen's memory when Brie stopped short.

"Look!" They had come to the top of a rise. Collun drew a deep breath. A mighty forest stretched both east and west below them, as far as the eye could see. The Forest of Eld.

Collun felt a wave of unease as he gazed down. Perhaps they should have taken their chances on the high road after all. But the kesil had said to stay away from it, and Brie knew of a path. . . .

"Is it possible the Scathians also know this path of yours, Brie?" he asked.

"It is possible," she admitted, "but not likely. It is a very old path and has fallen into disuse over the last twenty years or so. I learned of it from a woodsman who kept very much to himself. I did him a service and he repaid me thus."

The Ellyl suddenly spoke, an alert look on his face. "You say you are being pursued by a company on horseback?"

"Yes," answered Collun.

"I hear them," responded Silien.

"I don't hear anything," said Talisen.

"Ellylon have very good ears," the Ellyl replied.

"How far behind us?" asked Brie. "Can you tell?"

"Some distance. But they are coming fast."

Without another word Brie urged the mare into a run. The pony labored to keep pace as they sped down the slope of the moor.

They kept up a steady pace, and by twilight they had reached the forest.

"I'm afraid we will have to leave the horse and pony behind," Brie said, dismounting. "The forest is too dense. I hope they will be able to find their way back to the Traveler's Rest." Collun swung off the mare, and he and Brie began unpacking their belongings from the animal's back.

"Perhaps I can assist them," said the Ellyl, as he and Talisen also dismounted.

"How?"

"I know a song of returning. It guides lost animals back to their homes."

"Can you really do that with a song?" said Talisen, his eyes wide. "Will you teach it to me?"

"I don't suppose you know a song that will rid us of Scathians altogether," Brie said, pointing suddenly at the horizon.

Outlined against the darkening sky and standing at the very spot where the companions had first sighted the Forest of Eld rose more than a dozen figures on horseback.

Though the riders were far away, they were clearly Scathians. And the tall, cloaked figure was almost certainly the morg. They began to move forward, swooping down the hill at high speed.

"Have they seen us?" Collun asked.

"It is hard to know. The dark and the trees may obscure us. But the path should be close by," Brie said, scanning the edge of the forest.

"Silien, can you send animals anywhere you wish with your song?" asked Collun suddenly, his eyes on the riders on the moor.

"Within reason," replied the Ellyl with a half-smile.

"What about back to the high road?"

"Yes, I could do that."

"In this light it may throw the morg off," said Collun. "If he sees the animals heading toward the road, he may be fooled into following them."

"Yes," said Brie, her voice edged with excitement. "It might work. That is, *if* the Ellyl truly can sing such a song."

Silien crossed to the two animals. Talisen tried to get close to listen, but the Ellyl waved him away. While Brie began searching for the forest path, Collun anxiously watched the progress of the riders. It was getting more and more difficult to see in the twilight.

He could faintly hear the music of Silien's voice, though he could not decipher any words.

Suddenly the animals bolted, galloping along the forest's edge, away from the travelers.

"Well done!" cried Talisen.

"They will go as far as the high road, then will follow it back to this inn you spoke of," said Silien. He looked paler than before.

Collun could no longer see the Scathians. Night had fallen and the moon's light was dimmed by cloud cover.

"This way," Brie called out. She gestured for them to

follow. They walked quickly through the trees, moving in the opposite direction from the galloping animals.

They had been traveling no longer than an hour when Brie stopped short. She pointed at the faint beginning of a path.

Silien turned slightly and his face wore a listening expression. "It worked," he said simply.

They looked at him inquiringly.

"The riders have turned and are following the animals."

"Thank Amergin!" exclaimed Talisen.

"It may not take them long to discover they have been tricked," warned Brie. "Come." And she led them into the Forest of Eld.

As the others went ahead, Collun hesitated. Something about the forest filled him with a dread he couldn't shake. As he gazed fixedly at the path, the feeling of foreboding grew more and more intense.

Then he heard the harsh call of a bird. The sound was unmistakable. A scald-crow.

Collun ran blindly down the path. The cries of the scald-crow grew louder, echoing in his ears.

His three companions were far ahead of him on the path, though it had not seemed more than a few seconds that he had been standing alone at the forest's edge. He rubbed at the numb spot on his forehead as he ran. He had not felt the cold sensation in days, but he felt it now.

He caught up to Brie. "A scald-crow," he said breathlessly. "It may have seen me." Collun could read the alarm in her face.

They made their way as fast as they could through the darkness.

"Can we not have a torch?" asked Talisen after stumbling heavily over a tree root.

"Too risky," Brie replied.

They journeyed on silently, Brie leading them. Some hours before dawn they paused to rest, eating a quick meal. Then they slept until the sun rose, taking turns keeping watch. There was no further sign of the scald-crow.

After a light breakfast of bilberries, hazelnuts, and water, they resumed their journey. The sun filtered through the branches, and for the first time they could see their surroundings.

Everything, from the decayed leaves and pine needles at their feet to the wrinkled gray bark of the large tree trunks surrounding them, looked ancient, as though the forest had stood there since time began. It was also very quiet—unnaturally so. There were no birds calling to one another. There was only the soughing sound of a faint breeze stirring the leaves of the trees.

When the companions spoke, their voices held a dull, muted tone that weighed heavy on the ear. Even Silien's musical voice sounded flat, and Talisen's usually merry laugh began to sound melancholy. They soon stopped talking entirely.

The trees grew closer together the farther they traveled into the forest, and the denseness of the branches and trunks made the going difficult.

It quickly became impossible to see the sky through the close-woven ceiling of branches, and without the sun as a guide, they had to rely solely on the path winding before them.

The faint breeze died. The air was stagnant and

musty, as if it had been held in place by the canopy overhead for many hundreds of years. And perhaps because the air was so thick, they began to move more slowly. Their legs were heavier, and the packs they carried felt leaden.

The Ellyl and his faol seemed to be less affected than the others.

"We Elyllon breathe differently," Silien said when questioned by an irritated Talisen. "For example, we can stay underwater much longer than humans."

Collun suddenly realized that was what it felt like—like trudging along underwater.

"It was not so when I came through Eld before," Brie said in a puzzled voice.

"Was it a different time of year?" suggested Talisen. "Perhaps it is the weather."

Brie shook her head, unsatisfied.

As night fell, the focus of Collun's unease shifted from the possible pursuit by scald-crows and Scathians to the forest itself. The path became more difficult to follow and the trees took on contorted, frightening shapes in the darkness.

They called a halt and listlessly ate more bilberries and hazelnuts, washing them down with carefully apportioned swallows of water. They had not come across a stream since entering the forest. No one had the energy to speak, and for the first time during the journey, Talisen did not bring out his harp after the meal. They slept fitfully, and when they set out again, none felt rested.

Brie continued to lead, carefully trying to hold them to the path even though it kept thinning out and disappearing for stretches at a time. Collun began to feel the forest was conspiring to make them lose their way. He told himself he was being superstitious and irrational, but the silence and thick air made it hard to keep his thoughts clear.

As they stumbled on, Collun saw trees he had never seen before. There was one with the silvery bark of a birch, but the leaves were wider than the palm of his hand and were shot through with red veins like the croolachan vine. He saw trees with double trunks and even one with three trunks that wound around each other, looking, for one horrible moment, like three giant snakes writhing upward. There were trees with long, evil-looking thorns growing out of their trunks and trees overgrown with lichen, creating grotesque shapes.

They journeyed on in this way for two days, though to Collun it seemed he had been in the Forest of Eld for weeks, even months.

During the afternoon of the third day, Silien stopped abruptly. He looked as if he was listening very intently to something, then shook his head with a puzzled expression and resumed walking.

He did this several times, until Talisen asked in a querulous voice, "Just what is it you are listening to? The only sounds I can hear are the rumbling of my stomach and the crackling of my dry mouth."

Silien turned his silver eyes on Talisen and replied with a haughty look, "As I told you before, Ellylon can hear many times the distance of men."

"And what do you hear?" asked Collun, though the effort of forming those few words left him feeling drained. "Is it the Scathians?"

"No." Silien looked troubled. "I do not know what it is. Some kind of animal. Wait"—he held up his hand—"It comes faster now." His face was pale.

At first none of them could hear anything, but gradually their human ears could make out the crashing sounds of something moving through the forest. It was heading toward them.

The Ellyl's silver eyes were wide and staring, as if he could not believe what he was hearing. "Moccus!" he said, horror in his voice. The name meant nothing to Collun and Talisen, but Brie's face went white.

"It cannot be," she said.

Silien did not answer. He was already running.

"Climb!" Brie said, looking wildly around. Fara was already halfway up the trunk of the nearest tree. But most of the trees around them wore their branches high on the trunk, offering none low enough for them to grab. The crashing sound drew nearer.

The company scattered. As he ran, Collun saw a large shape hurtle into the clearing they had just abandoned. The glimpse he got as he fled filled him with terror. It was an enormous wild boar. It looked to be nearly six feet long and was all white, the color of bleached bones. Above the long pink-rimmed snout with its protruding yellow tusks there was nothing.

The boar was eyeless.

EIGHT

Moccus

When it reached the clearing, the boar ground to a halt and blindly sniffed the air.

Collun grasped his dagger. The stone seemed to glow in the dim green light of the forest.

The boar's snout suddenly swung in his direction. Then, pawing the ground with its thick front legs, it catapulted itself into motion, moving with a speed that belied its huge girth. It was headed directly for Collun.

Collun's legs pumped and his breath came in short gasps. The animal was getting closer and closer. Collun desperately scanned the trees he passed, looking for one with branches low enough for him to swing himself out

of the boar's reach. But even the lowest branches were too high.

The boar was closing on him. Collun realized he could never outrun it. He spun around, holding his dagger in front of him. The animal slowed, then came to a complete stop.

Collun watched in horror as the boar raised its hideous, eyeless face and once again sniffed the air. He could see black bristles standing out on the gleaming bone white skin. It slowly began to paw the ground, and flecks of foam dripped from the glistening pink snout.

Collun clutched the dagger tightly in his hand as if to wring courage from its handle, but it was hopeless. He did not know how to use a dagger.

Then, behind the boar, Collun saw Breo-Saight. Her bow was to her shoulder, and she let fly an arrow. It stuck in the animal's back. The boar gave a snort and kicked back with its rear legs. And then it charged.

Collun ran. He could feel the animal's hot breath on the back of his legs, and he desperately leaped up at the trunk of the nearest tree. There were no branches to grab, but fear gave him strength, and he shimmied several feet up the trunk and clung there, his heart racing.

The boar reared up and sliced at his legs with its tusks. Collun felt the skin on his calf open. He fought back a scream. Yet he managed to hold fast to the tree and was even able to inch higher up the trunk so that he was out of the animal's reach.

It circled the tree several times, rearing up at Collun, just missing his feet. It paused, sniffed again, and then stood still. Waiting.

Collun saw Brie again, this time with Talisen beside

her. Brie let fly three arrows in quick succession. But though they all found their mark, the boar just snuffled and twitched its thick white skin, as if flicking an annoying fly. It continued to wait.

Blood dripped from Collun's calf, and he felt himself weakening. He knew his arms would soon give out. The boar knew it, too. Collun thought he could hear Talisen calling out for Silien.

Brie's arrows had no effect. She shouted at the animal and waved her arms, trying to draw it from Collun's tree. She moved closer to the boar. It sniffed and turned toward her, but it did not move. Collun slid down an inch, the bark scraping his face and hands. His arms were aching and his leg throbbed.

Brie moved closer, a blade now visible in her hand. Talisen was not far behind. The boar moved a step toward them, its snout in the air.

"No," Collun screamed. "Go back!" He let go of the tree and hit the ground with a thud. The enormous creature deftly swung around on its short legs. There was only an arm's length between them. The boar charged again.

In desperation Collun hurled his dagger. Then the vast white body was on him, and the evil cloying smell of the animal's hot breath filled his nose.

Collun's last conscious thought was of Emer's face as she pressed the lucky stone into his palm.

Collun dimly perceived that something heavy was being rolled off him. His leg throbbed. For a moment he could not remember where he was. Then he heard Silien's musical voice and an abrupt reply from Brie. Collun opened his eyes and saw the still figure of the enormous boar lying on its side. He blinked twice, not believing what he saw. Out of the creature's forehead protruded the handle of the dagger that had been a trine. The lucky stone gleamed almost white.

A grim-faced Brie was pulling her arrows out of the boar's hide, using leaves to wipe off the red-black blood. Silien leaned over Collun's leg, peering at the wound in his calf. Talisen hovered anxiously behind the Ellyl.

"It is deep, but not too deep," Silien was saying.

"Is it . . . can it truly be dead?" said Collun weakly.

All three heads turned toward him in surprise.

"You are awake," replied Brie, relief etched on her face. "Yes. It is dead." She reached over and pulled the dagger from the boar's forehead. A trickle of blood flowed down over the grotesque eyeless face. Collun shuddered. Brie wiped the blade and handed it to Collun.

"You are a better marksman than I," she said.

Collun shook his head in wonder. "No. I just threw it. The blade found its own mark."

"This wound needs cleaning," said Silien, and Collun clenched his teeth as the Ellyl carefully swabbed the bloody gash. "I will cleanse it if you can find me water to heat."

"We are low on water, Ellyl." Brie's voice was cold. Through the fog of pain, Collun wondered why.

"You were about to tell us, Silien—what in Amergin's name was that hideous thing?" broke in Talisen. "You called it Moccus?"

The Ellyl nodded. He was holding a piece of cloth firmly against Collun's wound in an attempt to stop the flow of blood. "I was wrong," he replied. "Though not far wrong. Moccus was a giant boar, a legendary evil thing from the Cave of Cruachan. But it was black, not white. Do you know of the wizard Cruachan?"

"Of course. I know many songs about Cruachan," responded Talisen. "There was one I heard once about a giant boar, but it was from a bard who hit notes that made my fingernails ache, so I did not learn it."

"Do you know of Cruachan's cave?" asked Silien.

"The creatures came from the cave. But what were its origins?"

Keeping up the pressure on Collun's wound, Silien spoke. "When Cruachan carved his fortress in the Mountains of Mourne, there was one deep cavern that no one was allowed to enter. The wizard worked there, night and day, weaving spells, testing his powers against those of nature herself. Finally he found what he had been searching for: the ultimate power, the secret to making life. No one had done so before, nor has since.

"He used this power to create fantastic creatures, each one misshapen, powerful, and utterly evil. I do not know how many. Moccus, the black boar, was one; and there was a vast and evil Firewurme—Naid, it was called; and Arracht, half-man, half-bear; and others. It is said that ultimately one of his own creatures turned on Cruachan and killed him. But the legacy he left was an evil one, for these creatures roamed the land, mindlessly destroying all that stood in their path. The rivers of this country ran red with the blood of Ellylon and Eirrenians alike.

"It took the combined powers of Dil, Amergin, and Mannan to hunt down the creatures and seal them in the Cave of Cruachan. With the Cailceadon Lir, they wrought a powerful spell of binding at the entrance to the cave. It has held through time, and I did not think it could be broken, but when I heard the sound of what I knew to be a giant boar and sensed the evil that came from it, I thought only of Moccus. But, as you see, this boar is white—though, like Moccus, it is eyeless. Moccus did not need eyes; he had a sense of smell better even than Ellylon. This may be the mate of Moccus. His sow."

Collun's mind was hazy, and only scattered bits of what the Ellyl said filtered through. Brie had been watching Collun. She spoke abruptly, rising to her feet.

"I think our time would be better spent in finding water. And the path, which I fear we have lost."

"I will go," Silien offered, touching his ears. "I am well equipped for finding running water. And I shall look for the path as I search."

"And if you find it, it will no doubt be the last we see of you." Brie's voice was like a slap in the face, and Collun opened his eyes in surprise.

"Brie . . . ," Talisen protested.

She swung around to face him and Collun. "You did not see the Ellyl when the boar came. He fled, with no thought but of saving his own skin. And we all have heard much of the Ellyl's superior sense of hearing, but when we called to him for aid, he did not come."

The Ellyl's eyes widened in surprise. "Of course. I am young with many years yet to live. I have no desire to shorten my life on your account."

Brie gave a snort of disgust. "Nobly spoken. You see? Ellylon are not to be trusted."

"He saved our lives once before," pointed out Talisen.

"Yes, and I wondered then as I do now. Why did you

save us from the cro-olachan?" Brie turned again to the Ellyl, her eyes icy.

"I heard the music and your voices singing. It pleased me. I wished to see where it came from, and I found I had to uncover you first. Now I will see if I can find water, for I, too, am thirsty." And Silien left them, with an unperturbed smile.

"He has fine taste in music, you have to grant that, Brie," Talisen said, his eyes twinkling.

"I do not trust him," Brie said stubbornly. She then looked with concern at Collun, whose skin had turned a shade paler. His eyes had closed again.

"You judge the Ellyl harshly," said Collun through dry lips.

"Perhaps, but just to be sure I will also look for the path and for water." She left the clearing.

Talisen set about making a campfire, while Collun dozed.

Not long after, Silien returned. He was carrying two skin bags filled with water. "I found a brook," said Silien, "but it is dying and will not serve us long. Where is the Flame-girl?"

"She went in search of the path," answered Talisen.

The Ellyl's eyes flickered, but all he said was, "I hope she has more luck than I."

While Talisen held one of the skin bags up to Collun's lips, Silien brought a pan of water to a boil. He then opened a leather bag he wore at his waist. From it he drew out an assortment of items: a handful of small, dark green leaves; a wooden spool with a silvery, translucent thread wound around it; and a needle made of something black and shining.

Silien used the boiled water to cleanse Collun's wound and then the black needle. But first he told Collun to crush two of the leaves between his teeth.

"These will help you bear the pain," said the Ellyl. The leaves tasted bitter, but they numbed Collun's tongue and made him drowsy. Everything was muffled, including the pain in his leg. He wondered sleepily what herb it was.

Silien slid the gossamer thread into his needle and made a knot at the end. Then he expertly brought the two jagged edges of Collun's wound together and stitched his flesh as if it were a piece of torn cloth. When he came to the end of the gash, Silien tied another knot and cut the thread with his teeth.

Collun slept after that.

When he woke, he saw that Talisen and Silien also slept. Fara was pacing the clearing, looking uneasy, Collun thought. Brie had not returned. She had been gone long, and a stab of worry now pierced Collun's torpor. But his eyelids were heavy, and he was soon asleep again.

He woke again to the smell of a broth Silien was brewing over the fire. "Brie?" Collun said faintly.

"She has not returned," replied Talisen, bringing a cup of the broth to Collun's lips. Collun drank a few sips, then turned away.

"I am sure she'll be back soon," Talisen said, but he also looked worried.

"Someone is coming," said Silien, his eyes alert.

Soon after, Brie appeared in the clearing. She looked exhausted and discouraged. "I could not find the path," she said. "I will try again after some rest. How are you feeling?" she asked Collun.

He tried to speak, but his throat was dry and words would not come.

"We have to get him out of this cursed forest," said Talisen.

But Collun was too weak and feverish to travel, and they stayed in the clearing for a day and a night. They began to worry that there had been poisonous venom on the sow's yellowed tusks.

Brie made several more forays into the forest, but still could find no trace of the path.

"I don't understand it," she said upon returning from her last effort. "It is as if the forest wants to keep us here. I know it sounds foolish . . ."

Talisen was nodding. "No, I feel it, too. Like some evil spirit is watching us."

"We will find our way out," said Brie, abruptly getting to her feet. She glanced at Collun, who was awake and had been listening to their exchange. He struggled to sit up.

"We must go on," he said. "If . . . the forest . . . is closing in on us . . . we have to go somewhere . . . anywhere."

And so, not long after, they set forth. Without the path to guide them, Brie could only guess at the right direction. Talisen, Silien, and Brie took turns lending a shoulder for Collun to lean on as he limped along.

The forest seemed to get even denser as they moved forward. The gloom about them deepened.

They all felt unnaturally weary and stopped frequently, sinking to the ground with strength enough only to breathe. Collun was close to delirium. He slept at each stop and often woke sweating and wild-eyed, as if from a nightmare. They had filled every bag they had with water from Silien's dying brook, and they tried to conserve it, giving most to Collun.

Because it became almost impossible to distinguish day from night, they lost track of time, though Brie estimated that it had been four days since the attack of the boar. And still they could not find the path.

Then came a terrible moment. Brie abruptly stopped short with a sharp sound of dismay.

"What? What is it?" asked Talisen.

"We have passed this tree before. Yesterday. Or the day before. I can't remember." Brie pointed at a tree with an unusual bole that curved in the shape of a question mark. She dropped to her knees in exhaustion.

"You mean ... we've been going in circles?" Talisen moaned and leaned heavily against the tree. Silien gently lowered Collun to the ground, where the wounded boy promptly fell into a restless slumber.

"He cannot go much farther," the Ellyl said.

"None of us can," Brie answered. Listlessly they made camp. They were down to their last drops of water and had long since run out of food, subsisting on the few edible nuts and berries they were able to find.

"Lend me your harp, Talisen. Perhaps I can cheer us." The Ellyl held out his hand, and Talisen silently passed his harp to Silien.

Talisen asked dully, as though he could not remember why it was important, "You will sing an Ellyl song?"

Silien did not answer, but began to finger the harp strings. Beneath his hands the harmonies that shimmered forth were not like music as they knew it. The notes the Ellyl found were crystalline and pure, so pure they even penetrated the mantle of musty gloom that had oppressed them ever since they had entered the Forest of Eld.

Brie and Talisen both fell asleep.

The music wove its way into Collun's dreams. He was in a meadow back in Inkberrow. The tall grass brushed against his fingertips as he walked. A fresh breeze feathered his face, and there were purple wildflowers as far as the eye could see.

Silien sang on.

Abruptly Collun awoke. He saw that Talisen and Brie were just waking as well. Silien was watching them with his usual half-smile. His fingers were resting lightly on the harp strings.

"What did you do?" Brie's voice was sharp with suspicion.

"You needed sleep. Restful sleep. Do you not feel better for it?"

And Brie admitted she did. "I feel as though I have slept for days," she said in wonder.

"It was only several moments," replied Silien.

"You are a miracle worker, Silien," Talisen said. "But why didn't you do this before?"

"It takes much away from me," replied the Ellyl. "I keep that song as a last resort." And indeed Silien's face looked drawn and pale, as though the song had weakened him as much as it had strengthened them.

Collun saw that Brie was gazing at the Ellyl with a puzzled expression. He sensed she was confused by Silien—his coldness one moment and generosity the next.

"How do you feel, Collun?" asked Talisen.

"Better," he replied, though his leg still throbbed and his skin was hot.

"I'm afraid it will not last, but for a while the going will be a little easier," Silien said.

"Well, that's all very well and good," grumbled Talisen, "but I don't appreciate you knocking me out. I missed all the words to your song!"

"You would not have understood them," Silien responded. "I do not use words as you do."

They set out shortly after and made much better progress. But toward what, they knew not.

NINE

Crann

They had been walking a short distance when Brie abruptly stopped. "What was that?" she said.

"What was what?" asked Talisen.

"It was a flash of something—light, I think, only it was green..." She trailed off. "At least, I thought—" Her eyes stared ahead into the murk of the forest. "Yes, there it was again!"

The others peered in the same direction.

"I don't see anything," said Talisen.

"Nor I," Silien agreed, his voice soft with exhaustion.

"It was like the flicker of candlelight. And it was moving. I believe we should follow it," she announced unexpectedly.

"Follow it?" Talisen said. "Have you lost your wits? The rest of us can't even see the bloody— Oh!"

"You see it now?"

Talisen nodded slowly. "A will-o'-the-wisp," he murmured. "Brie, we cannot follow a will-o'-the-wisp. Surely you've heard tales of Gyl Burnt-tayle and how it leads travelers astray? We'd be certain to spend the rest of our days in the Forest of Eld were we to follow such a thing."

"I don't believe in superstitious tales," said Brie. "Nor do I believe it to be a will-o'-the-wisp. It is moving farther away. Come, or we'll lose it."

Talisen shook his head firmly. "I'll not be following Gyl Burnt-tayle..."

Collun listened to the two voices arguing back and forth, his eyes fixed on the irregular flashes of green light. Silien was sitting cross-legged beside Collun, his eyes closed.

"Let us follow the light," Collun said. He moved forward. Brie quickly stepped into the lead. Talisen helped Silien to his feet and, grumbling loudly to himself, fell in step with the other two. Fara brought up the rear.

So intent were they on keeping the elusive light in sight that they did not notice at first that the trees were thinning. But suddenly Talisen stopped dead in his tracks and, letting out an exclamation, pointed upward. They all looked up and through the branches of the trees, saw a patch of night sky. They had not seen the sky in days, or was it weeks? Collun no longer knew.

"We must be near the end of this blasted wood," said Talisen with a broad smile. "My apologies for doubting you and kindly old Gyl Burnt-tayle," he said to Brie, with a small courtly bow in her direction.

"I cannot see it anymore," said Brie, squinting at the trees ahead.

"Who cares? It has served us well. Come, on to Temair," Talisen said, putting an arm out to Silien, who was leaning against a tree.

As if to punctuate Talisen's words, a linnet somewhere nearby burst into song. The last time any of them had seen or heard a bird was the scald-crow Collun saw when they entered the Forest of Eld.

Through the fog of his fever, Collun felt a piercing burst of joy. To finally be free of this wretched forest! But his ears rang with a high-pitched buzzing sound, and his leg still throbbed. It took all his concentration just to set one foot ahead of the other. He paused for a moment to rest his leg, and his eye was caught by a small red finch winging to the top of a nearby tree. Unexpectedly Collun saw a flash of light in the night sky above. It was a different kind of light than the will-o'-the-wisp: a white angular thrust. Brie came up beside him.

"Do you need to rest?" she asked.

Collun shook his head then pointed to the sky. Brie looked up.

"Lightning," she said, with a puzzled look. "But I don't feel rain in the air. It must be far away."

A slight wind began to play with the dried leaves around their feet. The night air felt cool on Collun's hot skin.

Talisen noisily inhaled, then laughed. "I never thought I'd feel this way about a breath of fresh air.

Why, it tastes better than a mug of Job Wall's finest ale."

They pushed forward eagerly, unmindful of the far-off flashes in the sky above them.

Then suddenly, without any warning, a jagged splinter of light seared their eyes, and a dry thorn tree not twenty paces ahead of Silien was transformed into a pillar of hissing, leaping flame.

The tail end of a purple-white bolt of lightning shimmered through the flaming tree. Intense heat beat against the travelers' faces, and caustic smoke filled their mouths and noses.

Brie wrenched Collun's arm, pulling him back. They all began to run, retracing their steps into the forest. But the light breeze they had noticed earlier abruptly changed into a swirling, spinning maelstrom of wind that carried flame from tree to tree in the blink of an eye.

Before they knew it, a wall of fire was twisting around them in all directions. The dried leaves swirling up from the forest floor became flying motes of flame, like giant fireflies.

They kept running, trying to find a pathway through the fire wall as sparks rained down on them. An airborne ember scorched the hair on the right side of Collun's head. As they lurched one way and then another, they found they were trapped by a sea of flame rising up on all sides around them. They huddled together.

Suddenly Collun spotted something beyond the fire, something tall and green. For a moment he thought it was a tree that had somehow escaped the conflagration. But as he looked closer he saw that it was a man wearing a green cloak. The cloak billowed around his gaunt frame as the wind buffeted him. A gum tree nearby flared up with brilliant flame, and in the blinding light, Collun saw the man's face. He was an old man with a long, moon white beard, and his skin was deeply lined.

Collun had seen that face somewhere before. But where? Then a glowing cinder landed on his arm, and he had to beat at it frantically to keep from catching fire. When he looked back, he saw the old man had raised his arms above his head, one hand holding a long piece of wood, the other hand with the fingers splayed wide open.

The man's eyes were now closed, and he seemed to be concentrating deeply. His lips were moving, but Collun could not hear what he said. Then the green figure shouted at the top of his voice, "Muchtoir lasair!"

There was silence, then he cried out, "Fearthainne!"

And in that moment a drenching, powerful rain began to fall.

Collun and his companions looked at each other in wonder as great drops of water washed over their blackened faces and clothing. Huge billows of steam rose around them.

It was not long before the flames were completely extinguished and all they could hear was the hissing of damp, smoldering wood and the sound of the raindrops.

Collun's eyes were still on the old man, who had dropped his arms heavily to his sides. For a moment his body sagged. He looked ancient and ill.

But then his shoulders slowly straightened, and he stood erect again. His eyes looked directly into Collun's.

The kesil.

This figure in the green cloak was the wild man of the forest who had come into Collun's garden and told him he must leave Aonarach. Except that now his beard was smooth and untangled, and his cloak was clean and made of thick, rich cloth.

With an abrupt gesture the old man beckoned to Collun.

"He wants us to follow him," Collun said in a weak voice. The kesil had turned and was walking away from them with long, purposeful strides. Limping, Collun followed.

Brie, Talisen, and Silien exchanged glances, then fell into step behind Collun. Fara trotted along beside Brie.

They gingerly made their way through the twisted and blackened skeletons of burnt trees, their feet squelching through the soggy layers of ash and charred wood. Puffs of smoke wafted about their ankles.

They came again to the thorn tree that had been struck by lightning. All that remained was a jagged black stump. But not thirty paces beyond the stump the forest was miraculously intact, and were it not for the smell of smoke, they would not have known there had been a fire at all.

The kesil continued to walk. Collun focused all his remaining strength on keeping the green figure in sight. As before, the trees began to thin out. And it was not long before they were out of the Forest of Eld altogether.

Dawn was just breaking, and Collun could feel a faint warmth on his face from the autumn sun.

The old man had stopped at the edge of a large meadow and was waiting for them to catch up.

"Well met, Collun," said the kesil. He crossed to the

dazed boy, put his two hands on Collun's shoulders, and peered down at him. He said nothing for a moment, holding his eyes steady on Collun's. Collun could not read the old man's expression, but it had welcome in it, as well as concern.

The kesil spoke. "I see you took my advice and stayed clear of the high road." The corners of his mouth twitched slightly. "Only I might not have strayed into the deepest reaches of the Forest of Eld, were I you."

"A morg and some Scathians were pursuing us. Then there was a boar...and we lost the path. And the fire..."

"It does not matter. I found you yet. And perhaps some good will come of it."

"That's about as likely as a cuckoo song in January." Talisen stepped forward. "You are the kesil, aren't you? I must say, sir, you are not as I remember you."

The old man smiled and then spoke again to Collun. "You have chosen companions for your journey." He gazed around, lingering longest on the Ellyl and the faol. Then he gave a small nod as though satisfied.

Collun managed a faint smile. "In truth, they chose me."

The old man smiled back. "Even better."

"Who are you?" Talisen interrupted.

The kesil turned his blue eyes on Talisen. "I have had many names. Of late I am called Sen Crannach, but I answer to Crann."

"Crann?" Collun exclaimed. This was the name Emer had spoken. He opened his mouth to say something, but he was overcome by a wave of dizziness. He swayed.

Crann stepped forward, putting out a hand to steady

the boy. A trail of blood flowed down Collun's calf. The wound had reopened during the fire. The old man kneeled down and ran his long fingers over the silvery stitches in Collun's leg. "Ellyl stitchery...," he murmured to himself. He glanced up at Silien. "You do good work, though I can see you are young yet, Ellyl."

Collun thought Silien looked somewhat nettled by Crann's words, but the Ellyl said nothing.

"It looks ill. The boar did this?" the old man asked as he took a clean cloth and a small packet from inside his cloak. He rubbed salve on the cloth and held it against the wound. Talisen described the attack by Moccus's sow.

As Talisen spoke, Crann's face seemed almost to visibly age. Collun felt a cold stab of fear. When the old man spoke, his voice was weary beyond measure. "An eyeless boar...It is what I have feared. She has found a way to unseal the Cave of Cruachan."

He stared at the ground for several moments and then, recalling himself, he set about making a bandage of the cloth, affixing it to Collun's leg with two thin leather thongs. Then he rose to his feet and walked away from them. He supported himself with a long staff made of oak.

Crann stood motionless, looking up at the branches overhead. No one dared to speak.

Finally he turned back toward them and said with a deep sigh, "If it is done, it is done. We will make camp here."

They gathered wood for a fire, and Crann sparked the blaze with such ease Collun thought he must have used magic. He had not seen him use a teine stone.

The old man then passed around small dark blocks.

"Here, eat these." Crann smiled. "It is not mysterious, Talisen," he said as he caught the boy eyeing the block with curiosity. "Just honey, grain, and berries."

When they bit into their blocks, the taste was delicious. The sweet flavor of blueberries mingled with honey and cracked wheat. They ate quickly, thinking it would take many such blocks to make even a dent in their deep hunger; but, surprisingly, they felt full when they had finished just one. The buzzing in Collun's ears lessened, and his skin did not feel as hot.

"Your cloak," said Brie, "it is the same color as the light we followed. Did you send it?"

Crann nodded. "Until I could get to you myself. Although the fire very nearly outpaced me."

" 'Twas a narrow squeak, all right," said Talisen. "Are you a wizard?" he asked bluntly, licking the last crumbs from his fingers.

"I have been called so."

"Why do you disguise yourself as a kesil?"

"There are many reasons for disguise." His eyes rested lightly on Brie, and Collun realized that Crann knew her for who she was, too.

"There was a time when it was very nearly true," Crann continued, "when I was lost in madness, like a kesil. But that was long ago. And now, you need rest," said the wizard with a glance at Silien, whose eyes had already closed.

The exhausted travelers needed no further urging and all were soon quickly asleep.

Collun slept deeply for a time, but then his rest became fitful. Finally he rose and limped over to join Crann at the fire. The wizard was preparing a pan of hot chicory, sweetened with honey and apple.

"My mother spoke your name to me," said Collun slowly, as Crann poured him a cup of the steaming beverage.

"I know," the old man replied.

"She said you would explain."

Crann did not speak.

"Why did you come to me in the garden? What do you know of my mother and of Nessa? Why do the scald-crows follow us? And the morg?" Collun's words tumbled over one another.

Crann returned Collun's gaze, unblinking, but again Collun could not read what lay there. "Of your sister I know little except that she is in great danger."

"But she is alive?"

"I cannot be sure, but yes, I believe she is." He paused. "Your mother is very ill."

"More so than when I left?"

The wizard nodded, then spoke again, softly, and it was as if he could read Collun's thoughts. "It would avail you little to return home. Your sister is the one who needs you now."

Collun cried out, his voice shrill. "What is it? What is happening to me, to my family?"

Crann shook his head. "I made an oath to your mother and can say no more of her. Not now. But there are other things I can tell you, and, indeed, it has become vital that you know them. But first, I want to hear more of your journey since leaving Inkberrow. You spoke of scald-crows and of a morg?"

Collun related all that had befallen them during the past weeks as Crann listened closely.

"Urlacan. I have heard the name before." He shook his head, a grim expression on his face. "There is deep trouble in the land, Collun. Not just for you, but for all of Eirren."

"What's all this about trouble?" A yawning Talisen joined them at the fire. Crann poured him some of the sweetened chicory. Brie and Silien were awake as well, and after passing around more of the wheat-and-blueberry bars, Crann began to speak.

"Medb, the queen of Scath, grows restless with the peace forged fifteen years ago between Eirren and Scath. It is my belief she never planned to abide by the treaty. She agreed to it merely to give herself time. There is a hunger that drives the Queen of Ghosts. Like her ancestor Cruachan, she craves power—power over men and over nature herself."

Crann paused and rubbed his eyelids wearily. "As I said before, it seems that Medb has found a way to unseal the Cave of Cruachan. She waits now for the right moment, but with the power of the cave and its creatures behind her, she will surely destroy Eirren." The old wizard's voice was heavy with dread. "And Tir a Ceol as well," Crann added, his eyes on Silien. They all felt a chill and instinctively drew closer together.

"Surely there is something we can do?" demanded Talisen. "What of our champions? Our army?"

Crann shook his head. "For some time now Medb has been acting to remove that threat. I do not know if the news has reached Inkberrow, but in the past year many of Eirren's heroes have been murdered by faceless attackers. Or they have simply disappeared."

Collun felt Brie's body stiffen.

"We have heard of the disappearance of Cuillean," offered Talisen.

"Yes." The wizard's face was troubled. "Cuillean has not been seen in over a year. At first it was thought he had merely grown restless during peacetime and had taken to wandering, looking for adventure. But the time has grown long. It may be that he is dead. As are Laery and Conall and many others. I believe Medb and those that serve her are responsible for their murders."

Collun grew impatient. "But what has this to do with Nessa?"

"The scald-crows that follow you are from the Cave of Cruachan and, if I am right, they serve Medb. As does the morg."

"Of what interest is my journey to the queen of Scath?"

"You wear a blade on your belt. May I see it?" The wizard's voice was soft.

Collun silently handed him the dagger that had been a trine. The old man examined it, running his fingers lightly over the lucky stone. He handed it back, saying, "The blacksmith did good work."

Then his eyes shifted and he gazed abstractedly for several moments into the fire. Finally he spoke.

"Your mother gave you the stone in the handle." Though it had not been framed as a question, Collun nodded.

"Medb wants that stone."

Silien drew in his breath. The Ellyl's eyes were on Collun's dagger, and they glittered slightly.

"The Cailceadon Lir," he said softly. "Moccus's sow . . . I should have guessed."

Bewildered, Collun looked between wizard and Ellyl.

"The stone that lies in the handle of your dagger,

Collun," said Crann, "is the third shard of the Cailceadon Lir. Do you know of the Cailceadon Lir?"

Collun nodded slowly. "It is an ancient talisman. A
chalcedony. Talisen knows a song about it."

"Yes. Amergin used it to save Eirren from Cruachan
and his creatures," Talisen spoke up. "But that is all we
know of it."

"The earliest history of the chalcedony, or cailceadon
in the old tongue, is not known," began Crann, "but it
begins for us when an Ellyl named Lir found it lying
on the shore of the great Lake Erris. The stone was large
then, as large as his palm. When Lir found the stone
and lifted it, he felt a tingling in his hand and arms.

"I am not sure if I can explain this part so you will
understand, but there is something that happens in nature that is rare and unpredictable. It has to do with
convergence, with several things coming together in a
certain place over a period of time, and the effect is that
of concentration. The thing affected becomes more than
it was, denser and more powerful. This stone was such
a thing. I do not know where the chalcedony originally
lay—perhaps at the confluence of four rivers, or at the
center of the overlapping root systems of four trees. But
there was power in the stone. Wizards recognize and
seek such objects. We use them to focus and deepen the
power we already possess. My staff is such an object.

"Lir was not a wizard; not all Ellylon have the gift
of draoicht, or magic, as you call it. But Lir sensed something in the stone and believed it would bring him luck.
It did, and the cailceadon became a family treasure, to
be passed down to his firstborn, and every firstborn after
that.

"In the time of Amergin's rule it came into the hands of Lir's great-grandson, a man named Aed. And Aed had a close friend who was called Cruachan. Like Aed, Cruachan was Ellyl, and yet he had eyes that were not Ellyl. Instead of being all silver, there was a ring of brown around the iris.

"Cruachan was not at that time known to be a wizard, though he knew it himself. He was handsome and possessed great charm, but his charm masked an evil heart within. Aed showed his friend the cailceadon handed down by his ancestor Lir. Cruachan immediately sensed the great power in the smoky blue stone. He said nothing and did nothing, but he waited for his moment.

"Aed eventually wed an Eirrenian woman, which was not uncommon during that time. She bore him two sons. Cruachan was a frequent visitor and trusted friend and was even named athair, second father, to their firstborn son.

"But on the eve of the day on which Aed had planned to pass on the Cailceadon Lir to his eldest son, Cruachan came in the night and murdered Aed. He stole the stone and fled to a fortress he had secretly built for himself, high up in the Mountains of Mourne in North Eirren.

"There Cruachan was able to tap into the power of the Cailceadon Lir. He twisted the stone to his own evil ends. You already know the rest—how Cruachan used his power to forge the kingdom of Scath and to create his creatures. But Amergin was able to steal back the cailceadon.

"He and Mannan and Dil used the stone's power to call the creatures back to their cave and to seal them inside—forever, they thought.

"But the power unleashed in the sealing was so intense that the stone shattered. Into three shards.

"One shard was lost when it fell into the river that ran below Cruachan's cave. The two remaining shards were taken back to Eirren. One remains in a well-guarded spot known only to the king and queen of Eirren. It is one of the country's greatest treasures, though most Eirrenians do not even know of its existence.

"As to the second shard, Amergin took it with him on one of his voyages, where he foolishly lost it to a lady with more beauty than goodness. I believe that is the stone lying in the handle of your dagger, Collun."

Collun looked down at it in wonder. "But that all happened hundreds of years ago. How did my mother come to have the stone?"

Crann was silent.

"You cannot tell me."

"I must honor my vow to your mother."

"But how has Medb unsealed Cruachan's cave?" Talisen broke in.

Crann nodded grimly. "The lost shard of the Cailceadon Lir, the one that fell into the river—I believe Medb has found it."

"I still don't understand," said Collun. "What does the Cailceadon Lir have to do with Nessa? Where is she?"

"I do not know, but I think Medb has her."

Collun closed his eyes, tensing his body against the fear that coursed through him. "Where?"

"I do not know," the wizard repeated. "I have sought her, but as yet I can find no trace. It is you who must find her, Collun. Come. I cannot stay with you much longer." He kicked dirt on the campfire, dousing it, then began once more to walk.

They traveled at a brisk pace most of the day. Collun felt better—the buzzing in his ears was now completely gone, and his leg throbbed less. They made camp that night in a small glade of oak and hazel trees. Crann passed around more of his blueberry blocks.

"There is a path just over the next rise. It will take you to the road leading into Temair. It shouldn't take more than a few days to get to the city," said Crann.

"Oh, and I almost forgot to mention that on my journey toward the Forest of Eld, I chanced upon a band of Scathians with a morg leading them, a morg who sounds very much like your Mister Urlacan. They were traveling along the edge of the wood, looking for a path, I believe. But it happened that after I passed them, they were beset by bad weather." The wizard smiled. "A fog descended on them. It was so dense I am sure they could not see a hand's length before them. Not surprisingly, it caused a fair amount of confusion and fright among them, and the last I saw, they were headed east. By now they must be halfway to the Eastern Sea." Collun and Brie exchanged a look of wonder and relief, while Talisen laughed out loud.

"I hope they fall in," he said happily.

Before going to sleep, Crann inspected Collun's leg again. He removed the bandage carefully and traced the stitches with his long, dry fingers. As Collun watched, the translucent threads melted away. Crann then took stalks of something resembling purple nettles from inside the folds of his green cloak and rubbed them over the wound. Though it stung for a few moments, Collun felt an easing, as if a deep splinter were being pulled out.

Collun slept deeply that night. He dreamed that Crann sat beside him in the moonlight and said, "Be well, spriosan."

When they awoke the next morning, Crann was gone. He had left behind a small pile of the food blocks on a bed of leaves.

They easily found the path the wizard had spoken of and had a pleasant three-day journey, with the sun shining and a cool breeze at their backs.

As the sun sank on the second day, they came upon the road to Temair. The battlements of the city stood out against the darkening sky. They stopped for a moment and stared at it. Then Talisen let out a whoop of laughter.

"We made it," he said, clapping Collun enthusiastically on the back. "We made it to Temair!"

Collun smiled back at his friend but could not share his excitement. Nessa was not in Temair, and he did not know where to find her.

They made camp soon after, and the next morning embarked upon the road to the city. They encountered many travelers on the road as they passed through two villages that lay nestled in Temair's protective shadow.

Then they came to the gates of Temair. The city was surrounded by a massive wall of white stone. As they entered the gates, the noise inside overwhelmed them. It was the noise of voices raised, cart wheels clattering along the cobblestone pavement, and the squeals, honks, brays, and barks of the many animals that roamed the streets.

They made their way through jostling bodies. Everywhere they looked they saw something new. The buildings were mostly two-storied and constructed of the same thick white stone as the surrounding wall. They were hung with signboards advertising the services of candlemakers, weavers, furnituremakers, bakers. The small band of travelers passed a smithy, and though the sounds and smells were familiar to Collun, it was four times the size of Goban's.

Talisen stopped in front of the doorway of a harpmaker. He gazed transfixed at the signboard, which depicted an exquisite harp with a pillar carved in the shape of a salmon.

Silien seemed fascinated by this city built by men. His golden head swung from side to side as he took it all in. Collun noticed that the Ellyl and the faol received many openmouthed stares.

As widow of a slain champion, Collun's aunt Fial had been given living quarters in the royal dun, under the protection of the king and queen. Brie, who had been to Temair before, led the way. Then they rounded a corner and got their first sight of the dun. It was also crafted of white stone and was built on a steep outcrop of rock, rising high above the other buildings of Temair. A tall, castellated outer rampart encircled the dun itself, and entrance was provided through a massive set of iron doors. Three slender turrets of different heights surrounded one wide central turret. Collun was awed by the dun's vastness, and he steeled himself to approach one of the men who guarded the entrance.

Though he eyed their scorched and ragged clothing with curiosity, the guard cordially ushered them inside the gates when Collun mentioned the widow Fial. Staring at the silver-eyed Ellyl, he bade them wait. He returned soon after with Quince, the wiry, heavy-browed servingman whom Fial had sent to pick up Nessa in Inkberrow.

Quince recognized Collun. A shadow passed over his face, but he gave a terse nod of welcome and asked them to follow him. The guard reluctantly watched them go. He could hardly wait for his meal break to tell the other guards that an Ellyl and his faol had come to the royal dun.

TEN

Temair

Collun looked about him with interest as they passed through a serene grass-covered courtyard and then entered the dun itself. He had expected the inside to be dark, but it was full of light emanating from a number of windows cut high in the white stone walls. The ceilings were also high and covered with painted designs. They seemed to be the sort of pictures that told a story. Collun wished he could stop and look at them, but Quince was leading them on at a rapid pace.

Collun was surprised to see how clean and bright everything was, unlike their cottage in Inkberrow with its small windows and dirt floors. For the first time Collun thought about the choice Emer had made to leave

Temair and marry Goban. Why would she wish to leave this world of light and color?

After climbing a long flight of stone steps, they entered a large room. It was simply furnished with the exception of an exquisite tapestry that covered one entire wall. Worked in threads of silver, red, and green, it depicted Ana, the creator of Eirren, pulling the waters of her rivers up out of the Well of Connla. Silien immediately walked up to it, his eyes shining in appreciation.

As soon as he had closed the door behind him, the servingman turned and spoke to Collun. His face was unreadable.

"My mistress is very ill."

"I'm sorry," Collun replied with concern. "What is her illness?"

"It was the shock of the girl's disappearance that brought it on. She weakened then and has been wasting since."

"Who cares for her?"

"Myself. And the dun healers. But there is little enough to be done."

"May I see her?"

"Aye. But she will not know you. Why have you come?"

"I have come to look for my sister."

"She is gone."

"But where? Do you know?"

"Nay. Nobody does. She just disappeared." He paused, then said briskly, "I will set up pallets for you in the next room. There is a fire burning, as well as water for washing." Quince ushered them into the adjoining room, but Collun stayed behind.

"I would speak further with you," he said. The serv-ingman nodded, and after making sure the others had all they needed, he returned to the main room.

"The queen will wish to see you. Fond of the girl, she was," Quince said. "Can I get you something to drink or eat?"

"No," answered Collun. "But you can tell me about my sister. About what happened when she came here."

"Very well," responded Quince. "Neither the queen, nor anyone else, knew where the girl came from or who her people were. My mistress told them she was the daughter of an old friend with too many children, who lived in a small town on the southern coast. I was the only one who knew the truth, because I was the one sent to fetch your sister from Inkberrow. My mistress swore me to silence, and she told the girl when she came that she must never mention Inkberrow or her people while she was here."

"Do you know why?" Collun asked, remembering the words Emer had spoken when he himself left Inkberrow.

"Nay. But my mistress held her tongue, even when the girl disappeared. She pretended to send a messenger to the town Carrick on the southern coast, but secretly sent one to Inkberrow instead. She blamed herself for what happened to the girl." The man's face was drawn with worry. Collun could see he was devoted to Fial.

"Take me to her."

In his aunt's sickroom, Collun looked down at a pale face with purple rings under the eyes and lank gray hair trailing over the pillows. Fial's eyes were shut and her breathing shallow. Her mouth was thin, and her fingers lying on top of the bedclothes twitched occasionally. Collun barely recognized the plump, self-satisfied woman who had visited them in Inkberrow less than a year ago. "I know some herb lore," said Collun. "Perhaps...?"

"The dun healers have tried every remedy known in Temair."

"I understand," Collun replied. "Still, there is an herb called golden wood avens; I have been told it grows only in the southern reaches, below the Haw River. I have it with me."

Quince was silent a moment, then said, "Try your herb lore."

Collun quickly set to work and soon was pouring a posset of golden wood avens into his aunt's mouth. Quince watched him closely.

For some hours Collun kept a vigil by Fial's bedside, but she showed no change. Finally, at Quince's urging, he left the darkened room. He joined his companions, who were all fast asleep on the pallets Quince had set up for them. Fara was nestled at Silien's head.

Collun did not stop even to wash his face and hands, which still bore traces of soot from the fire in Eld. He took off his outer jersey and unlatched the dagger from his belt, stowing it carefully in his pack. Then he slid under a soft coverlet, his mind numbed by exhaustion.

They all slept late and woke to the smell of hot grannach, which Quince had brought for their morning meal. Fial's condition was little better that day, although after several more doses of Collun's posset, Quince claimed her breathing was easier and deeper.

Midway through the afternoon, Quince told Collun that the queen had been informed of his arrival, and as the servingman had predicted, she wished to meet

Nessa's brother. The king had recently departed with a small army for the border between Eirren and Scath to investigate the rumors of trouble there. His two eldest sons had accompanied him.

As Quince ushered him through a set of carved doors leading into the queen's rooms, Collun had a sudden longing to be back in Inkberrow, kneeling in his garden with dirt under his fingernails and the sun on his neck. He did not know how to speak to a queen.

They entered a large, bright room with brilliant and unusual cloth hangings covering most of the walls. A tall woman holding a muddy boot rose from a chair to greet Collun. She had green eyes and long red-brown hair that sprung wildly from her head. There were smudges of dirt on the pale skin of her cheeks.

"You are Nessa's brother. Collun, is it? Welcome to Temair." With a warm smile she made a move to grasp his hand, but then realized her hand was as muddy as the boot she held. "Forgive me. I have been riding, and I must have been thrown into the mud a dozen times. Please sit." She gestured toward a chair. She sat across from him, setting down the boot and wiping her hands on a cloth.

"I am deeply concerned about your sister, Collun. I am fond of Nessa, and I think she was happy here. We did everything in our power to find her, but we turned up nothing."

"I thank you for all you did, Your Majesty," said Collun awkwardly.

The queen gave a smile. "Please, call me Aine. So, you have come all the way from Carrick, on the southern coast? It must have been a long journey."

Collun did not speak for a moment. To speak the

truth would mean breaking his promise to Emer. Finally he simply nodded. After all, it *had* been a long journey.

"Nessa did not go back there, back to her family?"

Collun shook his head, feeling foolish and tongue-tied. Though her manner was warm, Collun could not forget he spoke to the queen of Eirren. It made him uncomfortable to be dishonest with her.

"It was such a blow to everyone here. And there have been so many troubles of late." The queen's green eyes wore a worried look. "And Fial? She is no better, I understand."

Collun shook his head again.

"I am glad you have come. She has no kin, you know. Her husband, Lud, died in the Eamh War."

Collun's hands shook slightly as he asked, keeping his voice carefully neutral, "Had Lud no family?"

"He did once, but they are all dead as well. He had a lovely sister. Emer, she was called. She and I were great friends. She died long ago. I still miss her." The queen's face was sad. Collun's heart beat faster, and he was about to speak when a young man came sweeping through the door.

The newcomer was strong-limbed and handsome, with a natural grace and air of authority that had the immediate effect of making Collun feel clumsy.

"Mother, Lord Bricriu has just arrived in Temair," he announced to the queen before his eyes fell on Collun.

Aine looked surprised but not displeased. "Gwynedd, I want you to meet Collun. He is brother to Nessa. Collun, my youngest son, Gwynedd."

The youth took Collun's hand in a muscular grip. "Welcome, Collun. Your sister is sorely missed. We must have uncovered every stone between here and Bricriu's dun in our search for her, but to no avail." The young man looked fierce, as though he took their failure personally.

"Bricriu," said Collun. "Fial wrote of him."

"Lord Bricriu took a special interest in Nessa when she arrived in Temair," said Queen Aine. "He offered to host her coming-of-age banquet. And we were all gathered at Bricriu's dun, which is less than a day's journey from Temair, when the tragedy occurred. Among all of us, I believe Bricriu took it the hardest. I am glad he has chosen this day to visit, for it will give you a chance to meet him. I am sure he will wish to lend you his assistance. As do we all."

"Yes," chimed in Gwynedd. "If there is any way I can be of service, do not hesitate to ask."

"Thank you, Prince," Collun responded stiffly.

"It grows late," said the queen, rising from her chair. "I hope you and your companions will join us tonight in the banquet hall."

"Thank you, Your Maj—Aine," Collun said, flushing and wishing he had Talisen's easy way with words.

"Oh, and Collun," Queen Aine said, a spark coming into her eyes, "I have heard an Ellyl travels with you."

"Yes."

"I have never met an Ellyl," mused the queen. "Will you tell him I am greatly looking forward to it?"

Collun nodded. He then followed Prince Gwynedd back to Fial's quarters, where they parted with another bone-cracking handshake and Gwynedd's enthusiastic pledges of assistance in the quest.

"The queen has invited us to the banquet hall

tonight," Collun told his friends, who were gathered in the main room. "She looks forward to meeting an Ellyl," he added with a glance at Silien.

"Is your queen beautiful?" the Ellyl asked.

Collun thought of the tall woman with the unruly hair and the muddy hands, and he hesitated. "I think so. She is very kind."

"Dining with the queen," broke in Talisen, giving a strum to his harp strings with a flourish. "If they could only see us back in Inkberrow."

Brie spoke quietly. "I will not join you tonight, if you will excuse me."

"Why not?" asked Talisen.

"I would be more comfortable here sharing bread with Quince. Please give my apologies to the queen."

Collun looked at Brie with curiosity, but her face was shadowed and revealed nothing.

At the appointed hour, which was marked by a short fanfare of trumpets, Collun, Talisen, and the Ellyl made their way to the banquet hall. Fara had surprised Silien by choosing to stay behind with Brie.

The banquet hall was a long rectangular room alight with hundreds of candles and hung with enormous tapestries. Many long wooden tables were already lined with members of the court, who filled the room with the sound of their chatter and laughter. The queen had set aside places at her own table for the new arrivals, and she rose now to greet them.

She was much altered from when Collun had last seen her. Her wild hair was now smooth, and it flowed from her head in shimmering, flame-colored waves. It was bound at the top by a circlet of sparkling green gems that echoed the color of her eyes.

Silien bent toward Collun, saying softly, "Your queen is indeed beautiful. How could you have thought otherwise?"

Collun introduced the queen to his two companions. She was gracious to Talisen, but her eyes quickly sought out the Ellyl.

"Welcome, Silien," she said to him. "This is a moment I have wished for since becoming queen. It is wrong that our races should be separated by a conflict as old as it is foolish."

Silien took the queen's offered hand. "I cannot speak for all Ellylon," he said, "but it is an honor to meet you, Queen Aine."

Aine smiled. "Collun," she said, turning toward him, "there is someone who wants to meet you." She put her hand on the arm of a man who stood by her. "Lord Bricriu, may I present Collun, brother to Nessa."

Bricriu was an elegant man, dressed in a luxuriant cape of red and black. He wore a closely trimmed black beard, and his face held a keen intelligence. Collun had felt the nobleman's deep-set eyes on him even before the queen made her introduction.

Lord Bricriu made a slight bow, saying, "Well met, Collun." There was sadness in his voice. "I would tell you how grieved I am by your sister's disappearance, but I choose not to, for I do truly believe she will be found safe and well. You have come to Temair in search of her. I wish you to know that your quest is mine. I shall do everything in my power to assist you." He gestured to the seat beside him.

"That is very kind of you, sir," Collun replied, sliding into the offered seat.

"It is nothing. It was I who failed to keep her safe in

my home." He paused. "I have an idea. Why don't you come with me to my dun? As soon as possible—tomorrow, even. Perhaps there we can begin the search anew."

The queen's son Gwynedd, who sat nearby, overheard Bricriu's words. He rose to his feet. "Hear, hear, Bricriu. Come, let us raise our glasses to Collun and to his quest." Servingmen quickly provided wine for the new arrivals, and everyone at the table drank.

Abruptly Prince Gwynedd set down his glass and leaned across the table toward Collun, his expression alive with purpose. "Collun, what would you say to an additional companion on your journey?"

Collun did not reply immediately, confused by the prince's words.

"What are you saying, son?" asked Queen Aine.

"If I am not to be allowed to join my father and brothers at the border, then I would assist Nessa's brother in his worthy quest. It was an act of infamy to abduct an innocent maid who was under the protection of the royal court. It bodes ill for Eirren." The prince's handsome face was flushed.

"What you say is true, Prince," said Bricriu, "but did not your father charge you to watch over your mother while he and your brothers were gone?"

"Nonsense, Bricriu," interrupted the queen with a laugh. "I do not require a keeper. Indeed, Gwynn and I argued far into the night over who was to go to the border and who was to stay behind—next time I will go. You must do as you choose, son, but I believe your place for now is here. Should the news from the border be dire, we would need to mount an army quickly."

"Perhaps, but no doubt you would say I was too

young to fight," replied the prince, a stubborn set to his jaw. "What say you, Collun?"

Collun, his mind in turmoil, did not know how to reply. He found himself nodding, a stiff smile on his face. What else could he do? The prince was indeed generous, offering himself as companion on a difficult journey. Collun knew he should be grateful.

"That's settled, then," said the queen, darting a last look at her son. "Shall we eat?"

The food was extraordinary. Collun sampled many dishes he had heard of but never tasted and many more that were completely unknown to him. There was honey-roasted lamb served with sloe preserves; there were succulent artichokes to be dipped into sunflower oil mixed with chervil; and there was a whortleberry fool tart with buttercups on top for decoration. Talisen had three servings of the tart. The violet-and-elderflower wine was delicious, and Collun drank more than he was accustomed to. It made him sleepy. He found himself leaning back in his chair and listening with only half an ear to the lively talk that swirled around him.

Rumors of war with Scath formed the main topic of conversation. The Eirrenians feared Medb was once again planning to invade their country.

"It is unfortunate that Cuillean has disappeared. We may need him in the months to come," said Lord Bricriu grimly.

"I fear Cuillean must be dead," stated a man with a thick russet beard. "Otherwise he would be here."

"I don't know," responded a second man. "In the months before he disappeared, Cuillean used to stand in the ramparts of his dun looking out at the sea. I saw him there myself, and I say he may have built himself a boat and set out to explore the western waters."

"Aye," said yet another man.

"And mark my words," continued the second one, "he will return to Eirren when we need him most."

Voices began to rise in heated debate over whether the hero Cuillean was alive or dead.

"There is yet another possibility," cut in Bricriu's smooth voice. "It is a rumor I have heard among my men, though I for one do not believe it for an instant."

"What is that?" queried the man with the russet beard.

"That Cuillean has betrayed Eirren and gone to Medb, the Queen of Ghosts."

This provoked a chorus of outraged dissent, and the queen's steady voice finally cleaved through the uproar.

"Such rumors do not deserve the dignity of a response, much less a public airing." She cast a quick, reproachful glance at the elegant nobleman.

Bricriu bowed his head deferentially. "I am in full agreement with you, my queen, but is it not true that a rumor ignored will run wild like heathfire? Is it not better to acknowledge it right away and put a stop to it?"

The queen replied evenly. "Perhaps. However, I cannot see that, in this case, your gossip has served any useful purpose. Cuillean was our friend." She paused, and a smile replaced the stern look on her face. "But enough solemn talk for one evening. Shall we have music?" She turned to the Ellyl. "Perhaps you would honor us with a song? We have heard much of Ellyl music."

Silien shook his head slightly with his usual half-smile. "I think not, Your Majesty, though I do not wish to appear ungrateful. I am weary and out of practice. Perhaps another time." The queen nodded graciously and gestured to the court bards.

The rest of the evening was filled with song and story. The bards were gifted with dazzling skill, each one with a repertoire that amazed Collun. He noticed Talisen was unusually silent; his face wore a fierce look of concentration.

Later, as they made their sleepy way back to Fial's quarters, Collun asked Talisen what he had thought of the night's entertainment.

"Oh, they were fair enough," Talisen responded breezily. He lapsed into silence for a few paces, then burst out, "That's nonsense, of course. They were extraordinary! But Collun, I have found out tonight from that posturing prig I was seated next to that to truly become a bard one must attend a special school called the Eisteddfod. It is only after four years of lessons, seven days a week from dawn until dark, that one can presume to call oneself a bard. Most of those bards who traveled through Inkberrow are called gleemen here in Temair, and they are much scorned. They cannot make songs and have never been to this accursed Eisteddfod." Talisen's face was more downcast than Collun had ever seen it.

"Not that I haven't the talent to be a true bard," Talisen added with a flash of a grin. "That goes without saying. But to spend four years shut inside some gloomy school building! I might just as well be back in Farmer Whicklow's pigsty."

The next morning Collun rose early. At Quince's request, he prepared several batches of the herb posset with which he had been treating Fial. He worked in a corner of the sick woman's room while she lay in her bed, still lost in a restless half-waking, half-sleeping state. A knock came at the door. Quince entered with a thick, folded piece of vellum in his hand.

"This has just arrived for the mistress. It is from Inkberrow. I thought you should be the one to open it."

Drying his hands on a cloth, Collun took the folded vellum from Quince. He recognized Goban's handwriting and got a queasy feeling in his stomach. His hands shook slightly as he broke the seal. He opened the letter.

"Fial," it began in Goban's awkward hand, "Emer is dead."

ELEVEN

Lord Bricriu

The room suddenly tilted, and Collun had to put a hand on a nearby table to steady himself. He stared blindly at the vellum. He thought of Emer's face as it had been the last time he saw her. He had known then that she was dying. He should not have left Aonarach. Now both Emer and Nessa were lost to him.

Collun focused his eyes to read the rest of the letter.

Fial,
Emer is dead. The boy Collun left here several
weeks ago, bound for Temair. If he should arrive
there, tell him what you will. It is no more a
concern of mine.
                    Goban

Collun's limbs felt frozen. He rubbed the numb spot on his forehead and wondered why he could not cry.

He suddenly became aware of Quince's voice. "What is wrong?"

"It is bad news," Collun replied, his voice sounding faint and high-pitched in his own ears. He cleared his throat. "My mother, Fial's sister by marriage, is dead." He walked woodenly to the small fire burning in Fial's fireplace. Collun thrust the thick goatskin vellum into the embers and watched, clenching his ice-cold fingers as it smoldered and finally burst into flames. A rancid smell permeated the room. On the bed nearby, Fial moved restlessly, but she remained unconscious.

Quince watched Collun, sympathy in his dark eyes. "May I bring you something?"

Collun shook his head. He turned and slowly walked into the outer room where his friends were gathered. Talisen and Silien were playing a game with dice, and Brie stood by the window gazing out.

Talisen looked up and, alarmed by the sight of Collun's chalk white face, laid down the dice he held. He quickly crossed the room to his friend's side. "What is it? What has happened?"

"She is dead," Collun replied dully.

"Who? Nessa?"

"No, Emer. My mother is dead."

From her spot by the window, Brie swung around to face Collun. "Emer?" she said sharply. Her face was almost as white as Collun's, and she stared at him as if at a ghost.

"Yes," Collun replied without looking at Brie. His lips felt dry.

"Here. Sit." Talisen gently nudged Collun into a chair. "Bring him something. Quickly!" he hissed at Quince, who had followed Collun into the room. The servingman nodded and went out. Talisen sat on the arm of the chair and tried to rub some heat into Collun's hands.

Collun sat still. His mother was dead, and his father's words hung before his eyes: "It is no more a concern of mine." Goban was dismissing Collun from his life as if he were a worn horseshoe. Collun had long known his father had little love for him, but to be swept aside so finally, so unexpectedly, caught him like a blow to the stomach. He had no home now. Nowhere to return to. And still he could not cry.

Quince returned with a flagon of thick amber liquid that burned Collun's throat as it went down. The paroxysm of coughing that followed brought his thoughts into focus. They were due to leave soon for Lord Bricriu's dun, and he still had to finish making the herb possets Quince had requested for Fial. He rose to his feet, feeling strangely calm. "Please do not speak of this to anyone," he said, voice flat, and then left the room.

As he crushed the leaves of the wood avens plant and sifted them into a bowl of broth from the dun's kitchen, Collun could hear voices through the open door.

"Why did you react so to the news of Emer's death?" asked Talisen. "You turned pale as a cloud."

There was no answer for a moment, then Brie spoke. "It must have reminded me of my own mother's death." Her voice was without expression. "Why has Collun never spoken the name of his mother before this?"

"She wished it so," Talisen replied. "I do not know why." There was another pause. "I thought you were only a babe when your mother died," Talisen went on, his voice speculative.

"Losing a mother is hard no matter what your age."

"Yes," responded Talisen. "Perhaps I am the lucky one. As far as I can remember, I never had a mother to lose."

Then Quince entered Fial's room. He closed the door behind him, shutting out the sound of the voices.

"Can I help?"

Collun shook his head. While Quince built up the fire, Collun crossed to Fial's bedside and looked down at his aunt. Her breathing was more regular, but still she did not awaken. He suppressed an urge to reach down and shake her by her thin shoulders. Collun was sure she knew the truth behind all the secrets Emer had kept hidden. He gazed at her half-expectantly, but the sick woman did not stir, and with a sigh, Collun returned to his work.

By midday they were ready to depart. The queen generously provided them with horses from the royal stables.

Collun had decided he would not speak to the queen about Emer now. But if he should ever return to Temair he would go to her at once and tell her everything. Now that his mother was dead, Collun could not believe she meant him to continue this silence. But first he must find Nessa—and Crann, too. His mother had told him to go to Crann when she died.

As they set out, Collun introduced Brie, still in her boy's raiment, to Prince Gwynedd and Lord Bricriu.

Bricriu looked closely at Brie. "Your face is familiar to me, Breo-Saight."

"I do not believe we have met before, m'lord," she replied.

"No, but..." His gaze dropped to the bow that Brie wore slung over her shoulder. A look of recognition came across Bricriu's face. "I know that bow! Unless I am much mistaken, I knew your father. Was he not Conall, the great champion of Eirren?"

Gwynedd, who rode nearby, peered at Brie. "Yes! I see the resemblance myself. But," he added in a puzzled tone, "Conall did not have a son."

Brie kept her lips tightly closed and motioned with her reins as if to move away from them. Collun saw that her cheeks were flushed.

Bricriu moved his horse up, blocking Brie's. "If you are not Conall's son, then how did you come by his bow? There cannot be two bows bearing the design of a Sun Bear." Bricriu's voice turned soft. "Unless you were one of his murderers?"

Brie drew up her reins and twisted in her saddle, facing Bricriu. Her eyes were blazing and her hand flew to the dagger she wore at her waist.

"No. I thought not," Bricriu responded with a conciliatory smile. "Indeed, I can see your father in your eyes, especially when the battle light comes upon them. You are Conall's daughter, are you not?"

Brie's mouth opened slightly, then she quickly clamped it shut.

Talisen laughed from behind. "Your disguise wears thinner and thinner every day, Brie."

Prince Gwynedd urged his horse up next to Brie's.

"You are Conall's daughter? Well met, Breo-Saight!" he said warmly. "I was a great admirer of your father. He was almost an uncle to me. How is it that he never brought you to Temair?"

"He did, several times, when I was very young. After that I chose not to accompany him. I grew up wearing breeches and running wild," she explained. "I would not have fit in at court."

Gwynedd gave an engaging laugh. "I know. For myself, I would much rather be off hunting or journeying than wasting time on dancing and feasting and acting polite all day. But tell me, Brie—may I call you Brie?" She nodded. "Are the arrows you carry of your own design? And what kind of feather do you favor?"

As the prince and Brie launched into a lively discussion of bow and arrow construction and design, Collun felt the stirrings of an emotion he could not name. Something about the self-assured prince and the sound of his voice affected Collun the same way as the noise of iron scraping iron. He felt ill-humored and awkward on top of the large horse. Grimly he reminded himself that it was an honor to be accompanied by the prince of Eirren.

The companions journeyed well into the night to reach Bricriu's dun, and they were hungry and tired when they arrived. They were provided with rooms and baths, after which Bricriu bade them join him for a late meal before retiring.

Just as they were sitting down to dinner, a serving-man bent to whisper in Bricriu's ear. A troubled expression came across the nobleman's face.

"Prince Gwynedd, I'm afraid a message has just arrived for you from Temair. It appears that the queen wishes you to return immediately. No reason was given, only the message that it is urgent."

"A messenger just arrived?"

"Yes. And both the poor man and his horse are dead with exhaustion. I hope there has not been bad news from the border."

"I shall leave at once." The prince rose to his feet.

"Of course, if you wish it. But do you not think you ought to wait until the morning? You are weary from the long ride . . ."

"No. If my mother thinks it urgent, then I must go. Collun," Gwynedd said, turning to him, "I am sorry to leave, but I hope we will meet again. Good luck to you." And he gave Collun's hand a last crushing grip. Then he bade the others farewell. Collun thought the prince's smile lingered longest on Brie.

Lord Bricriu called for food and drink. They were in a small room with a fire crackling in the large stone fireplace, seated on rust-colored cushions around a low round table. Lanterns of red glass gave the room a dim orange glow. The food was savory and elegantly prepared, and it was served by a throng of attentive serv-ingmen who all wore rust-colored hooded cloaks and white gloves.

Though he was clearly concerned about the abrupt departure of the prince, Lord Bricriu was a charming host. He, Talisen, and Silien did most of the talking. Collun was still numb from the news he had received in Temair, and Brie was characteristically silent.

After some worried speculation about the queen's ur-gent message for Gwynedd, the conversation gradually shifted to the heated exchange of the night before about Cuillean.

"I regret my part in it," Bricriu said. "I should not have repeated the rumor I heard. My own feeling is that, though a body has not been found, Cuillean must be dead. He would not stay away so long, not with our country on the verge of war.

"And I also fear that he met his end in much the same manner as his friend, Conall," Bricriu added grimly, with a sympathetic look in Brie's direction.

Brie did not respond, but Collun saw the muscles in her face tighten.

"It was a heinous crime and a tragic loss for all of Eirren," the nobleman continued, his eyes still on Brie.

"What were the circumstances, if you do not mind my asking?" Talisen asked Brie.

She did not reply, and Bricriu answered for her. "There were no witnesses, as far as I know, but those who discovered Conall's body say it was surrounded with the footprints of at least twenty or more men on horseback. But perhaps"—Bricriu looked over at Brie—"it is too painful for you to speak of your father's death?"

Brie shook her head. "The wound has healed," she said woodenly.

"He was outnumbered, then, by twenty to one?" said Talisen in revulsion.

"Twenty or more," replied Bricriu. "From the markings on the ground and all the blood that was spilled, Conall plainly hewed down a goodly number of his attackers. They took their dead with them, of course. But Conall died as he lived"—Bricriu gazed again at Brie as he spoke—"a courageous and honorable champion of Eirren."

Brie bowed her head but did not respond to his words. Bricriu then called for dessert, and as the servingmen cleared their plates Collun tried to catch Brie's eye. Her mouth was set in a tight line, and a small muscle near her left eye jumped spasmodically. She would not meet Collun's gaze, though he knew she was aware of him.

Ever since they had left Temair, Collun and Brie had spoken little. At first he thought it was because the prince was monopolizing her attention, but several times he had gotten the distinct impression she was avoiding him. Once, he had even turned toward her to ask a question and caught her staring at him with an expression that looked very much like hatred. It was gone a second later, and he thought he must have imagined it. Surely if she truly felt that way, she would not stay with them. But still he could not shake the memory of that look.

He looked down at the plate in front of him and saw they had been served an array of sweetmeats as well as a pie of pumpkin and currants, which Talisen was already devouring. With the dessert came cups of steaming mead. The mead had a nutty, slightly bitter taste.

Bricriu rose to his feet and raised his cup. "A toast before we retire. To the quest we begin tomorrow and to our success in bringing back the maiden Nessa, safe and well. Drink up." As they all dutifully drank the nutty mead, Collun noticed Bricriu's eyes fastened on him. They held an expression he could not fathom.

Collun suddenly felt uneasy. The orange light in the

room was giving him a headache, and his mouth felt dry. He'd become very tired, his head heavy and his limbs sore from riding the queen's horse. He tried to protest when a servingman refilled his cup, but he could not seem to move his tongue. In a daze he watched the gloved hand pouring mead, noticing almost idly that the wrist protruding from the glove had gray skin. With great effort he raised his eyes to look up into the hooded face. A pair of slitted yellow eyes gazed steadily back at him. Collun's body stiffened, and he groped in his fogged memory for the name of the creature with yellow eyes.

He started to rise to his feet, thinking to warn his host. The last thing he remembered was Bricriu's bright gaze on him with that same indefinable expression.

TWELVE

The Labyrinth

When Collun regained consciousness he was aware of an overwhelming thirst. His tongue felt huge in his mouth and seemed to be covered with fuzz, like the underside of a witch-hazel leaf. He was lying on a hard, cold surface, and as far as he could tell, he was virtually encased in rope. It was thick and prickly and began at his ankles, then circled his legs and body, binding his arms tightly to his sides. The tips of his fingers were tingling, and if his eyes were open or shut, it made no difference. There was only darkness.

He knew immediately that Bricriu had betrayed them. It had been a morg who served the mead; perhaps all Bricriu's servingmen were morgs. And in a flash

Collun understood the strange expression on the nobleman's face. It was a look of sly amusement, as of a cat toying with a dying mouse. And Collun also realized then that Bricriu himself must have been responsible for his sister's disappearance.

His stomach cramped suddenly, and he let out a small moan.

"Collun? Is that you?" It was Brie's voice, and she was nearby.

"Yes. Are you bound, too?" His voice was hoarse.

"Yes. We were drugged. The mead, I think." He heard her move. "The Ellyl is next to me. Unconscious still. I do not know what has happened to Talisen or Fara."

The darkness was abruptly filled with the sound of Talisen retching. When the noise finally subsided, he groaned. "Where in Amergin's name are we? I feel like someone has been kicking me in the stomach for a month."

"The mead we drank was drugged," Collun explained.

"Lord Bricriu . . . ?" Talisen asked in disbelief.

"Yes," Brie answered, her voice grim. "Before I lost consciousness I overheard Bricriu order the morgs, who were disguised as his servingmen, to take us down to his dungeon. We now lie in the darkness below the dun. Collun, Bricriu said, is to be taken north in a day or two while the rest of us are left here to die. I heard one of the morgs say there are many tunnels down here but no escape."

Talisen let out an oath, his voice shaking slightly.

"Bricriu must be in league with Medb," Collun said, his tongue still thick in his mouth.

"How will he explain our disappearance?" asked Talisen, clearing his throat.

"There probably was no messenger from Temair last night," suggested Brie. "Bricriu made it up in order to get the prince away. And Lord Bricriu will no doubt tell the queen there has been another tragic disappearance."

As Brie spoke, Collun strained to loosen his bonds, but he could not. He was bound as tightly as if it were the cro-olachan vine that held him.

"Fara," Brie suddenly said. Collun heard a low-pitched rumbling from the faol's throat.

"Fara is beside me," said Brie. "She is unbound. Can you help us, Fara?"

There was a short silence. Then Collun could hear a soft rustling sound.

"What is she doing?" asked Talisen impatiently.

"Her teeth are sharp," was all Brie said, and before long Fara had chewed through all their bonds, including those of Silien, who had not yet woken.

Collun quickly checked to see if his dagger was still attached to his belt. It was. That surprised him. He wondered if Bricriu had not been told why Medb sought him, or if he had just been very confident Collun would not be able to escape his bonds.

"Do you suppose all Ellylon sleep as much as this one does?" said Talisen as he groped away from them in the darkness. "Here's the door," he cried out. "And it isn't locked!"

They heard him stumble and then give an excited yell. "My harp! And our packs..."

Collun quickly found his teine stone inside his pack. He hoped to spark a fire so they might see where they were, but nothing in the damp cave was dry enough to provide kindling.

"Help me wake the Ellyl," said Brie. "We cannot stay here. Bricriu and his men may return at any time."

They sprinkled water from a skin bag onto the Ellyl's face. Brie slapped his wrists, and gradually Silien returned to consciousness. He was groggy and disoriented. It took some time before he was able to walk. They slowly made their way out of the dungeon.

"I would make light to guide us," the Ellyl said, his voice fuzzy, "but I do not have the strength. Lord Bricriu must have used the herb meliot to drug us, and meliot makes me ill, too ill to make a light. I will try again later." Then he dropped to a crouching position. They could hear a rumbling sound from Fara's throat. It reminded Collun of the purr of a large cat. They remained quiet until the rumbling stopped and Silien rose shakily to his feet.

"Fara tells me the dungeon ends at the beginning of a labyrinth. The other way leads back up into Bricriu's dun."

"What kind of labyrinth?" asked Collun.

"It is Ellyl. We must decide quickly," said Silien. "Fara says there are two morgs guarding the entrance to the dun."

"I don't see that we have a choice," came Brie's voice through the darkness. "Even if we could get past those morgs, if we try to escape through Bricriu's dun, we will almost certainly be captured."

There came the dull banging sound of a door opening

and then shutting. It was followed by the hollow echo of footsteps approaching.

"Is it to be the labyrinth?" whispered Silien.

"Yes," Collun whispered back, filled with misgivings.

They moved forward as quickly and quietly as they could in the darkness, feeling their way along the damp, cool rock of the tunnel walls. They passed a number of doorways; more cells, Collun guessed.

"The labyrinth begins up ahead," whispered Silien.

"You said it is Ellyl?" Talisen said softly.

"Yes. Fara knew it at once. I have heard of it but know little beyond this . . ." The companions drew closer to hear Silien's hushed words as they walked. "It is called Misteir Dearthair and was fashioned long ago by two Ellyl brothers. These brothers both wished to wed the same maiden, who, it was said, loved them equally and could not make the choice between them. She was fond of puzzles, so the brothers came up with the idea of a labyrinth with two ways out. One would lead to the first brother and one to the second. Whichever way she took would lead to the Ellyl she would marry. It took one year to build, so intricate was its design." Silien paused, out of breath.

"The maiden never found the way out. They believe she fell and injured herself deep within the twists and turnings of the labyrinth. She was dead before they could find her. After that the labyrinth was sealed. It was forbidden to enter it." Silien stopped speaking.

"No doubt Bricriu purposely built his dun over it," Brie mused.

"Handy for constructing a dungeon," added Talisen, "as well as a convenient graveyard." He laughed wryly. "Though hopefully not for us."

"I don't like it," Collun said, reverting to his earlier feelings of misgiving. "If the Ellyl maiden could not find her way out, how can we ever hope to?"

"It begins here," said Silien.

Suddenly they heard the sound of muffled shouts and doors banging. The morgs had discovered their escape.

They plunged forward into the labyrinth. They made several turnings, still feeling the way along the walls with their fingers and choosing at random the path to take.

They lapsed into silence. Collun found it eerie, walking without sight. He remembered old Neggan, the blind weaver back in Inkberrow. Collun had never thought before about what it must be like, living in darkness as she did. He understood now why she wove elaborate stories into her cloth. They must have brought some color and light into her dark world, even if she could not see them.

"There was a riddle," Silien finally broke the silence, his voice a faint whisper. "It was given to the maiden to help her find her way out. It provided a clue to the puzzle. I never learned the riddle, nor its answer..." His voice trailed away, then came again, softly, "Fara remembers only the first line of it. 'I go naked in winter yet feel no chill.' That is all."

"A riddle, eh?" said Talisen, his voice eager. "Well, then, I should be able to get us through this labyrinth in no time at all. 'I go naked in winter...' Just give me a few moments." He began muttering to himself. The rest of them lapsed again into silence.

After what seemed an eternity of groping in the dark, of doubling back from dead ends and starting over,

Silien gave a soft sigh and said, "I can go no farther." He slipped to the ground where he stood and was immediately asleep.

"We will have to carry him," said Collun. He and Talisen hoisted Silien up, draping one of the Ellyl's arms around Collun's neck, the other around Talisen's. Brie moved into the lead with Fara at her side.

As he walked, Collun thought about the riddle fragment. He considered asking Brie's opinion, but he hesitated. The strain was still there between them. He had tried many times to identify its cause, but he could not. Nor could he bring himself to ask her.

After several hours of carrying Silien, Collun and Talisen began to tire. They dragged on for some time but finally had to rest. They laid the Ellyl gently on the tunnel floor. Talisen went a short distance away to concentrate on the riddle. Collun could hear Brie breathing nearby. He took a step toward her, then stopped.

"Brie?" Collun said tentatively.

"Yes?" Her voice was cold. Collun could hear Fara's purr and guessed that Brie was stroking the animal's back.

"Why do you journey with us?" Collun blurted out.

"In our present circumstances it would seem I have little choice," Brie responded dryly.

"But why did you stay with us after we got to Temair?"

Brie didn't answer for a moment. "Did you want me to leave you then?"

"No!" Collun exclaimed. "That is, we have, uh, come to rely on your bow."

"I see." He could hear her move away from him.

Collun reached out to stop her, but then let his arm fall back to his side. He felt a numbness inside him, and for some reason the words in Goban's letter came back to him.

Collun felt his way back to the Ellyl. "Silien?"

"Yes." He was awake.

"How do you feel?" Collun queried.

"A little better," the Ellyl replied huskily. And suddenly he began to sing. At first his voice was so soft that Collun did not even recognize it as singing. It was like the time in the Forest of Eld. The song had no rhyme, it told no story, it did not even have recognizable words—yet somehow Collun knew it was a song. It painted pictures of fire and smoke behind his eyes, and when it was done, the darkness was gone. A soft pink light glowed in Silien's hand. He held it before him so they could see the place where they stood.

It was a tunnel carved of rock, just higher than the tallest of them. They stood at a turning. There was a drawing on the wall just below eye level.

As they walked forward they found more drawings. They were spaced at irregular intervals, and at each turning there was a picture. The designs depicted many different things—a ring-tailed mouse, a blade of grass glistening with moisture, a salmon leaping high above a stream. Each one was exquisite. The spray of periwinkle next to Collun was so lifelike he felt he could reach over and pluck it.

"Ellyl drawings," said Silien.

"They are beautiful," replied Talisen.

"I wonder if they were drawn for decoration only," said Brie.

"You mean you think they may be clues, like the riddle?" queried Talisen. "By Amergin, the answer is on the tip of my tongue! I have heard it before, I am sure. 'I go naked in winter . . .' Are you sure Fara can remember no more of it, Silien?"

"I am sure." The Ellyl's voice was hollow with fatigue. "Fara has no patience for riddling. Let us move ahead. Perhaps the pictures will tell us more." Silien held up the light in his hand and they walked on. They came to several turnings and randomly chose the way to go.

" 'In winter . . .' " Talisen was still muttering irritably to himself. "I would swear I *know* this riddle. I heard it once in a song." He slid his harp around again and began to finger the strings. "I can even picture the face of the bard who sang it to me. He was very old, and his voice had more cracks than the plates Farmer Whicklow used to throw at me."

They passed the painting of a spindly legged lamb, then a cluster of ripe huckleberries. Talisen gave a sigh and for a moment stopped playing. "I cannot concentrate for all the clamor my stomach is making. By chance, does anyone have food with them?" No one replied. "I thought not," he responded gloomily.

They came to another turning and paused. Collun absently ran his finger around the edge of the silver-green leaf etched onto the stone beside him. His eyes fell on a small pile of what he thought were rocks. But when he peered more closely at them, he gasped. It was a pile of bones.

He tried without success to stifle the horrible, unbidden thought that flooded his mind. Ever since he had woken in the darkness of the dungeon, he wondered if

Nessa had been there, too. And what if, like them, she had escaped into the labyrinth and gotten lost in the pitch-black twistings and turnings? He knelt down by the small pile.

"Those have lain here a long, long time," came Brie's voice from over Collun's shoulder. "Too long."

"Are you sure?" Collun stared down at the grisly heap.

"Yes. If they were your sister's, they would still have some flesh on them," Brie said, her voice matter-of-fact and still distant. She moved away.

"Yet they are too new to be those of the Ellyl maiden for whom the labyrinth was built," said Silien, holding the light over the bones. "Some other victim of Lord Bricriu's treachery, perhaps."

Suddenly Talisen's random playing took on form and he let out a triumphant laugh. "I have found it," he said, his voice loud with excitement. "Listen. It is not exactly the same, but it is close enough.

> " 'In spring I am gay,
>   in handsome array.
>   In summer more clothing I wear.
>   When colder it grows,
>   I fling off my clothes,
>   And in winter quite naked appear.'

"There," Talisen finished with a flourish. "Can you guess the answer? It is simple, really."

There was a short silence.

"A tree, of course," Talisen cried out impatiently.

"But what does it mean? Could the labyrinth be fashioned in the manner of the roots of a tree?" asked Brie.

Collun had been listening with half an ear, his eyes still fastened on the bones. But then something stirred in his memory. The picture at the turning. It had been a leaf. A mulberry leaf. He stood and crossed to the design. He stared at it.

"Perhaps it points the way out," he said more to himself than the others.

"What?" asked Talisen.

"Where the leaf of a tree is, perhaps that is the turning we are to take."

There was a silence, and then Brie said thoughtfully, "And perhaps because there were two brothers, there are two kinds of leaves."

"This is a mulberry," said Collun. "I remember seeing leaves of hawthorn, ash, and rowan earlier."

"There may be dozens of kinds of trees. How do we narrow it to the two we seek?" queried Talisen.

"Perhaps it lies in the riddle," Collun suggested.

"I don't see how..."

"Nor do I," confessed Collun.

"Well then, let us just choose one at random," said Talisen. "Although..." He paused. "You realize, don't you, that while one leaf may indeed lead us to freedom, another may lead us right back to Bricriu..."

There was another silence. Collun's eyes strayed to the pile of bones, and he shivered slightly.

The light in Silien's hand had grown dimmer, and they all noticed that his limbs were trembling with fatigue.

"What leaf is this?" asked Brie. Her voice was overly loud and echoed in the passageway.

"Mulberry," answered Collun.

"Then let us try mulberry," said Brie.

They began to move down the passage marked by the mulberry leaf, but Collun hesitated, reluctant to follow. "'In spring I am gay...,'" he murmured under his breath. "'In spring'...spring...winter..."

"Collun?" Talisen called back to him.

"I am coming," Collun said. He moved forward to join them. "What of this: The riddle names spring and winter. Perhaps the two trees we seek are ones that flourish in those two seasons..." He trailed off. Spoken out loud, his reasoning sounded unimpressive.

But Brie immediately spoke up. "It is well thought. Come, let us look for spring and winter trees."

Silien's light had grown dangerously low by the time they had narrowed their search. They chose the silver fir for the winter tree, as it was the only evergreen they found, and the hawthorn because of its vibrant spring blossoms.

"And now," wondered Talisen, "which of these lovely trees do you suppose leads to freedom and which to Bricriu's dungeon?"

Nobody spoke.

"Let us choose the fir. 'Twas my mother's birth tree," said Collun abruptly.

And so they took the turning with the silver fir markings. As they continued on, they passed several turnings that bore the design of a hawthorn leaf, but they went straight on. At first, the tunnels kept slanting downward, and Collun began to fear they had chosen wrong. Silien was growing weaker and weaker. He could not muster strength even to talk. All the energy he had was focused on the dwindling ball of light glowing in his palm. If the Ellyl's light was to go out, thought Collun, they would be lost. They were all exhausted, hungry, and more than anything else, thirsty. They had finished the water in their skin bags some time ago.

Finally the way began to slant upward, and they felt a glimmer of hope. But going up took more effort.

And then, without warning, Silien's light faded. He had stopped for a moment and was leaning up against a wall, staring blankly down at his hand. The light guttered, like a candle, and then went out, plunging them into total darkness.

THIRTEEN

Nemian

Collun laid his hand on the tunnel wall to orient himself. If Silien was to fall into one of his long sleeps now, they would never escape the labyrinth. They'd die of dehydration. He fought down the panic that began to rise in him. They could be entombed in these narrow tunnels forever, tons of earth and rock lying between them and the open air. He saw again in his mind the pathetic pile of bones, and his throat closed up.

His hands shaking, Collun groped his way back to the Ellyl to see if he was asleep. He found Silien still upright, breathing shallowly. When he spoke, his voice was a cracked whisper, difficult to understand. Finally,

though, Collun was able to make out the words "goat's thorn," the name of one of the herbs Collun carried in his wallet. He used it to heal coughs and sore throats.

Collun fumbled with the opening, and in the darkness his fingers sifted among the different herbs. He pulled out several leaves and smelled them to be sure they were goat's thorn.

"What is it?" asked Talisen through the darkness. "Has Silien fallen asleep?"

"No," Collun answered shortly.

He could hear Silien crush the leaves between his teeth. The Ellyl coughed several times, then they heard a faint humming sound. Collun realized that, once again, Silien was singing. His voice was thin and cracked, but the pink light slowly rekindled in his hand. It was not as bright as before, but it gave off enough light to see the drawings on the walls.

Collun and Talisen again supported Silien as they resumed moving forward, their minds and bodies numb.

And finally, almost without warning, they came to the end. They rounded a turning marked by the familiar silver fir marking, and in the flickering pink light they saw a rotting wooden barrier, about chest high, with ivy growing between the cracks.

Collun and Talisen put their shoulders to the door, and the sound of rotted wood splintering filled the tunnel. They scrambled up through several layers of decayed vegetation and finally emerged into a small copse of fir trees.

It was nighttime. Hundreds of stars twinkled above. The travelers gazed about numbly, taking deep breaths of the crisp autumn air. The Ellyl had already fallen asleep beside the tunnel's entrance; Fara settled quietly at his head.

Brie moved forward, following the sound of running water. She led them to a small, clear brook. They dropped to their knees and gratefully scooped handfuls of freezing water into their dry mouths. It made their teeth hurt and their stomachs ache with cold.

They filled their skin bags and took them back to Silien. They were able to wake the Ellyl just long enough to give him several deep draughts of the water.

Brie went off with her bow and soon came back carrying a small badger. Collun started a fire with his teine stone. The smell of roasting badger was torture to their empty stomachs as they waited for it to cook. The meat was tough and stringy but tasted delicious. They spoke little as they ate. And then they slept.

Collun awoke during the night. He sat up, chilled by the cold night air, and rekindled the fire. The moon was bright, and as he held his hands over the fire to warm them, he gazed at his sleeping companions.

Their faces were ashen with fatigue. Deep circles were etched under their eyes. Talisen's boots had holes in the soles, and Brie's clothing was dirty and worn. In his deep sleep, Silien looked more like a corpse than a living thing. The bones stood out under his skin, revealing the lines of his skull.

Collun felt a tightness in his chest. He could not allow his friends to go on endangering their lives.

He lifted his hand and absently rubbed the spot on his forehead where the scald-crow had brushed him. It seemed such a long time ago. But when his face was cold, as it was now, the numbness came back.

He knew they would not willingly let him go. He would have to slip away while they slept. He knew he should leave right now. They were all so deep in slumber that he would be able to get a good head start before they discovered he was gone. If only he were not so weary . . . Perhaps just a few moments of sleep. Then he would formulate a plan.

Collun woke abruptly to the call of a wood thrush. He had let himself rest much longer than he intended. Wisps of ground mist hung about their campsite, and he could see the sky lightening in the east. He silently began to gather his things.

Brie let out a small cry in her sleep, and Collun gazed over at her. She looked even paler than she had the night before. Suddenly her eyes flew wide open, and there was an almost savage expression in them. She seemed to be staring directly at Collun.

"Emer," Brie said, her husky voice urgent. "And your father . . . I have to tell you." Slowly her eyes shut, and she shifted her position on the ground. Her arm fell away from her neck, and Collun saw a dark shadowed area on the white skin. Then the shadow moved.

Collun froze.

Clinging to Brie's neck, just under the right side of her chin, was a black creature. Collun's first, irrational thought was that it was a scald-crow like the one pecking at Nessa's neck in his dream. But it was too small to be a scald-crow. It looked like a large black moth. Its body was squat and thick, and its black wings were as long as Brie's neck. They flapped open and shut slowly and rhythmically.

Collun dropped his pack. It made a thud as it hit the

ground. Should he try to brush the creature away or grab it and pull it off? He was afraid to touch it. What if it had the same freezing poison in its wings as the scald-crow? Uncertainly he reached for his dagger. But if he tried to stab it, he might hurt Brie. Collun was torn with indecision as he stared down at Brie's neck.

"What is it, Collun? What's wrong?" Talisen said sleepily, rubbing his eyes, looking over at his friend in bewilderment.

Collun did not hear him. He bent over Brie, shifted his dagger to his left hand, and gritting his teeth, he wildly swatted at the loathsome creature, trying to knock it off Brie's neck. His hand skidded off the tips of its wings, and he felt ice-cold pain shoot up his fingers.

The creature swayed slightly but held fast to Brie's neck, its wings flapping faster. Collun shifted his dagger back to his numb right hand. The stone in the handle glowed slightly in the dim light of dawn. He would have to risk cutting Brie. He swept his dagger down. This time he made direct contact. The thing was dislodged.

Collun let out an involuntary cry as pain froze along his arm. His fingers went so numb that he could not bend them.

The creature let out an unearthly, high-pitched screaming sound and flew up into Collun's face. He stumbled back, switching the dagger from his useless right hand to his left. The creature's cry grew even more shrill as it circled and flew again at his head. Collun got a glimpse of a grotesque, swollen face, a face that was neither human nor animal, with small slitted eyes the color of blood. He ducked and once again blindly thrust his dagger into the air. The unearthly cry reached a deafening pitch and then suddenly stopped. Something fell at Collun's feet. The creature flew up into the air and disappeared.

His heart pounding, Collun dropped to his knees beside Brie and anxiously looked into her face. Her eyes were closed. There was a round black mark on her neck. Sheathing his dagger awkwardly with his left hand, Collun laid his left forefinger at the pulse point in Brie's neck. To his relief a faint heartbeat thrummed under his touch.

"Brie? Wake up, Brie," he said, shaking her gently. But she did not respond. Talisen came to his side.

"What was it?"

"I do not know. It left this." Collun pointed to the round black mark on Brie's neck. "Its eyes were like the scald-crow's. I cannot wake her," Collun added, his voice bleak.

Something caught Talisen's eye, and he leaned over to pick it up. "Look," he said. "Ouch. It's cold." He held it up for Collun to see. It was black and made up of many small, shiny feathers, but the feathers were not soft. They were knife-sharp.

Collun took the black piece in his left hand. It was indeed ice-cold to the touch. He had to hold it with the end of his sleeve pulled down over it. "It looks like the tip of the creature's wing. I must have cut it off somehow."

"What's wrong with your arm?" asked Talisen suddenly.

"The thing did it ... When I touched it, it was cold, like this, but colder." He indicated the black piece in his hand. "It went into my hand and up my arm." He bent over Brie again and tentatively touched the black mark on her neck. It, too, was cold to the touch and hard like a crusted wound.

Collun crossed to Silien and tried to wake him, but he could not.

It was a long, dismal day. Collun would not leave Brie's side. He sat watching her face anxiously, feeling for her pulse every so often. At one point, Fara left her post at Silien's head and came to where Brie lay. She peered into Brie's face and let out a cry. With her long pink tongue the faol began to lick the girl's forehead, methodically working her way down to the chin. When Fara had finished, Collun checked Brie's pulse. He could have sworn it had grown slightly stronger, but still he could not rouse her.

Talisen heated some water from the nearby stream and tried bathing Collun's hand and arm, but they remained numb.

The Ellyl finally awoke long after dark. He was still weak, but fully alert. They quickly told him what had happened. He knelt beside Brie, examining the mark on her neck. Then Talisen showed him the tip of the creature's wing.

Silien closely examined it for what seemed to Collun an eternity. "It is Nemian," he finally said.

"What is Nemian?" Collun asked, filled with dread at the tone in the Ellyl's voice.

"Nemian is from the Cave of Cruachan. Like Moccus's sow. Nemian can be one or it can be many, but wherever it goes, it leaves behind death. It cannot be killed. I did not think it could even be injured. The wizard Crann was right, Collun. The stone in your dagger must be the Cailceadon Lir."

Collun nodded impatiently. "Perhaps. But what has this Nemian done to Brie?"

"I do not know, but I believe it has poisoned her blood."

"Will she die?"

"Yes."

"No!" Collun cried. "There must be something we can do."

"I can try," shrugged the Ellyl, "but it will avail her little." Silien kneeled again by Brie and laid his hand over the black mark on her neck, his own face still gaunt with fatigue.

Collun heard the song but faintly. Yet he felt a flickering of hope, and the tips of his own numb fingers tingled slightly.

When the song was done, Brie's eyelids trembled. Then slowly her eyes opened. Collun felt a surge of joy, but then he saw the expression in her eyes. There was nothing there; no sign of recognition, only a terrifying blankness.

FOURTEEN

The Ellyl Wind

Collun sat by her and said, "Brie? It is Collun. How do you feel?" But she did not respond. He laid a hand on her forehead. It was still freezing cold to the touch. He gave Silien a questioning look.

The Ellyl shook his head. "She is alive. She can move her limbs. I can do no more." He was already lying on the ground, eyelids drooping. "Just a short rest," he mumbled, and his eyelids fell shut.

Collun and Talisen tried to feed Brie some nuts, but she would not chew them. The best they could do was to pour water into her mouth, which she swallowed, more by reflex than choice.

While Silien slept again, Collun decided they must

get Brie back to Temair. Perhaps there they would know what to do. All thoughts of setting off on his own were forgotten.

When the Ellyl awoke, Collun told him his intention.

"It will do no good," said Silien, shaking his head. But Collun set his mouth in a stubborn line.

"We go to Temair," he said. Silien shrugged.

When morning came, they got Brie to her feet and found she was able to walk, although she moved sightlessly, like a sleepwalker. One of them had to be at her side always to guide her steps.

Collun chose an easterly direction, thinking to circle Bricriu's dun and then travel south toward Temair.

The day wore on and they made little progress from the copse of silver fir trees. Then they came to the crest of a small hill and Silien suddenly halted, a smile on his face. "There is a river near," he said.

Stepping briskly, he fell into the lead, and by late afternoon they came to the banks of a large, noisy river. "The River Ardagh," said the Ellyl with the tone of one meeting an old friend.

As they sank down onto the spongy turf at the river's edge, they watched Silien take out a length of translucent thread. To the end of it he attached a small glittering object and cast it into the water. It wasn't long before the riverbank around him was covered with flopping, silvery fish. Talisen kindled the fire, as Collun's right hand was still useless, and after Silien had cleaned the fish, Talisen roasted them over the flames. The hot fish melted in Collun's mouth.

They tried again to feed Brie, but she would not move

her jaws. Collun made a broth of fish, water, and herbs to pour into her mouth.

As Collun lay down to sleep that night, he noticed the Ellyl sitting on the very edge of the riverbank, Fara at his side. Silien was gazing fixedly at the flowing water. Ever since they had come to the river, his face had worn a distracted, hungry look.

Collun remembered Silien telling them Ellylon loved water, and many of the ways into Tir a Ceol were by water. Collun wondered, as he drifted off into an exhausted sleep, whether the Ellyl was homesick.

When Collun woke in the morning, Silien still sat by the river. Next to him was a makeshift basket made of reeds, filled to the top with fish. Fara was leisurely cleaning herself. Collun walked over to the Ellyl. "You have been busy."

"Yes," replied Silien. "I wanted to leave you with a supply of fish. The road back to Temair is a long one."

Collun was about to thank the Ellyl when the meaning of his words sank in. He stared down at the basket of fish. "You are leaving us?"

"My home is not far. I do not know if my father will have me, but I decided to return. I have been gone long."

Talisen overheard Silien's words. He sat upright and said angrily, "You're deserting us?"

"I can do no more for the Flame-girl."

"Silien," Collun cut in, his voice higher than usual, "is there nothing that can save Brie?"

"No." The Ellyl paused. "Nothing in your land."

"What do you mean, nothing in our land?"

"Except perhaps for your Crann, who comes and goes

as he chooses, there is no one in Eirren with the power to heal the Flame-girl. If she were Ellyl..."

"Yes?"

"There might be a way, *if* she were Ellyl."

"Can you not use the same method on Brie?"

Silien shook his head. "I do not know the way. Only the elders of Tir a Ceol know it."

"Then take us with you to Tir a Ceol," Collun said, his voice loud.

Silien was startled, but he shook his head again. "They would never agree to heal one of your kind."

"Are you sure?"

"I am."

"Take me to them anyway. Perhaps if I could speak with them..."

"You would be destroyed if you even tried to enter Tir a Ceol. And I, too, no doubt, for bringing you."

"Take us, Silien," Collun pleaded. "I will say I forced you, that you acted against your will."

The Ellyl only smiled.

Then Collun was angry. "Brie was right all along. You are capable only of feeling for yourself. You would let her die, as you would let anything weaker than you die, if helping meant danger to yourself."

"It is foolish to act otherwise," Silien responded coolly.

"Then you are a coward." Collun turned away, tears of anger stinging his eyes.

Silien was unmoved. "Call me what you will. I wish to return home, and I can think of no reason to take you with me." He bent to place a cover on the reed basket.

Collun walked back toward Brie, his good hand clenched tightly in frustration.

"I understand your point of view," he heard Talisen say to Silien. Collun spun around in disbelief.

"After all," Talisen continued, "you have said that no one in hundreds of years has dared to bring a human into Tir a Ceol. To be the first," Talisen paused, "why, it would be an act of infamy. Ellylon would speak of it for years hence."

Silien straightened. There was a speculative look in his eyes. He gazed across the water.

"Think of what your parents would say..."

"I have no mother," Silien said distractedly, still staring at the river.

"Your father, then. Why, he would never let you live it down. To bring a human into Tir a Ceol. Of course, it's unthinkable."

Silien shifted his gaze to Talisen. He gave his half-smile. "You are indeed the clever one, harp-player. Very well, I will take you into Tir a Ceol, if only to see the look on my father's face." He turned and walked off toward a nearby stand of trees.

Talisen let out a whoop and danced an impromptu jig around the remains of last night's fire. "Did you hear, Collun? We are going to Tir a Ceol!"

"Thank you, Talisen," Collun said to his friend.

When Silien returned, he bore an armful of branches. He sat down and patiently set to work stripping them. Collun asked what he was doing, and he replied, "On my own, I can swim to my home. But you are human and cannot. I must build a curragh to take us into Tir a Ceol."

"We will help you."

Silien nodded and put Collun to work stripping the leaves and twigs off the branches. At first it was awkward, working without his right hand, but Collun soon learned the knack of holding the branch between his knees, steadying it with his right shoulder, and using his left hand to pull off leaves.

It took them a day and a half of hard work to build the boat. Often, as they labored, Collun could hear Silien humming under his breath. Collun guessed the melody held Ellyl magic, for the work went much faster than it otherwise would have.

As he kept a watch over Brie, Collun stripped the hazel rods. Silien and Talisen went to hunt for game. They came back, exhausted but triumphant, bearing a large kine between them. They skinned the animal, saving the meat for dinner, then stretched the hide out on the ground to dry in the weak autumn sun.

When there were enough hazel rods, Silien used a piece of the translucent thread to mark out a large oval on the ground. He stuck thirty-two rods firmly into the ground at regular intervals around the oval. Next he wove more hazel branches through the stakes, making a pattern of sturdy wickerwork. With Talisen's help, the Ellyl then bent the long hazel rods over so they met and lay side by side, where they were securely bound with more of Silien's thread.

Silien carefully placed several large rocks on top of the structure to help it set, and Talisen laughingly asked if the Ellyl planned to carry them all in a giant basket. But Silien just smiled and carried the dried kine hide down to the river, where he let it soak overnight in a shallow pocket of river water.

The next morning Collun watched while Talisen and

Silien stretched the now-pliable hide over the upside-down basket and, when they were done, helped them lace it all around the edge with the Ellyl thread.

Then Silien set to work carving a tiller out of a large ash branch. He sang as he worked, and his hands flew over the wood. Soon he had not only finished the tiller but had fashioned two oars and a bench for sitting.

By the next morning the boat was ready. It was a sturdy little craft, and Talisen dubbed it *Wave-sweeper*.

Brie's body had shrunk in the time it had taken them to build the boat. She no longer had the strength to sit up. The dark spaces under her eyes cut more deeply into her face, and her skin felt like ice to the touch. It was the gray of approaching death.

They carried the boat down to a muddy shelf by the side of the river and loaded it first with their few belongings. Then they carefully laid Brie in the bottom. She lay there without a sound, her dead eyes staring at the sky.

Collun awkwardly stepped into the boat, and Silien and Talisen cast off. The river current immediately grabbed at the little vessel.

Holding tightly to the side of the boat with his left hand, Collun watched the land on either side of him slide by. He had never been on a body of water this large before.

Wave-sweeper suddenly slipped around a bend and was caught up in a rush of foaming white rapids. Silien guided the boat skillfully. The white water did not last long, and soon afterward the river emptied into a lake. If the river had seemed large to Collun, it was nothing compared to the broad expanse of water that stretched before them now. It was green in some places, brown in others, and everywhere overlaid with silver, like the Ellyl's eyes, where the sun caught it.

"This lake is called Ullswater," said Silien.

"It is large," replied Collun. "Is your home near?"

"Very near." Silien smiled. "The porth—or entrance—to Tir a Ceol lies underneath."

Collun's eyes widened. "Underneath?"

"We enter there." And he pointed straight ahead, over the water. "There is a cavern," he added, since all that was visible to them was a thin finger of land.

Silien got out the oars and began to row the boat across the lake. Compared to the headlong rush of the river journey, they now seemed barely to move at all. But then Silien began to sing, and the little boat skimmed over the water at an even, fluid pace.

Then Collun noticed the sky was changing. The sun went under a thin bank of clouds and stayed there. The light took on a yellowish cast, turning the water yellow as well. The breeze died completely, and the air became heavy and still. Silien looked up at the sky uneasily.

"Is there a storm coming?" Collun asked.

Silien did not answer.

The sky continued to darken, and the yellow light became more and more unreal. Their faces had all taken on the sallow color of toadflax blossoms.

Collun looked down at Brie. Her eyes had closed. Collun felt for her pulse, his own heart racing. He found it, but it was thready and irregular, more so than before. He prayed she would hold on long enough for them to cross the lake.

Then the boat slowed. Collun saw that Silien had set

down the oars. The Ellyl took hold of the tiller with both hands, his knuckles white. He told them to get into the bottom of the boat and hold fast. Barely were the words out of his mouth when the first blast of wind hit them. It was as if a giant hand had come out of the sky and given them a mighty blow. As he ducked into the bottom of the boat, Collun was almost swept into the water, his breath snatched away.

Silien said something they could not hear over the wind. Then he shouted, "My father. He is angry."

"What do you mean? Where is your father?" called out Talisen.

"He is below. He has sent Daoine Ellyl, the Ellyl Wind."

"Who is your father, Silien?" Talisen shouted as loudly as he could.

"He is king. King of the Ellylon," Silien replied, his eyes scanning the whitecaps that now covered the lake's surface. Waves slapped against the sides of the boat, rocking them up and down wildly.

"Your father is king?!" yelled Talisen. "Why didn't you tell us before?"

Silien cast a brief glance at Talisen and gave his half-smile. "It did not seem important. Get your head down."

Soon *Wave-sweeper* was being tossed from the top of great peaks of water down into deep troughs, where the water rose like yellow walls around them. The wind was driving them toward the opposite shore at a terrifying pace.

Then a wave larger than the rest loomed over them. It almost seemed to reach out for the boat. With a sickening lurch it flipped *Wave-sweeper* over, throwing them all into the churning, bitter-cold water.

When he came to the surface, Collun took in a deep breath of air and looked around wildly for the others. Through the spray he caught sight of Talisen's dark head. He was next to the upended boat. Collun thought he could hear Silien's voice shouting. Then he went under again. Yellow water flooded his mouth and nose. He kicked upward desperately. It seemed to take forever to find the surface. When he did, a wave immediately slammed into the side of his head, and he was under again. His frozen arm dangled uselessly in the water. Even if he had been an experienced swimmer, this foaming morass would have been too much for him. As it was, he knew it was only a matter of time before his legs would not be strong enough to keep lifting him to the surface.

The next time he came up he was closer to the shore and farther from the upended boat. But he was able to see that Talisen and Silien had gotten Brie on top of it and were somehow lashing her on. Then Collun saw a wave crash into them. When he next caught sight of the boat, Talisen and Silien were no longer visible, but Brie remained on top. Waves of yellow water washed over her. Collun wondered if she was still alive.

Then, above the wind, Collun heard a voice. It was loud, and it sounded angry. In the confused nightmare world of seething water and wind, Collun thought he must be imagining things. Who in Eirren was possessed of a voice loud enough to make itself heard over this howling, yellow storm? But still he heard it, and it was coming from the shore. He saw something tall and green standing on the land. At first he thought it to be a tree. Then he saw it was Crann.

Another wave propelled Collun closer to the shore. As he surfaced, gasping what felt to be his last breath, he saw Crann's mouth form a circle. His cheeks were distended. Collun had the sudden wild thought that the wizard was somehow sucking the great wind into his own gaunt body. He half expected to see the old man's throat balloon up, swelling like a frog's during mating season. But of course it did not.

And then the wind began to die. The waves started getting smaller. Collun didn't have to fight so hard to keep his head above water.

He looked again toward Crann, who raised his arms above his head, as he had in the forest, and shouted the words, "Siochain gaoth!" Suddenly the wind was gone.

Crann dropped his arms and turned toward Collun. The boy kicked feebly, moving forward in the nearly calm water.

By the time he reached the shallow waters of the lakeshore, Collun's legs had no strength left in them. The wizard lifted him out of the water and chafed his arms with the green cloak. Crann noticed that Collun's arm hung limp, but he said nothing. Collun lay without moving, listening to the sound of waves quietly lapping against the shore.

"Look," the wizard said. The upended boat with Brie on top was moving through the water. It wasn't until it was almost to shore that Collun realized Fara was dragging the boat, holding it by a length of rope clenched in her teeth.

Talisen and Silien soon appeared, and before long they were all gathered on the shore.

Collun kneeled by Brie. "Is she . . . ?" he asked Crann.

"She lives, though not for much longer. We must go." Crann's voice was stern, and Collun heard anger underneath his words.

The wizard lifted Brie into his arms and began to lead them.

They walked over a rocky headland covered with long grass and cattails. Crann led them inland toward a low-lying ridge of land.

They were approaching the opening of a large cave. Without hesitation, Crann ducked his head and entered. The others followed. Crann paused briefly to spark a fire and make a torch from a length of dry wood he found lying on the cave floor. He gave Talisen the torch to carry.

Silien spoke, his voice echoing in the cavern. "Do we go to Tir a Ceol?"

"Yes," answered Crann shortly.

"Do you know the way?"

"I do." Crann bit the words off, his voice sharp.

Silien shook his head. "I do not think . . ."

The wizard turned on him with a swish of his green robes. His eyes burned. "I do not care what you think, Ellyl."

Silien stared back at Crann for a moment, then shrugged. The wizard gently hoisted Brie's wasted body over one shoulder. Gesturing for Talisen to hold the torch high, Crann walked into the tunnel that gaped before them.

FIFTEEN

Tir a Ceol

The path they followed sloped smoothly downward, and they moved forward steadily. The air in the underground passageway was surprisingly warm, and their clothes dried quickly. No one spoke; all they could hear was the echoing sound of their footsteps. Collun was tired, his head throbbed, and he was hungry, but it did not matter; Crann led them now.

For a long time they followed the green figure with the dying girl in his arms. And finally they came to a cavern that glowed with a dim light. Crann told Talisen to extinguish his torch. The cavern walls were gray and rough like those of the path they had been following,

but at the other end was a wide tunnel carved of smooth white rock. Crann led them inside.

When they reached the end of the tunnel, two Ellylon stepped into their path. They looked much like Silien, with golden hair and silver eyes, and they carried white shields and short swords made of metal that gleamed blue in the soft light. Silien stepped in front of Crann. The two Ellylon deferentially moved back, letting the company pass. Silien silently took over the lead.

They passed through many caverns, all made of the same smooth stone and illuminated by a soft white light. At first Collun could not see the source of the light, but then he noticed a glowing white stone set in the corner of one of the caverns they passed through. After that he saw each cavern had a white stone set in a corner. As he passed one, he ran his hand over it. The stone gave off no heat, only light. It reminded him of the glow of a firefly.

At first they saw few Ellylon, but soon they passed into a cavern that appeared to be different from the others. Clusters of radiant gems were arranged in seemingly random patterns along the walls. They shone with colors richer and more dazzling than Collun had ever seen. He could not gaze at them long without having to look away.

Many Ellylon were gathered in this cavern. One in particular was clearly the king. He was old, with hair that matched the silver of his eyes. It fell in smooth waves from his large brow and down his neck. A circlet of the gems ringed his forehead. Even at a distance, Collun could see a resemblance between Silien and the king, mostly in the proud way they held their chins.

Crann turned to Talisen and wordlessly passed Brie into his arms. Then he approached the king, covering the distance between them quickly on his long legs. He stopped and, looking the king in the eye, said, "I am Crann."

The Ellyl king gazed at the wizard for several long moments without speaking. "Wizard of the Trees," he said finally, his voice soft and deadly. "You took a great risk coming into my kingdom."

"I come in peace. With a girl who is dying."

"What is that to me? She is a human." The Ellyl king's face held no pity, and Collun's hope dimmed. "Why do you not heal her yourself, Wizard of the Trees?"

"She has gone beyond my reach, Midir," replied Crann. "As you well know."

"Father, the Flame-girl...," Silien began, stepping forward.

The king turned toward Silien and the younger Ellyl's words died on his lips. His father's eyes burned with cold fury. "How dare you bring humans into Tir a Ceol!"

"I do as I choose," responded Silien, his head erect, and for the first time since Collun had known him, Silien's pale cheeks were flushed.

"Enough!" Crann's voice echoed through the cavern. The wizard had thrown off his hood. His eyes were lit with anger, and he held his oaken staff high.

The Ellyl king's expression did not change, but he rose from the seat of polished white stone on which he sat. Crann towered over the Ellyl.

"Is this, then, what Ellylon have become? It was not always so." Crann's voice held contempt.

"Having compassion for humans was the weakness of my ancestors. It almost destroyed us," replied the king.

"You speak of a forgotten war with a foolish human king who is long dead. And because of this you would arbitrarily dispense death with your Daoine Ellyl. You have become as cruel and merciless as any shadow creature Medb has called out of Cruachan's cave. Or even as Medb herself."

The Ellyl king's eyes flickered. His voice when he spoke was dangerous. "I would not be compared to the Queen of Ghosts."

"And what separates you? What reason had you for wishing these humans dead?"

"We want no part of humans. They were trespassing."

"They came with your son. Invited by him. And would you have killed him as well? Have you so many sons that one more or less matters not?"

The king was silent a moment. He glanced at Silien, and his voice was chill. "My son swims as the fish swim. But Silien chose to leave his kingdom, to live among humans. He is no son of mine."

Silien responded, his voice as cold as his father's. "If I am to rule one day, then I choose to know why things are as they are. I would *know* humans before I shun them." He paused. "I met the queen of Eirren, Father, and she was as full of grace as any woman of Tir a Ceol."

The Ellyl king looked at his son with a mixture of outrage and curiosity. "You were not content to merely roam among them, but you must consort with their queen?"

Crann spoke then, his voice low and deadly serious.

"If you wish for Ellylon to survive in the days that come, you must not only meet the king and queen of Eirren, but you must find a way to join your might with theirs. Even as we speak, Queen Medb gathers a host of evil that will destroy all in its path. And I promise you, Ellyl king, Tir a Ceol will know the taste of fear."

The Ellyl king gazed at Crann, his mouth set. "How do I know you speak the truth?"

Talisen suddenly cried out and dropped to one knee, his eyes on Brie's wasted face. "I think . . . she is dying." His voice was choked. Collun quickly came to his side and sought Brie's pulse. He could not find it.

And then Fara, who had also silently glided to Brie's side, let out a long, penetrating cry. Collun felt tears come into his eyes.

The king's head came up at the sound of the faol's cry. He stared steadily at Fara, who let out another low sound. The king gave a slight nod. He raised his hand. Two Ellylon came at once and lifted Brie out of Talisen's arms. They left the cavern soundlessly. It all happened so fast that Collun didn't have time to react.

Then Crann spoke in a quiet voice. "Thank you."

Collun's heart leaped within him. He did not know why the Ellyl king had decided to help them, but he wanted to shout aloud his happiness.

"I would speak with you more," the king said to Crann. "Silien, take the humans away, then return here."

As he and Talisen followed Silien, Collun asked the Ellyl, "Where have they taken Brie?"

"To Slanaigh and to the healing waters. Slanaigh will try to heal her." Silien's eyes fell on Collun's arm, which still hung limp at his side. "I had better take you to him as well."

Silien gave Talisen over to an Ellyl woman he called Ebba. Her face was tranquil, and she had long golden hair, which was brindled with gray.

Collun followed Silien through a number of caverns, then along a winding corridor, and down a steep flight of steps. They ducked their heads to enter a dark, warm room that smelled like the darkest, richest earth in which Collun had ever worked. A single light flickered from a thick candle.

When his eyes adjusted to the dim light, Collun saw an Ellyl seated by the side of a large, still pool of water. He was gently dipping Brie's emaciated body into the water, his hands holding her under the armpits. The Ellyl was very old, though his pale, translucent skin was unlined. He looked slight, almost fragile, but he held Brie effortlessly. He sang. His voice was feathery and ancient, but the melody was true.

The water Brie floated in was the color of milk. Small, rainbow-hued bubbles dotted the surface. Just looking at the water made Collun's body relax. Silien gestured for Collun to sit, and as soon as he did, he became drowsy. As he drifted off, he saw the healer lifting Brie's head out of the water. White beads of liquid dripped off her dark eyelashes.

At first Collun couldn't remember where he was. But he felt peaceful and warm. He blinked several times.

He lay in darkness. Something soft pillowed his head and a coverlet of feathers lay over him. He sat up, trying to remember. Brie. The white pool. The Ellyl with the translucent skin.

Then he suddenly realized. He could feel the tips of

all his fingers! And his right arm moved when he wanted it to. He curled his hand into a fist, and he laughed out loud.

He lay there for a long time, savoring the warmth. Once, when he reached up, almost by habit, to rub his forehead, he found that it, too, had been healed. There was no more numbness.

Finally he sat up, thinking it was time to find out where he was and what had happened to the others, when someone bearing a candle entered the darkened room. At first he thought it was an Ellyl because of the way its hair shone gold. But the hair was cut short. And then the candle came up to the face, and Collun saw it was Brie.

Without thinking, he gasped. He did not understand. Why was her hair gold now when before it had been black? Was it the Ellyl waters, and was his own hair gold now as well? He reached up and touched his head in confusion.

Brie laughed. "Do not worry. Your hair is as it was," she said, smiling. "Mine has always been yellow. I used black walnut leaves to color it, to make me look more like a boy. The Ellyl water washed all the stain away. My eyes and lashes were always dark, like my mother's."

Collun gazed at her without speaking. She was still gaunt and pale from her ordeal, but her eyes were her own again. She looked young. And beautiful. She wore a simple white shift that fell almost to the ground. He had not seen her in women's clothing before. He stood, feeling suddenly shy.

"How is your arm?" Brie asked.

"It is healed."

"I am glad." A strained silence came up between them.

"Talisen must be pleased beyond measure to be here in Tir a Ceol," Brie said with a smile. "Perhaps he will finally learn an Ellyl song."

Collun nodded, his mind searching for words.

"Is something wrong, Collun?" Brie asked abruptly.

"No. Nothing," Collun mumbled, his eyes averted.

"You are angry with me. For the way I behaved to you . . ."

Collun blushed. "No, it's just—it's your hair," he blurted out.

Brie looked startled. And then they both burst into laughter. Collun's confusion drained away.

"Are you well, Brie?"

"Yes. The white water healed me."

"What was it like before? Your eyes were so empty, but I kept wondering if you could see or hear us."

"I could hear voices, yours in particular, but it was distorted, and I could not always understand the words. I was cold all the time, and I saw everything through a cloud of gray. Then toward the end the gray began to turn black, and I heard a hollow voice calling to me. I did not want to listen, but it kept calling and calling and pulling me toward it." She shuddered. "Then suddenly it stopped. I began to feel a warmth growing in my body. It started in my toes and worked its way up. It felt . . . wonderful." She closed her eyes and smiled. Then she swayed and abruptly sat down on the bed.

"I still feel shaky," she said.

"Of course." He sat beside her. She looked so frail. Collun had a strong urge to wrap the feather quilt around her and to rub her thin arms with his hands to warm her. But suddenly that same feeling of shyness washed over him again and all he could do was say stiffly, "Can I get you something?"

Brie opened her mouth to answer, but the door opened and Ebba, the Ellyl woman with the calm eyes and brindled hair, came into the room.

"That's enough talking for now. You need your rest, especially you," she added with a stern look at Brie.

Brie rose and began to follow, but then turned back toward Collun. "I came to apologize. I have acted unfairly toward you since we left Temair. There is more I would tell you—that I would have told you if the creature, Nemian, had not come when it did. But Crann has asked me to wait." And then she was gone. The door swung shut behind them. Collun sank back on his soft bed, his thoughts racing.

During the next two days they slept, ate, and slept some more, as they recovered their health and strength. Collun, Brie, and Talisen each had a separate room, but the rooms were joined by a common one where they met for meals. The food they were given was different from the food they knew, but they soon developed a taste for it. A particular delicacy of the Ellylon, brisgein, was made of stalks of heather and silverwood. They found it to be surprisingly delicious. Fish was also a staple of the Ellyl diet and was prepared in a variety of ways.

They often heard music coming from other rooms. Whenever it began, Talisen would grab his harp and try to pick out the melodies. He asked Ebba if she would teach him a song, but she told him she did not have the gift for music.

Ebba was the only Ellyl they saw at first, except for an occasional visit from Silien, who told them that Crann and the king were deep in discussion, barely pausing for meals.

Ebba was an artist who worked with an unusual white clay with streaks of light blue running through it. She showed them samples of her work, and they were impressed by the grace of form and line she had achieved. The subjects of her art were from nature: a fish with unusual, trailing fins; a plate depicting the sky after a summer storm; a puffball bending in the wind.

"How do you know of plants and clouds, Ebba, when you live below the ground?" Talisen asked at the evening meal on their second day in Tir a Ceol.

She laughed. "Ellylon move freely between land and water. We have devised many ways over the years of obscuring our presence from you."

"How?" queried Talisen in some disbelief.

"Dense fogs, hidden valleys, unscalable mountains, to name only a few," she replied placidly as she heaped more brisgein on his plate. "Silien is one of the few Ellylon in many hundreds of years to move undisguised among humans." She paused. "Though there are many young Ellylon with the same curiosity. Silien is merely the first to have the courage to risk the wrath of the elders."

Crann came to their quarters just as they were finishing the meal.

"You look well," he said, gazing at them. "Better, at

least, than the last time I saw you," he added with a brief smile in Brie's direction.

"When do we leave here?" asked Collun.

"We have only just arrived, spriosan."

"But Nessa..."

"I know. But what I am speaking of with the Ellyl king affects you and your sister, Collun."

An Ellyl appeared in the doorway. "A message from Midir, wizard. He says to come immediately. There is news from the north."

"Very well." The wizard turned to go.

"Crann...," began Collun, his voice edged with worry.

"Be patient, spriosan. By evening of the third day from today, I will return. Then we will make plans. In the meantime, gather your strength." And the wizard was gone.

The next morning Ebba took the three of them out of their quarters and guided them through some of the caverns of Tir a Ceol. Fara came with them. The Ellylon they saw looked at them with curiosity but stayed aloof from the human visitors.

Ebba told them they were free to explore as long as they did not disturb the Ellylon and were back in time for the evening meal. Talisen immediately headed toward the nearest cavern from which music emanated. Fara reached up a paw and batted Brie's leg. Then the faol set off. "I think I am meant to follow. Would you like to join us?" Brie asked Collun. The boy shook his head. He stood irresolutely as he watched them disappear into the next cavern. Ebba walked up to him.

"There is a cavern near here that might interest you."

The Ellyl woman led him silently through a series of caverns. "Here," she said, entering one that was much larger than any Collun had yet seen.

In the center lay a long oval pool of silvery water, and ranged around it was a herd of Ellyl horses.

Collun had heard stories of Ellyl horses—that they were unmatchable in power and speed and too wild to be ridden by humans; though it was said that the hero Cuillean rode an Ellyl horse.

Many of the horses were grazing on a soft green-and-white carpet of something that Collun had at first thought to be dappled moss. When he bent to get a closer look, he found it was made up of millions of tiny green-and-white flowers. The delicate flowers grew in the shape of trefoil and smelled sweet, almost like honey.

"It is seamir, their favorite food. It grows very quickly so there is always plenty for them to eat. Now I must return to my work." Ebba left the cavern.

Collun continued to gaze about him in awe. The animals resembled Eirrenian horses but were shorter and leaner and somehow more graceful. Their tails were long, almost brushing the ground, and there was a sheen to their coats like the surface of the silvery pool.

As Collun knelt to touch the carpet of tiny flowers, a pair of flared nostrils suddenly appeared by his hand. Hardly daring to breathe, Collun pulled up a clump of seamir and offered it to the horse. The animal nosed the boy's hand and then, giving Collun the sense a great favor was being done him, delicately cropped the clump from his palm.

It was a beautiful animal, white with blue-gray markings. It had hooves that gleamed like silver, and its eyes were large and lit with fire from within. Collun offered up another clump of flowers.

When he told her later of his encounter with the white-and-gray horse, Ebba was astonished.

"The horse you describe is called Fiain, or the Wild One, and it is called so because no Ellyl has ever been able to tame him. I myself am considered one of the most skilled with the horses in Tir a Ceol, and Fiain will not let me within a foot of him. Have you a special way with horses, Collun?"

"Indeed not," the boy replied. "I once had an accident with the old farm horse at Aonarach..." He trailed off under Ebba's skeptical look.

"He speaks the truth," said Talisen, entering their quarters. "But Collun, listen to what has happened to me today." Ebba left the room to finish preparations on their meal. "At first the Ellyon hung back from me. They even stopped playing their music," Talisen said. "But I challenged one of them to a riddling contest, and that broke through their reserve. Ellylon love riddles, even more than I. We played games, danced, ate food, and finally they let me listen to their music. First, though, they explained to me about the different types of music in Tir a Ceol.

"There are two kinds," Talisen explained in an animated voice. "One is the ancient music that works what we humans call magic. The Ellylon call it draiocht. Only a select few have the gift for, and are trained in, draoicht. You see, the Ellylon believe that in the same way all things bear a name, so does each thing bear a song. A song unique only to it. There are songs for rocks, for clouds, for men, and for animals. To learn and be able to sing that song gives power. You remember when Silien kindled the light in his hand in the labyrinth? He used the song of a flame. Even an Ellyl with the gift takes many years of training to learn the songs and to sing them well. Amergin, they told me, was the only non-Ellyl ever to learn draoicht, and he only understood very little.

"The other kind of Ellyl music," Talisen continued, "is like the music we know in Eirren, except that it is *more*—more beautiful, more wrenching. This kind they call ceol, and it is my belief that ceol is the kind of music the ancient bards of Eirren knew. The kind that can make you weep, laugh, dance, and even sleep. And it is the kind that I am going to learn. One way or another, Collun, I am going to learn this ceol music." The expression on Talisen's face was resolute.

Collun did not see much of Talisen in the next two days. He would return to their quarters only to eat an occasional meal and to sleep, though he seemed to do little of the latter. Every time Collun woke in the night, he could hear harp music coming from Talisen's room.

Ebba was teaching Brie the Ellyl way of carving wood, and Collun watched as she worked on a new bow. Ebba supplied her with a soft, white wood, perfect for carving. And through the curls of wood shavings, a delicate, long-necked bird began to take form. It was a tine-ean, Ebba said, a flame-bird.

Collun felt restless, anxious to resume his search for Nessa. He found himself returning to the cavern of the horses. At each visit he and the white-and-gray horse went through the same ritual. As the horse nibbled the flowers from his hand, Collun couldn't help wondering what it would be like to ride such a magnificent animal. But he could not imagine the proud horse allowing anyone to climb on his back.

On the afternoon of their fifth day in Tir a Ceol, Talisen came to Collun's room and sat wordlessly in front of him. He closed his eyes and let his fingers play over the strings of his harp. Collun listened with pleasure to the delicate, haunting tune, and when Talisen had finished, he complimented him enthusiastically. "You have learned an Ellyl song!"

"Several," Talisen replied carelessly. "But this was not one." And suddenly there was an uncharacteristic shyness in Talisen's manner.

"But that did not sound like a song I have heard. Something you learned in Temair?"

"No. Collun, I made this song myself." Talisen's face glowed.

Collun's eyes widened. "You mean . . . ?"

"Yes. I have learned how to make songs, and without going to any stuffy school with a name that sounds like a sneeze."

Collun was filled with pride for his friend. "I am pleased for you, Talisen."

"And well you should be." Talisen laughed. And he was the old Talisen again, full of impossible boasts and carefree laughter.

The evening Crann had promised to come, Silien appeared instead. He said the wizard had been delayed and would be there the next morning.

"I came to say good-bye," said the Ellyl. "Much has happened in the past few days. I am bound for Temair, where, on behalf of my father, I will propose a comhairle, a council, with King Gwynn and Queen Aine."

Talisen let out a sound of wonderment. "This is indeed an historic event."

Silien nodded. "I must leave now. Time is precious. But I wish you well on your quest," Silien said, gazing at Collun. Collun thought he read sympathy in the silver eyes.

"I hope to meet you again." The Ellyl shook each of their hands gravely. Then with his familiar half-smile, he turned and left the room.

That night Collun had trouble getting to sleep, and when he did, he dreamed of the pile of bones in the labyrinth. He woke up, shivering uncontrollably.

SIXTEEN

Hero's Son

The next morning after breakfast, Collun began to pace the stone floor. "Where is Crann? What can be keeping him?" he said. To distract him, Brie said she would teach him an Ellyl game called ficheall that Ebba had taught her. It was played with a board, dice, and small figures carved of black spinel. Collun reluctantly sat, and they began to play. Talisen watched, harp in hand, and he made them laugh with a song he improvised about Farmer Whicklow and his enormous appetite for partridge pie.

The door abruptly swung open and Crann entered. Wearily he lowered himself into a chair that was too small for his long body. He took up one of the small

figures from the game board and began absently to roll it between his fingers.

"You look terrible," said Talisen.

"Thank you," replied Crann dryly.

"Have you and the king not paused for rest at all?"

"Midir is proud and strong-willed, and my tongue is not so graceful with words as once it was. Still, he finally sees the darkness that threatens and the need for an alliance with Eirren," said Crann.

"Surely that is good news," remarked Talisen.

"Yes," replied Crann. "But there has been news that is not good, I'm afraid. An Ellyl who lives underneath a lake in upper Scath arrived a day ago to seek counsel from his king." Crann paused. "It is the Firewurme. The Ellyl spotted it off the shores of the Northern Sea. It is worse even than I had feared. Medb has called up the Wurme—or Naid, as the Ellylon call it."

Collun felt a chill. Silien had spoken of a Firewurme when he was telling them about the wizard Cruachan, and Collun remembered stories told to him as a child about a monstrous white Wurme that had laid waste to Eirren in the days of Amergin.

"The Firewurme," Crann continued, "was Cruachan's most powerful, most deadly creation. It destroyed countless Eirrenians and Ellylon alike. It was the Wurme that ultimately turned on Cruachan and killed him when he could no longer control it.

"I had hoped Medb would not dare awaken the Firewurme, but she has grown more reckless and arrogant than I had believed possible. If she chooses to let the Firewurme loose, then there is little hope any of us will survive its coming.

"As Silien no doubt told you, Midir has agreed to a comhairle with the king and queen of Eirren. I doubt not the Eirrenians will be eager for such an alliance."

Silence filled the room. Crann gazed fixedly at the small spinel figurine in his hand, then looked up at Collun. "But I did not come to speak of this alone. Collun, the time has come to tell you all."

"Do you wish us to leave?" asked Brie, half rising.

"That is up to Collun," replied the wizard.

"Stay," Collun said. "Is it because Emer is dead that you can now speak?"

The wizard nodded. "I am released from the oath I gave to her." He paused. "Give me your dagger," Crann said abruptly.

With a bewildered expression Collun reached for the dagger at his waist and passed it to Crann. The wizard laid it on the table amidst the spinel figures and the dice. The stone in the handle glowed faintly, as it had the last time Crann held it.

"As I told you in the Forest of Eld, I believe this stone to be one of the three shards of the Cailceadon Lir. The fact that it killed Moccus's sow and injured the creature Nemian confirms my belief." Crann paused. "As I also said, it is my guess that this is the shard that Amergin lost on one of his sea voyages. Collun, did your mother ever tell you where she got the lucky stone?"

Collun shook his head. "I have been trying to puzzle it out. What happened to the shard after Amergin lost it? To a woman, you said?"

"Yes. And she, in turn, sold it to an adventurer and explorer who called himself Lleann. Like Lir before him, Lleann recognized this stone would bring luck to him and to his family. So he, too, began a tradition of passing it on to his firstborn child, and each succeeding generation did the same."

"Then Emer is a descendant of Lleann?" Collun asked.

The wizard shook his head, and Collun saw a look pass between him and Brie.

"Then Goban . . . ?" Collun asked in confusion.

"Collun," Crann interrupted. "What do you know of the hero Cuillean?"

Puzzled, Collun answered slowly. "Only what I have learned from Talisen's songs. And then I heard more in Temair. Why?"

"Tell me what you do know."

"Let's see . . . That as a youth he showed great courage and prowess. That he was a hero in the Eamh War . . ." Collun trailed off.

"That he loved a lady and lost her shortly after they were wed," spoke up Talisen. "Remember the song 'Lady of the Silver Fir,' Collun? It has always been one of my favorites."

"Yes, I remember. He mourned her death for many years. And then, most recently, it is said that he disappeared, a year ago or so, and may be dead."

"That is all?"

Collun nodded slowly. "My mother did not like songs of the Eamh War or of Cuillean. She lost a brother in the fighting, and the pain ran deep."

"Once," agreed Talisen, "Emer heard me singing a song of the war and of one of Cuillean's most spectacular battles, and she bade me never to sing it or any others like it on the farmhold Aonarach."

The old wizard was quiet for a moment, as if gathering his thoughts. "Before he went off to fight for Eirren in the Eamh War, Cuillean did indeed love a maiden. He pledged himself to this maiden, and she to him, and when he returned from battle, they were to be wed. In the songs about them she is called Eilm, or the Lady of the Silver Fir. But her true name was Emer."

Collun felt the hairs on the back of his neck rise. He stared at the wizard's moon white beard.

"Emer was the daughter of a powerful lord, Fogal. She had two brothers, one older and one younger. The younger, Neill, was his father's favorite, the apple of his eye. Neill worshiped his sister's betrothed, the hero Cuillean. He wished to be exactly like his idol. Though he was young—barely older than yourself, Collun—he ran off to join the army in its northward march to fight Medb. Neill was brave, but he was also impulsive and unschooled in the ways of war. Despite Cuillean's efforts to watch over the stripling—indeed, putting his own life in danger more than once—Neill was one of the first to die in the Eamh War.

"When his father received word of Neill's death, he went half mad with grief, and in his madness Fogal blamed Cuillean. He withdrew his blessing from the proposed marriage between Emer and Cuillean and forbade her to see him. When Cuillean returned from the war and found himself barred from the maiden he loved, he acted in haste and anger and, with a handful of men, assailed the dun of Emer's father. Under the cover of darkness he stole Emer away, killing several of Fogal's men. Cuillean took Emer off with him to his dun by Siar Muir, the Western Sea. There they were wed.

"Fogal was now left completely alone, his own wife long dead, both sons dead in the Eamh War—the elder killed in the waning months of the fighting—and Emer taken from him by Cuillean, whom he now saw as his most bitter enemy. He gathered an army and waged battle with Cuillean. Fogal was ultimately killed in the fight, and it was Cuillean himself who killed him.

"Emer stayed with Cuillean for a year after that, but the pain of seeing her father killed by the man she loved, on top of the deaths of both her brothers, proved to be more than she could bear. Finally she left Cuillean, taking with her their newborn son." Crann paused.

"You are that son, Collun."

Collun's breath stopped for a moment. He felt as if he must be in a dream. Numbly he watched the wizard's lips move. Collun did not speak, and the wizard continued his tale, his eyes carefully watching the boy.

"Emer hid her true identity and found peace in Inkberrow, a small town some distance from Temair and Cuillean, and from the life she had known. She met the local blacksmith, and he became her friend. When she told him her story, he offered to live with her as husband and be a father to her son. They never were wed, as Emer was already wife to Cuillean, but they let the people of Inkberrow believe they were married. Emer found she was expecting another child, and though Goban knew the baby was also Cuillean's, he felt a special attachment to the girl-child he himself helped into the world.

"At first the union between Emer and Goban was a healing one. The blacksmith helped Emer to forget. But somewhere inside she still loved Cuillean, though she could not admit it even to herself. Goban sensed it, and it ate away at him. It turned his feelings against Cuillean's son.

"Before leaving Temair, Emer went to her only living relative, her elder brother's widow, Fial, and told her what she intended to do. By threatening to kill herself rather than remain with Cuillean, she forced Fial to tell everyone at court that Emer had been found dead—that she and the baby had both been drowned trying to cross the River Haw. A few bedraggled remains of Emer's belongings were produced as evidence, and the story was believed. Cuillean was heart-stricken and hid in his dun, refusing to see anyone for months.

"There were only two people besides Emer and Goban who knew the truth: Fial and myself. I had been a friend to both Fogal and Cuillean. At first I, too, believed Emer was dead. It was only by accident that I discovered otherwise. It has long been a practice with me to disguise myself as a kesil. One day my travels took me through the town of Inkberrow. Passing your lonely farmhold Aonarach, I caught a glimpse of a woman's face that was familiar to me. Her hair had turned gray, and she looked careworn. I almost did not recognize her. But when our eyes met, I saw the Lady of the Silver Fir. Emer recognized me as well, despite my own appearance. She was terrified I would give away her secret.

"I told her of Cuillean's grief and tried to convince her to return to him, but she would not. She had made an oath to the goddess Eira, she said, and would not break it. She begged me to tell no one that I had seen her, and finally I agreed. And I pledged to say nothing of her children's true parentage, to them or to anyone.

Only if she was to die, and I deemed it important to their safety, was I to be released from the oath. Fial had been made to swear a similar pledge."

"Why? Why didn't she tell us?" asked Collun, his voice barely audible.

"It is difficult to explain. The pain of losing her brothers and then seeing her father killed by the man she loved altered Emer. She came to despise violence and war, and she sought to protect her children from this world—a world that, in her eyes, was embodied by Cuillean, the man she had once loved above all.

"She also told me that in a moment of her deepest pain, she had had a vision of the goddess Eira. Eira, she said, told Emer that any children she had that were begotten by Cuillean would meet the same fate as Emer's father and brothers if Emer did not leave Cuillean forever. That was when she swore to take you away to a place where you would be safe and where she would never tell you of your true identity.

"But Emer did not know there were events unfolding, with their beginnings in the distant past, that would make it impossible for her children to remain safe and hidden in Inkberrow.

"You see, it is Cuillean who is descended from Lleann. And like his ancestors before him, Cuillean intended to pass the lucky stone on to his firstborn. To you, Collun. Cuillean, of course, knew nothing of the chalcedony's true origin. Nor did Emer. Before she fled his dun, Cuillean had given it to her to fashion into a pendant or arm circlet for you to wear, and she took the Cailceadon Lir with her when she left. So, you see, as far as Cuillean knew the stone was lost in the River Haw with Emer and their child. It did not matter to him, for in his grief he swore he would never take another wife; therefore, there would be no other child to whom to pass the stone.

"But the cailceadon was not lost in the River Haw. It was in Inkberrow, and Emer did pass it on to Cuillean's son when she thought the time was right. As far as she knew, it was merely a lucky talisman that had been in her son's father's family for generations."

All eyes were on the dagger lying on the game board before them.

"I do not know when, but sometime after the Eamh War, Medb must have discovered the first of the lost shards of the Cailceadon Lir," continued the wizard. "When this stone was whole it bore the power to seal the Cave of Cruachan and defeat its creatures. Is it any wonder then that Medb conceived a desire to possess all three shards? To make whole the original Cailceadon Lir?

"The Eirrenian shard of the stone is too well hidden for her to trace, though I advised the king and queen early on of the danger so that they might augment the cailceadon's security if necessary.

"But, and I do not know how, Medb discovered the other shard was in Cuillean's possession. He used to wear it in an armband of silver, and perhaps the traitor Bricriu saw it. But before Medb could go after Cuillean's stone, Bricriu relayed the news that Cuillean no longer had it. That in fact it lay at the bottom of the River Haw where Emer and Cuillean's firstborn child had drowned. This must have been a blow to Medb. But then, many years later, Nessa came to Temair.

"It surprises me that Emer allowed Nessa to leave Inkberrow, much less journey to Temair. Her vows to protect the two of you were so deeply felt."

"Once Fial made the offer, Nessa would not listen to Emer. She was determined to go," replied Collun.

Crann nodded. "Emer must have hoped enough time had passed that no one would see the resemblance. Indeed there was none between the girl and Cuillean, and little between mother and daughter, except in the eyes. Queen Aine felt an immediate liking for the girl, yet did not know her as the daughter of her old friend. But Bricriu, with his sharp eyes, saw the resemblance. He noted the few slips of the tongue Nessa no doubt made about her family and the village she came from, and he relayed his suspicions to Medb. The two must have guessed that Emer had had another child, and if a second one lived, so might the first. Even if the firstborn son had died, perhaps Emer herself still lived and had given the chalcedony to her daughter.

"The Queen of Ghosts must have ordered Bricriu to find out what he could from the girl and then, depending on what he learned, to abduct her. If she did not have the stone herself, she might know where it was, or, indeed, serve as bait for the true holder of the stone— her elder brother, if he still lived. Medb knew Cuillean, and she knew that any son of his must come to save his sister."

Collun's cheeks were burning.

"But why didn't Medb come for Collun in Inkberrow?" asked Talisen.

"She did. Once she found out from Nessa where Collun was, she sent Urlacan. But Nessa must have held out against Medb for a period of time, hence the delay. You had left Inkberrow by the time Urlacan got there. He was doubling back when he found you at the Traveler's Rest."

"Where is Nessa, then?" Collun asked, his voice barely audible.

"She is being held somewhere in Scath, I believe. Not at Medb's fortress, Rathcroghan, according to a source I trust. But that is all I have been able to discover."

"Why would Medb keep her alive?" Collun said the words with difficulty.

"I do not know, but it is my guess that Medb deems a live hostage more valuable than a dead one. Perhaps, also, she has some idea of using Nessa to flush Cuillean out of hiding—that is, if he still lives." The room went still, and no one spoke for several moments.

"What is to be done?" Collun finally said, his voice hollow.

"The better question, son of Cuillean, is what is it that *you* choose to do?" said Crann. His words were formal and distant.

Collun's head whirled at the sound of his naming. "Son of Cuillean." Was it possible? He hovered between laughter and tears. That he was not the son of the man he had long called father—the silent, grim blacksmith who had shown him little love—was not a surprise. Indeed, he wondered why he had not guessed it before. But to find that he, a cowardly farm boy with dirt under his fingernails, was the son of one of Eirren's greatest heroes...If it were not so painful, he would call it the best joke he had ever heard.

He realized they were all looking at him. What was his choice? What other choice was there for him? He must finish what he had begun. "I would find my sister," he said simply.

Crann nodded, then fixed his bright gaze on Collun. "If you will have me, I would journey with you, son of Cuillean."

Collun felt a surge of relief. With Crann as companion, perhaps there was a chance of finding Nessa and bringing her back alive.

"And I would go with you, too, Collun," said Brie, her voice quiet but firm.

Collun opened his mouth to object, but Brie's dark eyes looked stubbornly into his.

"I'm coming, too, of course," said Talisen. He strummed his harp with a dramatic flourish.

Crann rose. "It is settled, then. We will leave tomorrow."

"But where do we go?" asked Collun, picking up the dagger from the game board.

"We go to Scath."

The wizard's words sent a shiver of dread through the group. "I have eyes in Scath and hope to know more of your sister's whereabouts by the time we reach its border." The wizard stood. He moved toward Collun.

"You have learned much today, spriosan." He rested his hand gently on Collun's shoulder. The boy could feel warmth emanating from the wizard's long fingers. Then Crann made a gesture of farewell and left the room.

Talisen was plucking the strings of his harp. "To think that all this time I was keeping company with the son of Cuillean! I will have to make a song about it."

Collun stood abruptly. "I want no such song," he said roughly.

"Collun . . . ," began Brie.

"You knew, didn't you?" Collun said, turning toward her.

"The very first time I saw you in the Traveler's Rest, I noticed the resemblance to Cuillean—the color of your hair and eyes. But you said you were the son of a blacksmith, and I sensed no guile in your words. Then I heard you speak your mother's name in Temair."

"Cuillean was a friend of your father, wasn't he?" said Talisen.

"Yes," replied Brie, her voice flat.

"This is astounding, is it not, Collun? A true adventure," Talisen continued, enthusiastically. "To find you are the son of a great hero, hidden away in Inkberrow for all these years. I never did like that old beetle-browed Goban. Son of Cuillean . . . !"

But Collun only felt blank inside.

"Just think what they'd say back in Inkberrow if they knew you were the son of Cuillean," continued Talisen.

Son of Cuillean, son of Cuillean . . . The words echoed in Collun's head. He rose. Brie gave Talisen a warning look, but he went prattling on.

"And all that time Emer was really wed to Cuillean . . ."

"Quiet!" Collun suddenly shouted, his voice cracking. Then he felt his stomach heave. He fled from the room. Leaning his forehead against the cold stone of the corridor wall, Collun retched until his stomach held nothing more.

SEVENTEEN

Fiain

Collun didn't know how he got there, but he was in the cavern of the horses, sitting by the pool. He cupped his hands and filled them with cool water to splash on his hot face. Then he idly began plucking handfuls of the flower turf. It was not long before the familiar white-and-gray muzzle dropped down by his hand.

The animal must have sensed Collun's turmoil for he was uncommonly patient, allowing the boy, for the first time, to stand beside him and run his hand along his mane. It was soft, not wiry and coarse like manes Collun had touched before. He had an overwhelming urge to bury his face in it, but he did not dare.

And then, again without knowing how it happened, Collun was astride the horse. His hands clutched Fiain's silky mane. They were moving through the Ellyl herd. They came to the end of the cavern, and Fiain took them through a passage to an even larger one. And then they were flying over the ground at a gallop. For a brief moment Collun was terrified, but then he abandoned himself to the dizzying sensation of motion and speed.

His legs were locked fast to the horse's body. He buried his hands and face in the streaming mane. Hot tears coursed down his cheeks. The horse moved with the fluid grace of a nighthawk, and Collun wondered if its hooves were even touching the ground.

And then, just as suddenly as it had begun, the ride was over. Fiain came to an abrupt stop. Collun tumbled off his back onto the spongy turf.

Collun looked up at the horse, who was grazing unconcernedly beside him. He had never seen a creature so magnificent, so lit with fire and strength. He could not believe he had ridden this horse, or that he would ever have the courage to do so again. Fiain raised his head and looked at the boy. Collun felt something nudge into his thoughts.

It wasn't a word or a sentence, but more like a feeling inside him. Yet it wasn't from within him. And it was laughter. Suddenly Collun realized Fiain was laughing at him, as Talisen might, or Brie. Then the horse turned, flicked his tail, and broke into a trot. Wiping the remnants of tears from his cheeks, Collun stood and followed. They had covered a large distance during their wild ride, and Collun was weary by the time they returned to the cavern of the horses.

He saw Ebba making her way toward him. Fiain went directly to the silvery pool and began to drink.

"Then it is true," Ebba said as she reached Collun's side.

"What?" asked Collun.

"That Fiain has chosen you. And now that I know your history, it does not surprise me. Fiain is one of the foals sired by the Gray of Macha. The Gray was the Ellyl horse that Cuillean found and tamed many years ago. Fiain will go with you when you leave."

Collun could not believe it. "But I cannot ride him."

"If I am not mistaken, you just did. Anyway, he will teach you, and I will help, if you like. Here he comes." And Fiain was indeed approaching, his regal head held high. He allowed Collun to mount him, with Ebba's help.

Collun spent the rest of the afternoon learning how to ride an Ellyl horse. Ebba was a patient but unrelenting teacher. There was no saddle, and Collun had to learn to hold himself on the horse with only his legs, as he had done instinctively during that first headlong flight. Nor did Ellyl horses wear bridles; they could be guided only by pressure from the knees.

"Eventually you and Fiain will be able to communicate without speaking," said Ebba. "And he will need no physical guidance." Collun nodded thoughtfully, remembering the silent laughter that had edged into his thoughts.

By the time he and Ebba left the cavern of the horses, Collun's legs felt like overcooked runner beans, but he glowed with pride because he finally had been able to mount Fiain without Ebba's help.

When he entered their quarters, Collun found Brie attaching feathers to a new set of arrows. But she worked with an absent air. Collun sensed she had been waiting to speak with him. She seemed reluctant to begin, so Collun told her of his day in the cavern of the horses.

"Fiain is the foal of the Gray of Macha," he said, his eyes alight, "the Ellyl horse that my fath—" the word felt strange on his tongue "—that Cuillean rode. It is amazing, is it not?"

Brie nodded, her eyes on Collun's face.

"Tell me about Cuillean," Collun said suddenly.

Brie was silent for a moment. "Cuillean was friend to my father. More than a friend; in truth, they were blood brothers. They swore an oath sealed by blood from their veins." Brie's voice had taken on a different sound; there was something hard and distant he didn't understand.

"Collun...There is something I must tell you..." Brie's voice trailed off. Collun waited.

"It has to do with my father's death. You heard the traitor Bricriu speak of the manner in which my father died. But there is more. You see, I was there when he died." And again that queer, hard tone came into her voice.

"When my father set off that day it was because he had received an urgent message from his friend, Cuillean. The message said to meet him in the Ramhar Forest. Cuillean did not give a reason, but they were blood brothers and so my father went.

"Soon after he had gone, I discovered that, in his haste, my father had saddled his horse with a bridle and reins that were badly frayed on one side. I had noticed the fraying the day before and had meant to set them aside to be repaired, but I'd forgotten. I was angry with myself and so decided to follow my father and take him a fresh set of tack.

"I followed the path I knew he would take, and when I came to the Ramhar Forest I heard the sound of men fighting. I approached quietly, and from the shelter of a copse of rowan trees I saw my father surrounded by more Scathians than I could count. He was on foot with his back to a tree. He had just lost his sword—and part of his hand with it." Brie's eyes closed and she had to stop for a moment before she could continue.

"His death was upon him. His wounds were deep and many. But his murderers were not content merely to take his life. They sought also to rob him of his honor. They tortured him, forcing him to grovel and beg for his life. Then they made him tell all he knew of Eirren's army and of Temair and the royal dun. And my father told them. In his pain and his fear of death, he gave up his honor. For that, I shall never forgive them."

Brie paused for a moment, her eyes glittering, then continued. "For a moment, as I watched my father die, I was lost in madness. I wanted to kill each one of those cowards with my bare hands. I cared not at all for my own life. But then my thoughts cleared, and I knew my death would avail my father nothing. I watched and listened and memorized each face, especially that of the man who led them—a Scathian wearing a patch over his left eye. I have sworn to avenge my father's death and the manner in which he died, even if it costs my own life."

She stopped speaking. Her face was so frozen with hatred that to Collun she looked like a stranger.

"What of Cuillean, my father? And the message that he sent? Was he not there?"

Brie did not answer for several moments. Then she turned her head and stared at Collun. Slowly her eyes came back into focus, and Collun recognized her again.

"No, Cuillean was not there. And the truth is, I blamed him. In my rage and sorrow, I looked toward the man who ought to have been with my father, to stand with him against the cowards who killed him. And Cuillean was not there."

"But where was he? Why had he sent the message?"

"I do not know. But it was around that time that Cuillean disappeared."

"Then perhaps the murderers got him first," Collun said slowly. He felt suddenly exhausted. To gain a father and lose him in such a short time was more than he could take in.

"Perhaps, though I saw no sign of it. It is more likely they used Cuillean's name to lure my father to his death." Her eyes were on Collun's drawn face. "Go to bed, Collun. It has been a long day."

"Is there more you would tell me?"

"No, except that it was my anger toward your father that caused me to act so to you, his son. When I heard you say that Emer was your mother, I knew then you were indeed the son of Cuillean, as I had guessed when I first saw you. I hated you for who your father was, but that was not right. You have been a friend to me. If you had not risked your own life with the creature Nemian, I would have lost mine. I hope you will forgive me," Brie added, meeting his eyes with a tentative smile.

"Of course." Collun's glance fell on her neck. There was still a faint shadow of the mark Nemian had left behind. Without even being aware of what he did, he reached up and gently brushed the mark with his fingers. Brie looked at him in surprise. He quickly pulled his hand away.

"I, uh, I think I'll go to bed now," he stammered.

"Yes. You must be weary," Brie responded. They bade each other good night awkwardly, and Collun limped off to his pallet in the next room.

When he woke the next morning Collun rolled over and let out a moan. His muscles ached from his all-day riding lesson. But Ebba glided into his room and calmly rousted him out of bed and into the common room, where the morning meal waited.

As they were finishing, Crann entered. "Come." He gestured to Brie and Talisen. "King Midir has graciously offered horses to all in our company. He has selected those that are gentle, but they are Ellyl horses and you will need help to manage them. Ebba has volunteered to instruct you."

Collun accompanied them to the cavern of the horses and watched as Brie quickly adapted to her mount. Talisen, however, was awkward and impatient and took several tumbles. Ebba finally suggested that he try singing a song to the skittish horse. "Ellyl horses love music as much as you do."

Crann's horse was a magnificent white mare named Gealach, a gift to Crann from the Ellyl king. The wizard needed no instruction in Ellyl horsemanship.

Then it was time to leave, and they had to say good-bye to Ebba and the other Ellylon they had met. The king came to see them off.

Brie stepped forward. She had resumed her boyish travel garb, but she'd left her hair yellow. On her back she wore her new bow, with the design of a flame-bird, or tine-ean as the Ellylon called it. The old one, her father's, she left with Ebba. She would be back for it one day, she said, when her journey was done.

She approached the Ellyl king. "I owe you much, King Midir. And your son, for bringing me here."

The king did not smile, but there was a glint in his eye. "Silien is as stubborn as his father. He will rule Tir a Ceol well one day."

Then Fara appeared from nowhere, threading herself between Brie's legs. The girl crouched and ran her hand along the faol's arched back. "Thank you, Fara," Brie said softly. "I hope we meet again." The faol looked up into Brie's eyes and made a low sound. Brie smiled, her eyes bright, then quickly mounted her horse.

Crann stepped forward and solemnly shook the Ellyl king's hand. "Midir," he said, "much rides on the outcome of the comhairle. Ellyl and human may be different in many ways, but at heart you want the same thing—to live as you will in a land you may call your own. If we do not meet again, I wish you and your people well."

"Are you sure you have made the right choice?" asked the Ellyl king with the air of one continuing a long-running argument.

Crann nodded. "I journey with the boy."

"There may be a greater need for you elsewhere in the weeks and months to come."

"I owe it to his mother. And his father."

"Then watch out for yourself, wizard," responded Midir gravely. "You are old, but you are not immortal."

"I would not have it otherwise," Crann rejoined with a quick smile.

As Collun mounted Fiain, he ground his teeth together against the pain in his stiff body. It was not much better when he sat astride the Ellyl horse. But Fiain assumed a rolling, steady gait, and soon the pain subsided to a dull throb. Collun grew used to it.

It took them longer to leave Tir a Ceol than it had to enter, because as Crann explained, the safest porth was near the Western Sea. Though this new route made their journey longer, the distant exit might throw off those who pursued them.

When they finally emerged from under the ground, Collun closed his eyes and drew in a deep breath, joyfully letting his lungs swell with the brisk autumn air.

Collun saw that the first frost had come and gone while they were in Tir a Ceol. Many of the leaves still on the trees were shot through with blazing oranges and reds. Collun drew his cloak more tightly around his shoulders.

By the campfire that night Crann took out an old map. It was etched on a piece of worn and stained leather, yet it was clearly drawn and easier to read than most maps Collun had seen. Crann's long finger traced the route they would take to Scath.

Just before he rolled the map up, Crann pointed to a dot on the western coast of Eirren. "This is where Cuillean's dun lies," he said, with a glance at Collun.

"Does no one live there now?" asked Collun.

The wizard shook his head. "It has stood empty for more than a year, though with all his wandering Cuillean spent little enough time in it even before he disappeared." He paused, then said briskly, "Come. I will show you how to make lasan."

"Lasan?" queried Collun.

"You are skilled with the teine stone, spriosan. But there is a quicker way to kindle a fire." The wizard bade Collun gather the wild fungus called agaric that grew on tree bark. Then he showed the boy how to make fire sticks using the agaric and small pieces of splintered wood. Crann called the fire sticks lasan. When he rubbed one across a rough surface, it burst into flame.

Once he saw how the lasan worked, Collun laughed. "I thought the fire you kindled so quickly came from magic in your fingertips."

Talisen had overheard the interchange and came to sit beside them. "What kind of magic do you have, Crann? How did you stop the Ellyl Wind? And bring the rain to quench the fire in the Forest of Eld? Were they ancient spells?"

Crann shook his head, still smiling. "My magic, as you call it, does not lie in some mysterious realm of spells and potions. It is like the Ellyl draoicht, and yet it is different. Ellyl power lies in the music of all things, animate and inanimate. Mine is rooted in nature, in living things. In flowers and grass and wind and rain. My power comes from the trees. The forest is my true home, where I was born, where I go to be restored, and where I shall return when I die. That is why I am called Crann, the old word for tree. What I am able to do, all that appears to you as magic, is only because of the trees."

Talisen gave a dubious nod. "I confess that I understood better the Ellylon's description of their magic. Perhaps because it's to do with music."

"Indeed," Crann replied, then said pensively, "I envy Ellylon, their gift for melody. My own efforts make a bullfrog sound lyrical." The wizard gave a wry laugh. "Ah well, perhaps one day..." He trailed off, reaching for his map.

They roasted a pheasant Brie had felled with her bow and glazed it with sweet honey the Ellylon had given them. The air was so cool they could see their breath. When they had eaten their fill, they lay by the fire, and Talisen took up his harp. Crann asked for an Ellyl song.

Talisen nodded agreeably, but when his fingers went to find the chords, they faltered. He tried again, a puzzled look on his face, and again his fingers were stiff and unyielding.

"I do not understand," he said. He closed his eyes and concentrated. His hands frantically scrabbled over the strings, but still no melody came forth.

He looked toward Crann with a bewildered expression.

"I wondered if they would let you keep their songs. I suspected not," Crann said, his voice touched with sympathy.

"What do you mean? Why, only yesterday..."

"Legend has it that if a human should ever learn an Ellyl song in Tir a Ceol, he will forget it the moment he leaves their land."

Talisen stared at the wizard. He suddenly tossed the harp aside in a burst of anger. "I might have known. Those deceitful Ellylon..."

"Did they say it was a gift that you might keep?"

"No," replied Talisen. "Nor did they say they would take it from me. I never thought..." He trailed off. "Wait. I wonder..."

He grabbed his harp again. His fingers flew over the strings, and the notes to a lovely melody began to emerge. He sang. It was a song of loss, and of regaining, and it reminded Collun of waves in the ever-moving, gleaming pattern of the sea.

When he finished, Talisen burst into laughter. "I will be a true bard yet," he said triumphantly. "Even if I cannot remember Ellyl music, I have still the ability to make songs of my own. It is one gift they could not take from me."

"Perhaps because they chose not to," said Crann in a low voice, but Talisen paid him no heed. He stayed up late that night tinkering with his new song. Collun lay on the ground, his cloak wrapped around him, and listened to the harp music. As he drifted into sleep, Collun thought about the father back in Inkberrow he had lost and the one he had gained, if Cuillean yet lived.

The next afternoon as they were traveling through a thicket of birch trees, Crann suddenly stopped. He gestured for them all to pause, and his face wore the look of one who listens deeply to a far-off sound.

"Someone follows us," he said tersely. "A rider on horseback. And he comes quickly."

Brie readied her bow, pulling an arrow from the quiver on her back. Collun and Talisen drew their daggers, while Crann sat unmoving on Gealach. Soon they could all hear the crackling sound of a horse's hooves traveling over the bracken. They waited, bodies tensed and weapons at the ready.

EIGHTEEN

The Lapwing

A dark horse with a rider crouching in the saddle burst through the thicket of birch trees.

"Hold, Gerran!" the rider said to his horse. The steed immediately came to a halt.

The companions looked, unbelieving, into the handsome face of Prince Gwynedd.

"At last!" said the prince. "I have been seeking you all this day and the last. I'd begun to believe that the Ellyl, Silien, had guessed wrong about your route to Scath. Well met, Collun!"

"Prince Gwynedd," Collun greeted him stiffly. He cast a darting glance at Brie.

"You are Gwynn and Aine's son?" asked Crann, moving his horse forward.

"Yes. And you must be the wizard Crann. It is an honor to meet you." Gwynedd bowed his head respectfully. "So, son of Cuillean—," the prince began, but stopped when he saw the expression of surprise on Collun's face. "Yes, Silien told us everything when he got to Temair. I can see the resemblance now."

"Did Queen Aine agree to the comhairle?" queried Crann.

"Most assuredly. All of Temair is buzzing with the news. It is truly an historic occasion."

"Why are you not there?" The words popped out unbidden. Collun hoped his tone did not betray him.

"I have come to rejoin the quest that the traitor Bricriu did his best to thwart. Silien told me of your journey to Scath. If you are to tangle with the Queen of Ghosts herself, you will need another sword."

"I hope it will not come to that," said Crann.

"What happened to Bricriu?" asked Talisen.

"When I returned to Temair and discovered the message was a hoax, we thought at first there had been some sort of mistake," related Gwynedd. "Bricriu has long been a friend to my mother and father. But when I went back to Bricriu's dun with a party of soldiers, we found it deserted. A search of the dun revealed evidence of Bricriu's collusion with Medb."

"So he has escaped?" said Talisen.

"No doubt he is in Scath by now," said Gwynedd.

"Come," interrupted Crann, "we must not delay further."

When they began moving forward, Collun noticed that Gwynedd gravitated naturally to a spot beside Brie.

She greeted him warmly. Collun forced himself to look away.

That night over the fire Gwynedd reported that the last news they had received from the border was ill.

"Rumors of an invasion are rife, and it has been several weeks since any messengers have been able to get through," said the prince. "Even before Silien arrived in Temair, my mother was preparing for war. The proposed alliance between Tir a Ceol and Eirren gives everyone new hope."

Crann nodded gravely. Then he turned to Brie. "Are you fresh enough to scout for us? We should not relax our vigilance."

Brie nodded quickly and began to move toward her horse.

Gwynedd jumped up. "She should not go alone."

"No," interrupted Crann. "Brie is an accomplished tracker and trail finder. And one is less easily spotted than two."

"Crann is right," said Brie, swinging herself onto her horse.

Collun watched as Brie rode out of sight, her hand upraised in farewell. He resented Prince Gwynedd's protective gesture—despite the fact he had had the same impulse.

Collun woke well before dawn. He scanned the campsite quickly. Brie had not returned.

Crann was keeping watch and sat by the fire, brewing a pan of chicory. He held out a steaming cupful as Collun sat beside him. Sipping the nutty hot liquid, he looked sideways at Crann. The wizard's face was drawn and troubled.

"Is something wrong?" asked Collun anxiously.

Crann turned toward him and smiled. "Do not worry, spriosan. I'm certain Brie is fine. She will be back with us soon."

Collun relaxed. "What is spriosan?" he asked.

"Ah, it is the old word for twig or little branch. I hope you do not mind it." Collun shook his head. Then Crann said, "You asked if something is wrong. The answer is yes. I have been thinking of the Firewurme. Collun, what do you know of it?"

"Only what you have told me."

"Perhaps it is time I told you more," the wizard said. "I hope you will never see it, but it is well for all Eirrenians to be prepared." He drew a breath.

"In form, the Firewurme is much like the earthworms you find in your garden, only it is the size of a dun. Its body is supple and wrinkled, and it gleams pale white. It has no teeth, nor does it breathe fire. But in the Firewurme's white skin there is death, for it secretes an oozing, colorless guam, or sram in the old language, and this guam burns without flame. It is said to strip flesh from bone in a matter of minutes."

Collun shivered at the wizard's words.

"It has a long black tongue," continued Crann, "which is also coated with the deadly sram, and the tongue moves with lightning speed. The Firewurme cannot be harmed through its skin. It is many layers deep and, like its earthworm cousin's, can regenerate itself. It is rumored that its only vulnerable point is the eye, but the creature's eyelids are as hard as stone.

"According to the Ellyl who came to Tir a Ceol from Scath, it appears the monster lies quietly and shows no sign of leaving the island in northern Scath where it now dwells. But if Medb plans to place the Wurme at the head of her army..." Crann sighed deeply. "Yes, I am troubled by the Firewurme. And frightened, spriosan. All the comhairles and armies of the land will amount to naught if the Firewurme comes to Eirren."

Collun refilled his cup, willing his hand not to shake.

Crann shifted his position on the log they shared. "I am frightening you."

"No," began Collun, his cheeks reddening.

Crann gave a brisk shake to his head. "It is well to be afraid. You should never be ashamed when evil frightens you, spriosan. It is what will make you strong."

"I don't understand."

"You will. At any rate, Medb knows what the Wurme did to her ancestor Cruachan. I cannot believe she would risk such a fate herself. It is my guess that she will use it as a threat, a show of force, and nothing more." But Collun thought the wizard did not sound convinced by his own words.

Crann was gazing into his cup of chicory. Then he set it down and reached into his cloak. He pulled out the leather map.

"Here, I want you to have this, spriosan."

Collun looked at the wizard, uncomprehending.

"I have little need of it," said Crann, "and if for any reason we should become separated..." Collun opened his mouth to protest, but Crann spoke quickly. "I do not foresee that happening, but humor me just the same."

Collun took the map.

Dawn was breaking by then, and the others awoke. After a hurried meal, they set out again. It was late in the afternoon when Brie rejoined them. She looked pale and exhausted.

"Morgs," Brie said. "Four of them. They are about a half day's lag behind us."

"No Scathians?" asked the wizard.

"Just morgs, and they are traveling at a leisurely pace."

Crann looked thoughtful. "Either they wait for reinforcements, or they have orders merely to follow us." He paused. "Morgs shun daylight. Unless these four are unusual, they will rest during the day and travel by night. I suggest we do the same so there can be no surprise attacks."

And that became the pattern of their northward journey—sleeping during the day and riding all night. Collun found he could not easily adjust to this.

He did, however, grow increasingly comfortable riding Fiain. They began to develop the wordless communication Ebba had spoken of, until at times Collun felt he understood Fiain's thoughts. And it was clear the Ellyl horse knew his, for only rarely did he need to guide Fiain with pressure from his knees.

Most often he and Fiain rode alongside Crann, while Gwynedd and Brie rode together at the front. Talisen brought up the rear, singing snatches of the songs he was composing.

Close to dawn on the fourth day of the journey, they crossed a stream that Crann identified as Trout Beck. They made camp not far from the stream, and the dawn meal consisted of fresh trout flavored with peppergrass. As they ate, Crann asked Talisen if he knew any songs of the Cailleach Beara, the Old Woman of Beara.

"I know one, but it is no favorite of mine," Talisen replied. "It is all about old age and loneliness. Although I do like the bit about the well," he added with a smile.

"Who is the Old Woman of Beara?" asked Collun.

"An old friend," said Crann, and his face held a softness Collun had not seen there before. "She was once well-known in Eirren. And at one time she lived near Trout Beck. Beara planted that apple orchard." The wizard gestured toward the beginning of a grove that stretched out of sight.

"You knew the Hag?" asked Talisen in some disbelief.

Crann smiled. "She was not called so when I knew her."

"Does she still live?"

The wizard nodded. "Though I lost track of her many, many years ago. In truth, she cannot die."

"She is immortal?"

"Not exactly, but she found a way of renewing herself. I never learned how. But there is a very old spell that enables a person to take his life out of his body and put it into a separate vessel. As long as that vessel remains safe, the person will live. I have long wondered if Beara found that spell. Her magic was powerful enough. Come, Talisen, let us hear your song of Beara. I am in the mood for memories."

Talisen wiped his fingers clean and took up his harp. The song was indeed sad, telling of all the lifetimes the Old Woman of Beara had lived through; the husbands she had watched grow old and die, one after the other; the children, grandchildren, great-grandchildren she had long ago buried and forgotten. Talisen paused.

"I told you it was gloomy," he said. "But here's the part about the well.

> *"Nine hazel trees spread their branches wide;*
> *In clear water spotted salmon glide.*
> *Past, present, and future to reveal,*
> *When Beara the secrets will unseal."*

Talisen broke off. "Is there indeed such a well, Crann?"

"There was," said Crann.

"What were its powers?"

"It revealed what was to come and what had already been. It could find that which was lost. It healed injuries. But it could also be very dangerous, if used improperly."

"Does the well still exist?" asked Talisen.

"I do not know. I heard long ago it had run dry. Now let us get some rest."

At first Collun slept deeply, but then he awoke and could not get back to sleep. The sky was overcast, obscuring the sun, but because it was daytime Collun could not shake his restlessness.

He got to his feet and stretched. His eyes fell on the apple orchard. He wondered if there were still good apples to be found. He took along an empty pack and headed for the grove.

There were hundreds of apples on the ground; many were rotten, but Collun found a few edible ones. He began to fill the pack, letting his thoughts drift. Nessa had had a great love of apples, especially roasted and slathered in butter, honey, and cinnamon. These apples were the kind that tasted best roasted.

At the foot of a tree Collun spotted a clump of comfrey. He remembered he was low on the herb and bent to pick some, when he suddenly heard a bird call out, "Peewit, peewit!" It was a cry of distress. He quickly turned, scanning the area. He saw a fluttering motion on the ground ten paces away. He moved toward the bird. It hopped away. Collun took another few steps and it hopped farther away from him. He tried to speak to it in soothing tones, but the bird kept moving out of his reach.

It was a bronze-green bird with a black throat and underbelly. It held its wing at an awkward angle, and Collun was afraid it was broken.

Collun was slightly out of breath from chasing the injured bird. He paused. He could not identify it. Its belly and "peewit" reminded him of the lapwing, but lapwings did not have golden eye markings.

Lapwing. A memory stirred in Collun. The deceitful lapwing. He suddenly laughed out loud.

The bird *was* a lapwing, a different species than the ones in Inkberrow perhaps, but like its southern relative it had been leading Collun on a merry chase. When he was young, he and Talisen had made a sport of finding and robbing birds' nests. They had never been able to find the lapwing's nest, until they had caught on to its tricks. The lapwing was a master of deception. It would feign injury to lure intruders away from its nest.

The lapwing must have realized Collun was on to him, for it suddenly flew up into the apple trees, its wing showing no sign of injury, and disappeared.

Collun retraced his steps, a grin on his face. Some fresh eggs for the evening meal would be a welcome treat. At first he doubted he'd be able to find where he'd been before the lapwing drew him away, but then he remembered the comfrey.

Sure enough, he spotted a nest in the tree right beside the one with the comfrey under it. After filling his wallet with comfrey, Collun shimmied up the trunk and took three of the six eggs, leaving some for the lapwing.

Nestled in among the eggs was a small apple. Collun idly wondered how it had gotten there, and because it was so perfect in shape and was a rich golden color, he pocketed the apple as well.

Once he was back on the ground he gazed up at the sky. Sunset was still far off. Yet he did not feel sleepy. He walked slowly among the apple trees, thinking again of Nessa. Eventually the orchard ended, and he emerged into a copse of trees. Spotting a slab of smooth rock in the midst of it, he sat down, removing Nessa's small book from his jersey pocket. He ran his fingers over the simple design tooled in the leather cover. Despite the fact they were being pursued by morgs and still did not know where Nessa was, Collun felt the first stirrings of optimism since leaving Aonarach. He knew it was because of Crann.

He replaced the book in his pocket and took a draught of water from his skin bag. Some of it dribbled onto the stone under him. The water quickly seeped into grooves on the surface. Collun peered more closely and saw there was something carved into the rock. It was lettering in the old language.

He suddenly experienced an odd feeling of breathlessness; a hushed expectant sensation he could not account for.

Then, as he bowed his head to make out the lettering,

he heard the faint splash of water coming from underneath. His breath still short, he dug his fingers around the sides of the rock. It was a square slab, fashioned by man, not nature. He tried to pry the slab up, but he had to do more digging around the edges until it was loosened enough to move. Even then he had to use a stick as a lever to help raise it.

He finally was able to slide the heavy rock off. Underneath was a pool of water. The sides were reinforced with white marbleized stone. The water rose to within a hand's length of the top. Collun could not tell how deep it was.

Suddenly a silver shape broke the surface. It was a salmon with spots standing out on its gleaming body. It glided back down, out of sight. A few moments later, it reappeared and was accompanied by a second salmon. Then they were both gone.

A man-made well with salmon swimming in it. Collun looked up suddenly. The trees around him were hazel trees, and he counted nine of them.

The boy drew a deep breath. Beara's Well. Was it possible?

Tentatively, Collun extended a finger and dipped it into the water. It was cool. It looked and felt no different from any other water.

His heart beating loudly, Collun put his finger to his lips.

NINETEEN

Arracht

Collun?!" Crann's voice echoed in his ear. Collun blinked several times. Crann was standing over him, his hand on the boy's shoulder. The wizard's face was unreadable in the twilight.

Collun blinked again. Twilight? When he had pried up the stone it had been the middle of the afternoon.

"What . . . ?"

"You found the well, spriosan. Did you drink the water?"

"Only a drop, on my finger. And then—"

"There is no time to tell me more. The morgs have gained on us." The wizard leaned down and slid the stone back over the well. He pulled Collun, still in

a daze, to his feet. The two ran through the apple orchard.

"I found him," Crann called ahead.

Soon they had left Trout Beck and the apple orchard far behind. The Ellyl horses were flying at the top of their speed.

"Brie was scouting . . . found the morgs coming up on us fast . . . ," Talisen shouted to Collun as they rode.

The moon had risen, casting an eerie brightness on the landscape. They were heading due west. Collun began to smell the sea.

It was well after midnight when they came to the coast. Crann gestured for them to slow their horses. They were on a rocky cliff high above the ocean. The moon's light dappled the endless moving expanse below with silver. It was Collun's first glimpse of the Siar Muir. He was awestruck.

Brie made another scouting foray and came back with the news that the morgs had slowed their pace and, strangely, that there were now only two in pursuit. Crann looked thoughtful.

Following the coast north, they maintained a moderate pace for the next several hours. Collun began to feel drowsy, as he'd had little sleep that day. He had to struggle to stay awake. Crann came up beside him.

They rode silently for a while, then Collun asked, "What happened to me by the well? The sun was high in the sky when I put my finger to my mouth, but when you spoke my name, the sun was setting. I remember nothing in between."

"The waters of the well are unpredictable. Only Beara knows their secrets." He paused, then said in a measured tone, "Did you bring anything with you from the well, or from Beara's orchard?"

"Only some apples and a few eggs. Why?"

"You did not fill your skin bag at the well?"

"No."

Crann shook his head. "I sense something strange. What sort of eggs?"

"The lapwing's. Oh, there was something else." He drew out the small apple he'd found in the nest.

Crann gazed unblinking at the apple for several long moments.

Collun grew uncomfortable. "What is it, Crann?"

"Guard it well, spriosan," the wizard said softly. "You have found Beara's life."

"You mean...?"

Crann nodded. "The spell I told you of. It appears I was right. And she used this apple as the vessel." The wizard abruptly turned away, peering ahead.

"The Forest Ceryddwyn," he said. Collun could see the outline of trees looming ahead.

"Morgs!" shouted Brie.

They turned to see two morgs streaking up behind them from the south and two more coming from the east.

"Fly," called out Crann, and the horses raced along the cliff side.

"Why do we not turn and fight, Crann?" yelled Prince Gwynedd. "We are five..."

"No," shouted back the wizard. "To the forest."

But as they came up on the Forest Ceryddwyn, they saw four more morgs on horseback waiting for them.

Collun wheeled Fiain around, reaching for his dagger. He saw a volley of arrows fly through the air, and one of the morgs behind them went down.

Crann had raised his oak staff. Gealach stood very still under him. The two morgs coming at them from the side were less than a hundred paces away when Crann shouted, "Stadanna Eacha!"

The morgs' horses suddenly seemed to lose their footing and tumbled forward, hurling the morgs to the ground. One did not move from where he lay, while the other rose shakily and bent over his horse, trying in vain to get the animal to move.

Crann, Gwynedd, and Collun turned to face the morgs coming from the forest, while Talisen and Brie grappled with the remaining morg, who had approached from behind.

"Don't let it touch your skin!" Crann called back.

Meanwhile Gwynedd, with an almost fanatical gleam in his eye, had drawn his sword. He was relentlessly urging Gerran forward. The horse's eyes were wide with fear at the sight of the oncoming morgs.

"Hold, Prince," cried out Crann. "Stay out of the way!" But Gwynedd did not heed the wizard's words and kept pushing Gerran on. Crann again lifted his staff high. He paused, trying to see beyond the prince to the advancing morgs. He opened his mouth to speak, but before he could get the words out, he was tackled from behind by the morg whose horse had gone down. The wizard was dragged off Gealach, who struck out vainly with her hooves.

Fiain pivoted. Collun lashed at the morg with his dagger, but his blows fell short.

Wizard and morg wrestled on the ground for several

moments. Then with his staff, Crann landed a mighty blow to the side of the morg's head, and the creature lay still.

Suddenly Fiain let out a shrill whinny. Collun was grabbed from behind. He looked down. The hand clutching his shoulder was disfigured by a blackened, puckered scar.

He heard a hissing voice in his ear. "I told you we would meet again." He was looking into the yellow eyes of Mister Urlacan.

The morg had shifted its damp hand to Collun's throat. The boy felt a torpor begin to steal over him. He was slowly being dragged off Fiain's back. But the horse kicked out savagely, dislodging the morg's grip.

Collun fell to the ground. The force of his landing knocked the breath out of him. His forehead struck sharply against a rock. He reached up to feel a jagged gash. Blood was running down the side of his face.

Wiping it away from his eyes, Collun saw that Gwynedd was surrounded by three morgs. The prince brandished his sword, keeping the creatures at bay, but one moved behind him. Collun let out a warning yell as he saw a long thin blade emerge from the folds of the creature's cloak. Gwynedd's horse bolted forward into the two morgs in front of them. The animal went down with a high-pitched bray of pain. The prince fell, too, a morg on top of him.

Crann was on his feet, striding toward the fallen prince, his staff raised once again. Collun could not hear the words this time, but there was a great flash of light. Two of the morgs lay still, the fronts of their cloaks blackened.

Collun glanced over to see Gwynedd, lying on his side, deal a death blow to the remaining morg, but the prince then crumpled and lay still.

At the same time, Urlacan had drawn an evil-looking blade and was bearing down once again on Collun. The boy rolled away from the oncoming horse's hooves. He got unsteadily to his feet, looking around for Fiain, who came up beside him. He tried to mount the Ellyl horse but stumbled and fell to his knees.

Brie and Talisen were riding to Collun's aid, and Crann, too, was striding toward them.

Urlacan's yellow eyes darted from one to the other of them. An arrow flew past his head and was followed by another, which struck him in the shoulder. He let out a grating, hissing sound of thwarted rage and abruptly swung his horse. The morg bore down on Crann, and before the wizard could react, Urlacan swooped, snatching the oak staff out of Crann's hands.

The morg rode a short distance, then turned his horse so he was facing them. Collun watched in disbelief as, with a great shout of pain and exertion, Urlacan snapped the piece of wood into two pieces. He threw them to the ground. Black blood was flowing freely from the arrow wound in his shoulder.

Then, twisting his body toward the Forest Ceryddwyn, he cried out, "Arracht!" He repeated the word in an even louder, more strident voice.

A split second later a large figure emerged from the forest. It lumbered toward them on four feet with a speed that was surprising given its girth. It looked like a bear, with shaggy black fur covering its body. But as it drew closer, Collun saw it had the face of a man. It was a hideous face, misshapen and swollen, as though it had been thrown together haphazardly. It was headed toward Crann, picking up speed as it came.

The wizard stood facing the creature Arracht. He made no move to retrieve his broken staff. Collun began to run toward him.

As it drew close, Arracht raised itself on its hind legs. Then it lunged at Crann. The sheer force of the creature's forward motion propelled the wizard backward several paces, but he stayed on his feet.

Arracht drove Crann still farther back, until they were standing near the edge of the sea cliff. Crann wrapped his long arms around the creature's neck, and the two stood so close together they almost merged into one.

Then with a booming sound, the ground under Collun's feet heaved, knocking him flat. When he rolled over and looked for the wizard again, Collun saw him, still locked in an embrace with Arracht, standing on the very edge of the precipice.

Then, in the flicker of a moment, they were gone.

TWENTY

Burial Cairn

Collun screamed. He ran to the edge and looked over, his whole body shaking in horror. He could see nothing of either wizard or creature. The sheer cliff on which Collun now stood plunged almost straight down to a jagged outcrop of rock far below. The powerful waves that crashed against the rock, sending up spumes of white spray, looked almost miniature from the height at which Collun stood. His eyes desperately sought for a way to climb down, but it was obvious that the sheer walls were unscalable. He cried out in anguish and spun toward Urlacan, his dagger in his hand.

He could see the morg clearly in the moonlight,

sagging on his horse's back. In a ragged voice Collun cried out, "Urlacan!"

The morg turned, and the triumph Collun saw in Urlacan's yellow eyes filled him with a feverish hatred. He began to run toward the morg, dagger upraised. The blue chalcedony glowed.

Urlacan painfully spurred his horse into motion and, pulling sharply on the reins, guided him back toward the forest. Collun let out a cry. He looked wildly around for Fiain, but even as the Ellyl horse came to Collun's side, the morg reached the forest's edge and was quickly lost to sight.

Collun stood still for a moment, ignoring the blood that trickled down his face. In a daze he turned his steps toward the sea cliff. When he got to the edge, he sank to his knees and looked sightlessly down at the crashing surf.

"Collun?" It was Brie. He turned and met her eyes. His own grief was mirrored there.

"He is gone," Collun said, his voice raw.

"Yes," answered Brie.

"How is Gwynedd?"

"Poorly. Gerran, the horse, is dead."

Collun stiffly rose to his feet. He crossed to the fallen prince. A long gash marked the right side of Gwynedd's body. It was as though someone had taken the sharpest of points and riven the flesh from the prince's ribs to his upper leg, where the wound was deepest. There was also a cut in the right side of his face. The handsome features were gray and distorted with pain.

Nearby lay the still figure of the dead horse.

Collun leaned over Gwynedd and gently inspected the

wound. It was deep. Collun did not know whether the young prince would survive.

After quickly tending to his own cut forehead, Collun kindled a fire and prepared poultices of comfrey leaves crushed to a pulp and mixed with hot water. When they were ready, Collun laid them along the worst parts of the prince's wound. They quickly soaked through with blood, and he set to work making a new batch.

Gwynedd became delirious. His skin was flaming hot to the touch. He let out low animal sounds, and the only word they could make out was the name of his dead horse. At one point they had to hold him down, his body writhing and twisting as he shouted Gerran's name over and over. The bleeding got heavier.

Collun quickly prepared a mild sedative from valerian leaves and forced it between Gwynedd's cracked lips. After that the prince was quiet, though his fever still burned.

The moon was now high above them. The bluff was cool, with a sharp wind blowing off the ocean. Collun prepared a pan of hot chicory to take off the chill. As he watched the liquid come to a boil over the red-hot embers, his mind kept going back to the two figures struggling at the edge of the precipice.

They had built their fire as far as they could from the bodies of the fallen morgs and tried not to think of the shrouded figures. The morgs' horses had long since bolted.

They sat huddled in front of their campfire, drinking the chicory and listening to Gwynedd's labored breathing. They took turns sleeping and watching the prince.

The next afternoon, while Brie kept watch, Collun and Talisen set about clearing away the dead morgs. They dug a wide, shallow grave and then dragged the creatures into it, careful not to touch their skin. Talisen wanted to make a funeral pyre, but Collun overrode him, and they covered the bodies with earth instead.

Then the two boys dug a grave for Gerran. Collun was glad of all the mind-numbing exertion. They lowered the large animal into the hole they had dug and covered him over with earth and grass. They piled a few rocks up into a cairn.

Then, where Crann had fallen, Collun buried the two halves of his broken staff and laid three white stones over it. He scratched Crann's name onto the top rock. Night had fallen by the time he finished. Collun and Talisen stood for a moment by Crann's cairn, the raw wind penetrating their cloaks. Then Talisen silently stepped away, returning to the warmth of the fire. He lifted his harp into his lap and began to pick out an elegy.

Collun's eyes blurred. He blinked rapidly several times. Looking out into the night, he listened to the sound of the sea under the harp song, and he thought of the old wizard. His long fingers. His tired, seamed face. His clear eyes. Collun could not believe that Crann was gone. He dropped to one knee. Tears slid down his cheeks. He knelt there, unmoving, until long after Talisen's song was done.

Finally Collun straightened and walked back to the fire. Brie was roasting a small badger, while Talisen sipped a cup of chicory. Gwynedd slept.

"I have decided," said Collun. Brie and Talisen

looked up, their attention caught by the tone in Collun's voice. "I will journey on alone to find Nessa," Collun went on. "The two of you must take the prince to Temair, where he can get the care he needs. Gwynedd can ride Gealach." Though his voice was edged with grief, there was a forcefulness to it that Brie and Talisen had not heard before. Talisen began to open his mouth to object, but reading the expression in Collun's face, slowly closed it again.

"How will you find Nessa?" asked Brie.

"Crann never told me how or where he planned to make contact with his spies from Scath. So I have decided to return to Beara's Well."

His companions looked at him blankly.

"There has been no chance to tell you, but back in that apple orchard near Trout Beck, I found the well."

"The one with the salmon and the hazel trees and everything?" asked Talisen in amazement.

Collun nodded.

"I do not believe you."

"It is true. And I am hoping the magic there will show me where Nessa is. Crann said the well can find that which is lost."

"And if it does not work?" Brie asked.

"I will go to Scath regardless. But I will not take this." He unclasped from his belt the sheath holding the dagger that had been a trine. "If I am captured or killed by Medb, then at least the stone will not fall into her hands. Take it with you to Temair and give it to Queen Aine."

Brie reached out to take the dagger. "Are you sure?"

Collun nodded, but he felt a sudden stab of loss as he let go of the well-worn handle.

The next morning as Collun sat by him, Prince Gwynedd's fever at last broke. His eyelids flickered open.

"Prince Gwynedd. Are you awake?"

The prince nodded weakly. He tried to speak, but Collun could not understand him. He leaned closer.

"Crann?" came the thin voice.

"He is gone, Prince," answered Collun, his own voice expressionless.

Gwynedd's eyelids fell shut and, keeping them closed, he spoke again. "And Gerran. He is dead, too."

Although it was not spoken as a question, Collun replied, "Yes." Gwynedd turned his face away. Collun silently placed his hand on the young prince's arm.

"It is my fault."

Collun could barely hear the muffled words.

"Do not try to talk. You were badly hurt."

Gwynedd kept his face turned away. After a while Collun decided he must have fallen asleep.

Collun left him then and went to the fire. "His fever has broken," Collun told Brie and Talisen. "But I do not know if he has the will to heal."

"His body is strong," Brie replied.

"He is not strong enough to travel, but we can't wait any longer. He must get to Temair. And Urlacan is out there somewhere. He may return."

"Yes," Brie answered.

They got the prince to eat a few bites of bread and some broth and then, in the late afternoon, hoisted him astride the Ellyl horse Gealach.

Before they rode off, they paid a last visit to Crann's cairn. Then, in a hoarse voice, the prince asked to see where Gerran was buried. As they paused by the fresh grave, Collun got a glimpse of Gwynedd's ravaged face. His heart squeezed with pity.

Collun and Brie had studied Crann's map before setting out. Collun had tried to give the map to Brie for their journey to Temair, but she refused to take it.

"I know the ways between here and Temair well enough. You are the one traveling into unknown territory."

The plan was to journey together for a short distance, and then Brie, Talisen, and Gwynedd would veer off at a diagonal, heading southeast toward Temair.

The time to part came quickly. Collun examined Gwynedd's wounds one last time. He freshened the prince's bandages, and then gave Brie and Talisen the rest of the comfrey leaves. Gwynedd was barely conscious but seemed to understand that Collun was leaving them.

"Good luck," Collun thought he heard Gwynedd whisper through dry lips.

Talisen clapped Collun on the back. "When you find Nessa of the black eyes, tell her I've learned a hundred new riddles and that I shall make a song just for her when she comes back."

Collun agreed to do as Talisen requested. Then the two friends looked at each other, and without words, they clasped hands.

Collun turned to say good-bye to Brie.

"I will guard the dagger that was a trine well," she said.

"Thank you," Collun replied. Their eyes locked for

a moment. Collun suddenly felt as though the small dagger was turning in his heart. "Brie . . . ," he began.

"Yes?" Her eyes were bright.

"Uh . . . be careful," he said lamely.

Brie nodded. "And you, too," she said, then swung herself onto her horse.

Collun mounted Fiain, and the Ellyl horse broke into a brisk trot. Collun lifted his hand in farewell.

As he came to the crest of a small hill, Collun took a last look back at the three figures. He felt a sudden surge of loneliness, but he set his jaw and focused his thoughts on what lay ahead.

At twilight he arrived at the apple orchard.

He and Fiain made their way to the copse of hazel trees. It was strangely silent; not a leaf stirred, not a bird called. Collun dismounted. The horse wandered off a short distance.

With a prickling sensation on his scalp, Collun slid the rock slab off the top of the well. A salmon darted in and out of sight. Taking a cup from his pack, Collun filled it with water. He hesitated a moment. Crann had said the waters of the well could be dangerous if used improperly. And just a drop had caused him to lose several hours of his life.

Resolutely he closed his eyes and concentrated all his thoughts on Nessa. He raised the cup to his lips.

"I would not drink that, were I you," came a deep voice.

Collun's eyes flew open. A tall, thin man dressed in black clothing stood before him. He was bald and had pale, unfocused eyes that gazed fixedly above Collun's head. The boy guessed the man was blind.

"Why not?" Collun asked.

"Well, I'm not certain, but it would either kill you outright or else drive you mad. One or the other," the man answered in an offhand manner.

Collun lowered the cup, his hand shaking.

"It is Beara's Well, you see. Only Beara can drink the water. Not even Mordu can drink."

"Mordu?"

The bald man pointed to himself. "Mordu serves the Cailleach Beara. And it is time for Mordu to prepare her dinner." He turned to leave. "Close the well when you go, if you please." Mordu began to walk away.

Collun slid the rock into place over the well. He scrambled to his feet and fell into step beside the blind man who walked as surely as a sighted person. Fiain followed behind.

"Would Beara help me, do you think?"

"Have you lost something?" Mordu asked, his eyes staring straight ahead.

"Yes. My sister."

"That was careless of you," Mordu said accusingly.

"It wasn't like that. She was kidnapped. And I go to rescue her. But I need to know where she is being held. Would Beara be able to tell me that? With the help of her well?"

"More likely she would turn you into an apple seed and sow you in her orchard," Mordu answered in a matter-of-fact voice. "But you can try. Is that an Ellyl horse with you?"

"Yes. Fiain is his name. The Cailleach Beara's magic must be powerful," Collun said nervously.

"She likes to show off," the blind man said with a

trace of scorn. "But old age has addled her," he added. "She forgets things. Like as not she'd think she was changing you into an apple seed, and you'd really turn out to be an apron. Or a swan. Now, that wouldn't be so bad. I've always liked swans."

"I would prefer to stay as I am," Collun responded.

"Suit yourself." Mordu shrugged. An old, derelict-looking house had come into sight. Mordu was heading toward it.

"Is this where you live with the Old Woman of Beara?" asked Collun.

Mordu nodded. "I would invite you in, but you did say you prefer your present shape . . . Besides, she's been in a foul mood all day." They were passing through a small grove of apple trees that surrounded the house.

"Why?"

"Says she lost something. But when I asked what, she says she can't remember. I told her to try the well, but she just barked at me. It's not easy." Mordu sighed. "Good evening to you, then." The bald man bowed and entered the hovel.

Collun stood irresolute outside the door. He did not like the sound of a foul-tempered hag with powerful magic and a penchant for shape changing. But he carried her life in his jersey pocket. If he was to give it to her, perhaps she would be grateful enough to grant him a favor. It was a risk, but what choice did he have? Blunder about Scath blindly on the off chance of running across his sister? Fiain gave a whicker.

"I won't be long," Collun said to the horse. He stepped up to the door and knocked.

TWENTY-ONE

The Hag of Beara

Mordu opened the door.

"May I see the Cailleach Beara?" Collun asked politely.

The blind man's face registered surprise, but he gestured Collun inside.

The room was dark, lit only by a few candles. The inside of the house was as run-down as the outside. Dust lay thick on the floor, and the furniture was broken and worn.

At one side of the room, Collun saw an old woman hunched over a large loom, her feet rhythmically pumping the treadles while her gnarled hands deftly worked the threads.

Collun had never seen a person so old. Her skin hung loose on her bones, with cascades of wrinkles spilling down her face. The color of her skin reminded Collun of dried-out apple blossom petals.

Collun's glance fell on the design in the cloth the old woman was weaving. When he saw what it was, he let out a low cry.

Against a background of a dark blue sky and an ever-moving sea, two figures stood locked in a deadly embrace. It was Crann and the creature Arracht.

It was the same nightmarish scene Collun kept seeing over and over in his head, both awake and asleep.

"How did you know—?" Collun stumbled out.

The hag's hands kept moving on the loom. "Beara knows. Past, present, and future. The morg called Arracht out of the forest, but it is because of the cowardly boy-child that the Wizard of the Trees is gone."

Collun gasped for air as though from a blow to his stomach. He stepped back a few paces, leaning against a table to support himself.

"Yes," the hag went on, her dry voice buzzing in Collun's ears. "Beara knows. It was because of you the wizard died. There is no one else to blame."

Collun's cheeks were flame hot.

"The boy-child knows Beara speaks the truth. The prince of Eirren lies broken, his horse dead. The wizard is gone. And why?"

Collun trembled, tears smearing his vision. He thrust his hand inside his jersey, feeling for the small golden apple.

"Because the cowardly boy-child was too frightened to fight his own battles. To find his own sister. And *this* is the son of Cuillean, the brave, the mighty champion. How proud he would be of his only son." The crone opened her toothless mouth, cackling with laughter.

Collun grasped the apple and snatched it out of his shirt. He held it aloft with a shaking hand.

When the hag's eyes fell on it, they narrowed slightly, but she continued to laugh, wiping the edges of her eyes with her gray cloak.

"Did the boy-child find a pretty apple in my orchard?"

"Lady, I would trade you your life for secrets from your well." Collun's voice was raised, but it cracked slightly.

"Would you indeed, boy-child? I am afraid I shall have to disappoint you. It is a pretty little apple. But there are many more in my orchard, just as pretty as that one."

A look of uncertainty passed over Collun's face.

"Ah, I see. The boy-child thought he had found something of value? Did the Wizard of the Trees tell you so? Well, he was wrong. My lapwing did her job well. It is a pretty apple, but I'm afraid it is quite worthless."

Collun lowered his hand and stared at the apple. It had been his last hope. Collun was filled with an overwhelming desire to throw it away from him. He drew his arm back, but before he let go of the apple, he glanced at the hag. She was still weaving, but her eyes watched him closely, avidly.

His body stiffened and he realized what he had almost done. The hag had sought to deceive him. Collun paused, spotting a knife on the table beside him. He grabbed it up and held the blade next to the golden skin of the apple.

The hag abruptly stopped laughing, and her dried-petal face went a shade whiter, but when she spoke, her tone was hard and taunting.

"Go ahead. Cut the apple in half. Kill old Beara. She has lived long enough. Too long. But you cannot do it, can you? The cowardly boy-child has not the stomach for killing. Not like his father. Not like the champion of Eirren, who would willingly die himself before he would allow others to fight his battles for him."

Collun let out a strangled cry. He set the apple on the table and raised the knife to slash the golden fruit. His whole body shook. Beads of sweat stood out on his face. He began a savage downward plunge, but at the last minute, his hand faltered and swerved to the side. The knife stood upright where it had landed, embedded deep in the wooden table.

With a choked sob Collun snatched up the apple and rolled it across the floor. It stopped at the hag's feet. She gave a crow of triumph and leaned over to grab the apple. Moving with surprising speed, she crossed to the table and set the apple on it and then pulled the knife from the wood. She lifted the blade and brought it down with a vigorous thrust, cleaving the apple neatly in half.

Collun stared, transfixed by the two halves of the apple as they rocked gently on their sides. Against the white flesh of the fruit, Collun could see a five-pointed star formed by the black seeds at the apple's core. He raised his eyes to look at the hag, but he could not see her. The candles had gone out, and it was pitch-black in the room.

Then a light kindled. Someone was lighting the candles again. It was the hag, Collun thought, as he watched the figure with a shawl pulled over its head move from candle to candle.

As the light grew brighter Collun realized the room had changed. The dust was gone, and there was no trace of the broken old furniture. Everything was new and clean.

The shawled figure kept lighting candles until the whole place blazed with light. Then it swung around to face Collun. His mouth dropped open. Underneath the hag's hood was the luminous face of a maiden. With a sudden rippling laugh she threw off the shawl and let it fall to the floor. She stepped gracefully away from it, her small nose slightly wrinkled.

"Musty old thing," she said in a voice that sounded of bells pealing through the dawn. She was dressed in a flowing garment the color of apple blossoms and had yellow-gold hair that fell in waves to her waist. She looked the same age as Collun.

The maiden gazed steadily at Collun and laughed her musical laugh. "Close your mouth at once, Collun, son of Cuillean. You look like one of my silver salmon." Collun clapped his mouth shut.

The maiden caught sight of herself in a mirror across the room and gave an admiring smile, tucking a stray lock of yellow-gold hair behind one delicate ear.

"Where was I? . . . Oh, yes, I was about to thank you. I let myself get too old this time." She shook her head with a worried frown. "I'd forgotten where my little apple was, although when I woke up this morning I knew it was gone."

"But the apple was cut."

"Of course. So my life could begin anew. Well, not exactly anew. I have been a baby once or twice, and I hated it. All sleeping and burping and nothing else really. So I skip over that now." Collun continued to look bewildered.

"Don't you see? It is the cycle of my life. The apple must be cleaved in half so that I may begin anew. Here it is, whole again." She removed something from the folds of her gown. It was the golden apple, and its golden skin matched the maiden's hair. It lay in her small white hand, and Collun could see that it was indeed whole and unblemished.

"But we are straying from the subject. Son of Cuillean, I would give you two gifts, as you gave me two gifts."

"Two, m'lady?" Collun answered in confusion.

"Yes. You gave me both your pity and my life. In spite of all I said, you gave me my apple. I was cruel, I know, but I could not help myself. I was angry about the Wizard of the Trees. He was once a friend to me. And you can't know what it is like to be so old. And so lonely." She gave a quick shudder.

"First, I will give you the knowledge that you seek. I will find out where your sister lies. My first meal shall be a fine silver salmon from the well. Mordu? Oh, Mordu?" she called into the next room. The blind man appeared.

"This boy-child found my apple, Mordu! And you will broil me a salmon with rosemary and chervil. Oh, and I must have some of your bread, Mordu. Your delicious bread! Now that I have teeth again . . ." And she flashed her perfect teeth in another radiant smile. "Quick, Mordu, bring me bread right now!" Mordu nodded and left the room.

"Where was I?" she asked again. "Oh yes, my second gift." Out of the folds of her gown she drew a small shining object. "It was given to me by a wizard. The Wizard of the Trees. Young and strong he was then. I believe you knew him as Crann." Her beautiful face grew sad. She held out her hand to Collun. Lying in her palm was a seashell. It was slightly larger than Collun's thumb and spiraled in pearly folds from the bottom, with a small opening at the top.

Collun took it in awe. He had not seen many seashells, but somehow he knew there were few as exquisite as this one. He carefully placed it in his pocket.

"Thank you, Lady."

She nodded distractedly, her eyes again on her reflection in the mirror. "I look a little pale, don't you think, son of Cuillean? Oh, I cannot wait to walk among my apple trees and feel the sun and wind on my face." The maiden stretched her lithe young body, reveling in its suppleness. Mordu reappeared, bearing a platter of bread and cheese. He placed it in front of the maiden. She gazed at it longingly, but she shook her head.

"If I start eating now, I won't be able to stop. First I must do as I promised. Mordu, where is my fishing pole?" Mordu found a pole by the door and brought it to her. "We shall have a moonlight fishing expedition. Come, Mordu. We will be back soon," she called out as they disappeared through the door.

Collun sat at the table. He took out the seashell and gazed at it. Crann had given this to the maiden, perhaps when he was a young man. Collun tried to picture the wizard in his youth and could not. Then he dozed, his head falling forward onto the table.

He woke to the sound of the maiden's laughter as she and the blind man reentered the cottage. Mordu disappeared into the kitchen with the bucket. The maiden crossed to Collun and said, "It won't be long."

She began to flit about the room, opening windows and raising curtains. Dawn light began to fill the room. The maiden blew out all the candles, then left the house.

She returned shortly with an armful of apple-tree branches covered with delicate pink and white blossoms, still closed from the night. She placed them in containers around the room. Collun stared at the greenery. It was winter in Eirren. Where had she gotten apple blossoms?

"There," the maiden said, eyeing the room critically. Collun crossed to the window. He drew in his breath sharply. The apple trees around the house were filled with blossoms. "How . . . ?"

"Spring is so much nicer than winter, don't you think?" the maiden said.

Collun nodded in a daze.

Mordu reentered bearing a plate. He set it on the table, and the maiden practically flew to her chair. She ripped off a hunk of bread and took a bite. As her jaws worked, she closed her eyes and a contented smile came over her face. "Oh, Mordu, you are a wonder!" Then she opened her eyes and looked at Collun, who had been watching her eagerly.

"Mordu, take the son of Cuillean to see your garden. I must be alone now." Mordu nodded and led Collun out the door. The boy breathed in the fresh warm air in wonder.

Behind the house lay a magnificent garden. Here, too, a perpetual spring seemed to hold sway. Collun forgot his fatigue as he took in all the varieties of brilliant, eye-catching flowers, as well as an exquisite garden of herbs. Reverently he crouched down beside a teeming patch of mint. He thought with longing of his almost empty wallet of herbs.

As if he could read the boy's mind, Mordu said in his deep voice, "You may take what you like. It grows quickly." Collun looked up at the tall man, who was staring straight ahead with his blind eyes.

"In truth?"

Mordu nodded. "But you need sleep. Tomorrow morning will be soon enough."

When they returned to the house, they found the maiden curled up on her wooden bed, fast asleep.

Mordu set up a soft, feather-filled pallet by the fireplace for Collun. The boy gratefully climbed in and slept deeply.

He awoke at midday, and Mordu prepared and served Collun a delicious dinner of fresh fish. It was not salmon, Collun knew, but the flesh was flaky and white and it melted in his mouth. There was also hot squash with orange skin, garnished with rich butter and tangy herbs.

He ate hungrily, and as he was finishing, Collun glanced at the slumbering maiden and whispered to Mordu, "What should I call her now? Has she a name, other than Beara?"

"You may call me Mealladh, son of Cuillean." The maiden sat up in her bed, yawning. "It is one of my early names. The Wizard of the Trees used to call me Mealladh." The maiden climbed out of her bed and padded over to the table in her bare feet. She sat down and began eating the last of the bread. Collun gazed at her anxiously, but she remained silent, munching the bread, her eyes distant. She spoke abruptly.

"The news I have for you is not good, Collun," Mealladh said. Collun's body stiffened.

"Is Nessa . . . ?"

"No, she is alive. But while I slept I saw where she is and who guards her." Silence filled the room. The maiden pushed the empty bread plate away from her with a frown. "Why can we not talk of something else? This is my favorite of your bread recipes, Mordu. Do you use goat's milk?"

The blind man did not answer.

"Bring me more. I cannot get enough."

But Mordu did not move. Collun stood, his heart pounding. "What is it, Lady? Who guards Nessa?"

"It is the Wurme," the maiden said finally.

"What?"

"The Firewurme, Naid, guards her. I am sorry."

TWENTY-TWO

Scath

Collun stared blindly ahead. The Firewurme.

The maiden shuddered and rose, moving across the room to one of the arrangements of apple blossom branches. She fiddled with it absently, then pressed her nose into the pink and white petals, inhaling deeply. "It is a loathsome thing. If I had known I would dream of the Firewurme, I never would have agreed to your request. Cruachan was an evil man. Evil." She shivered again and turned toward Collun.

"The Wurme guards your sister on an island off the north of Scath. The Isle of Thule. She is in some sort of cave. She looks ill and thin. Oh, how I hate bad news! Mordu, please bring me more bread. And apple wine."

She moved to the mirror on the wall and smoothed her hair. She turned back to Collun with a smile. "Well, it is a shame. But when you have lived as long as I, you see that one life is no more than a feather in the wind."

Collun looked away.

"Of course," the maiden continued, "it is disappointing to travel so far for naught, son of Cuillean. But you can return to your home now, knowing you have done all that you could."

Collun shook his head slowly. Home. He had no home. "Do you know the way to Thule, Lady?"

Mealladh looked at him in disbelief. "Thule? You do not think to go to Thule?"

"Yes."

"You know about the Firewurme?"

"Crann told me."

Mealladh shook her head. "Then there shall be no more talk of going to Thule. You are young, with many years to live." Mordu placed a platter of hot bread on the table. Collun closed his eyes and breathed in the warm, fresh aroma. Then he reluctantly opened them again. He drew Crann's map out of his jersey. Unrolling the old leather, he looked up at the maiden.

"Show me Thule."

Mealladh looked with distaste at the map. Then, peering closely, she laid her finger on a small dot off the north coast of Scath.

"But truly you cannot go there. You are welcome to stay with Mordu and me for as long as you like. There is much that Mordu can teach you of plants and growing."

Collun thought of the bountiful herb garden. He took a deep breath.

"I will go to Thule," Collun said resolutely.

The maiden exclaimed in annoyance. "Oh, I am tired, and you are making me cross! This is not the way I thought to spend my first day with teeth that can chew and knees that bend—dreaming of Wurmes and listening to stubborn boy-children." There was a hint of the hag's crackling voice in her last words.

"Mordu, tell me quickly, why should I not use my words of changing on the boy-child? I need practice, and when he goes to Thule, the Firewurme will destroy him anyway. Would he not make a handsome apple tree? I do so love apple trees."

Collun looked uneasily at Mordu, who was pouring a goblet of wine for Mealladh, his blind eyes fixed unseeingly over her head.

"The boy would indeed make a handsome apple tree. But you have so many apple trees already. And do not forget he brought you your golden apple."

"Of course he did." She sighed. "Very well. I will show you the way to Thule, boy-child. And it is a good way. It is easy to follow and avoids the places where the Scathians dwell. But it will have to wait until tomorrow. Perhaps you will have come to your senses by then. Now, bring me more bread, dear, kind Mordu."

Collun slept well that night. When he awoke, Mordu fed him a hearty breakfast of apple cakes and clotted cream. As he ate, Collun heard Mealladh outside, singing as she moved about her apple grove.

After feeding and grooming Fiain, who had been waiting patiently outside the house, Collun spent the morning in Mordu's garden replenishing his wallet of herbs. He found a large cluster of agaric growing on the roots of a nearby tree and spent several hours making lasan for kindling fires. He collected an extra quantity of the fungus to keep in reserve.

As his fingers shaped the agaric around the end of a shaved stick, Collun called to mind all that the wizard had told him of the Firewurme. As he remembered what Crann had said of the guam that burned without flame, his eyes fell on a clump of mallow growing off to the side. Something else stirred in his memory.

When he was young and just beginning to be interested in herb lore, an old woman had come to Inkberrow. She was said to have great skill with herbs and healing. Her face had frightened Collun at first because it was sprinkled all over with warts. One wart sprouting from her eyelid was so large she could not open her eye all the way. She looked as if she were constantly winking.

Goban had been furious when he found out later that Collun had traded four carrots, three sweet potatoes, and a prize yellow squash for the old woman's secrets.

And Goban had been right, for the things she had taught Collun turned out to be useless. Most of it was superstitious foolishness, such as how to tell a maid whom she would marry by thrusting a turnip root into the fire and seeing which way the sparks flew. There had been a few recipes as well for cure-alls, such as a concoction of moth wings and dandelion greens that was supposed to cure insomnia. He had tried one or two, and they had done nothing, so he discarded the rest. But he remembered there had been one for a salve that would miraculously heal insect bites and burns, no matter how severe. It had been made of mallow and several other ingredients.

"Mordu," he called to the blind man, who had come to the garden to gather herbs for the midday meal. "Do you know of a salve made from mallow that is good for healing burns?"

Mordu scratched his smooth head and thought for a moment. "Yes," he said slowly. "Mallow and leek and goat's thorn, the leaves only. I think that is all. No, some gentian as well. I have not used it myself but remember it from long ago."

"Equal parts?"

"Yes, except for the mallow. Two of that to every one of the others."

Collun plucked several large fistfuls of the musky-smelling mallow plant with its pink flowers, as well as a quantity of the other ingredients Mordu had mentioned. Whether such a salve would work against the Firewurme's burning guam he did not know, but it would do no harm to bring the ingredients along.

Mordu called him in for a delicious meal of pheasant and gillyflower pie. The maiden once again showered Mordu with praise and ate with such gusto that conversation was almost impossible.

When the maiden had taken her last gulp of wine, she turned to Collun. "Is it still your intent to go to Thule?"

"Yes, Lady."

She sighed. "Very well. Then I will show you the way. Where is your musty old map?"

They bent over the wizard's map. Mealladh's finger traced the route. "You will journey this way through the north of Eirren. When you come to this small river, you will know you are in Scath. Follow along here." Collun watched closely. "It will take you several days, at least. But eventually you will come to the River Omagh. After that it is simple. Just follow the Omagh to the top of Scath. There you will find Thule." She paused. "Now, Mordu has packed some items for your journey. Come."

She led Collun outside, and Fiain had indeed been laden with two leather packs filled with food, blankets, and two extra cloaks lined with fur.

The maiden then presented Collun with a large red apple. "An apple for an apple," she said with a flashing smile. "Though I have already given you far too much. I remember I had a soft spot for your father, as well."

"You knew Cuillean?"

"I met him once or twice, when he was young."

"Do you know where he is now?"

The maiden laughed. "You are allowed only one missing person per visit, Collun, son of Cuillean. Now go."

Thanking Mealladh for the apple, Collun tucked it safely in one of his leather packs and then mounted Fiain.

"Farewell, Collun," Mealladh trilled. "I wish you well on your quest."

Mordu stood behind his mistress and raised his hand, a solemn smile on his pale face.

Collun waved good-bye, and the Ellyl horse broke into a brisk trot, happy to be setting forth once again. Collun glanced back just before leaving the apple grove and saw Mealladh moving among her trees, weaving apple blossoms into her yellow-gold hair.

As he passed the copse of hazel trees, the wind began to blow chill once more. He pulled his cloak tightly around him. When they came close to Trout Beck, Collun spotted a thin curl of wood smoke rising above their old campsite. He cautiously guided Fiain toward the smoke. He could see a figure standing over a campfire. It turned toward him at the sound of Fiain's hooves on the ground. Collun's heart contracted.

It was Brie. She was alone.

He rode up to the fire and dismounted.

"What happened? Where are Talisen and the prince?" He shivered slightly in the cold wind.

Brie poured him a cup of hot chicory. Handing it to him, she said, "On their way to Temair. Not long after we left you, we came across a man on foot; his name was Poddup. He was a messenger from the king. He was traveling with an urgent message for the queen in Temair, but he had lost his horse and almost his life at the hand of Scathians. The tidings he bore were grave. Medb is planning a full-scale invasion in a fortnight. A war host has begun to gather."

"Has there been any talk of the Wurme, of Naid?"

Brie shook her head. "Why?"

Collun told her of Crann's fear that Medb would call on the Firewurme when she invaded Eirren. Collun also told Brie all that had happened in Beara's cottage.

Brie absorbed his story in silence, then said, "Perhaps

the Queen of Ghosts plans to summon the Wurme only if the need is great."

"And perhaps she knows even now that I go to Thule. But I must. It is all I know to do."

"Then you will need this." Brie drew Collun's dagger out and handed it to him.

Collun shook his head. "Did you not hear what I just said? If taking Nessa was part of a plan to lure me into bringing the stone to Thule, then I would be playing right into her hands."

"Perhaps," answered Brie. "But the more I thought about it, the more I felt the dagger and the stone belong with you, Collun. And I believe the wizard Crann felt so, too. Otherwise he would have cautioned you against carrying it into Scath."

"But . . ."

"We will not let the Queen of Ghosts get her hands on the Cailceadon Lir," Brie said, her voice confident. Collun slowly took the dagger from her. Then he stopped.

"What do you mean 'we'?" He gazed around the campsite. "And where is your horse?"

Brie smiled. "I did not come just to give you the dagger. I go with you to Thule, Collun. I gave the messenger Poddup my horse. He will guide Talisen and Gwynedd to Temair much more surely and quickly than I ever could."

Collun shook his head. "No. I would not ask you to face this kind of danger . . ."

"You did not ask me." She paused. "Anyway, the others are halfway to Temair by now. I'm afraid you are stuck with me."

Collun gazed at Brie, searching her face. Finally he nodded in acceptance. "But I face the Firewurme alone." Brie opened her mouth to protest, but Collun held up his hand. "If you do not promise me this, I will ride off and leave you to find your way back to Temair on foot."

Brie was silent for several moments. "Very well. I promise." She washed out the pan and cups she'd used and doused the fire. Swinging up behind Collun on Fiain, she said, "Talisen grumbled a good deal when I told him what I proposed to do. He accused me of wanting all the glory of the quest for myself, but finally he agreed it was for the best. They dropped me several leagues from here, and I walked the rest."

Fiain broke into a brisk trot, and the campsite was soon far behind them.

The wind grew more bitter as the day wore on. Though Collun could not be sure of the date, he knew it was near the beginning of the month of Ruis, and winter had its grip upon the land.

They had been traveling for three days when they came to a small river, and they realized they had passed into Scath sometime that afternoon.

The terrain grew rockier and the trees fewer, though there were occasional small clusters of pine and yew trees. As Mealladh had promised, the route they followed was uninhabited.

They came across a deserted village on the fourth day. Collun remembered Crann telling them that when Medb came to power, she had moved the Scathians from outlying villages and farms in order to exert her control more easily over them. Now most of the population lived in huge cities hewn out of black rock cut into the sides

of the Mountains of Mourne. The only farms that remained were spread out from the cities. The more remote areas were completely empty of people.

The weather was cold and overcast, but it stayed dry.
Their journey began to take on a sameness as they rode
all day and into the night, sleeping for only a few hours
before setting out again.

Collun began to feel an increasing sense of urgency.
Though he dreaded reaching their destination, he
pushed forward relentlessly.

On the morning of the fifth day of their journey,
Collun awoke from an uneasy sleep. Brie had already
risen and kindled a fire. They had taken shelter in a
deserted Scathian village. Collun's eyes nervously
scanned the dark shapes of the buildings, indistinct and
eerie in the dim light of dawn. He could see his breath.
He held his hands over the fire Brie had made. They
had not yet begun using the fur-lined cloaks Mealladh
had given him, but Collun could tell the time was fast
coming.

Brie poured him a cup of hot chicory sweetened with
a splinter of chocolate Mordu had supplied. Collun took
it from her gratefully, breathing in the steam that rose
from it. As he took his first sip, Collun heard the call of
a bird. Then he realized what it was that had awakened
him. His body tensed. A scald-crow.

TWENTY-THREE

The Blizzard

There was only one bird, but it had spotted them. It circled several times, with each circle dipping lower and tighter. Collun reached for his dagger, while Brie silently lifted her bow to her shoulder and notched an arrow to the string. Then, unexpectedly, the scald-crow spun off, winging away at high speed in an easterly direction. Collun watched until it had disappeared. Without a word, Brie doused the fire with the leftover chicory. They hurriedly packed up and mounted Fiain. The Ellyl horse sensed their urgency at once and set off at a gallop.

"I wonder how long it will take the bird to reach Medb's dun," Collun said, his heart pounding.

He scanned the sky. Outlined as they were against the stark landscape, he and Brie were easy to spot from above. He shuddered, remembering the ice-dark feeling of the scald-crow feather that had brushed his forehead months ago.

Brie pointed to the clouds. "Look. Snow blossoms," she said.

Collun looked up. Indeed the clouds had changed, taking on the shape of gigantic white flowers with streaks of gray radiating from their centers.

"A storm is coming," Brie said.

"Will it hide us?" Collun asked with a flicker of hope.

"Perhaps," answered Brie, but she sounded worried.

The first of the white flakes began to fall by late afternoon. They brought out Mealladh's fur-lined cloaks and put them on. The snowflakes were thick, and they clung stubbornly to eyelashes and hair before melting.

Their cloaks were soon damp, though they kept the rest of their clothing mostly dry. Brie and Collun snuggled into the hoods gratefully. The snow was piling up.

They came upon a dense bank of red-berry juniper shrubs and decided to stop there for the night. They dug out a small shelter beside the bushes, and though it was difficult to kindle a fire, they finally managed to get a small blaze going. Except for the apple Mealladh had given Collun, they were close to the end of their provisions. Brie was able to find little game in the snow.

Holding the map up to the flickering light of the fire, Collun and Brie estimated they were well over halfway to the Isle of Thule. But Brie was worried about the snow. There was danger in traveling through a blizzard, especially in a hostile land with little hope of shelter and food. She showed Collun how to make coverings for their hands by cutting up an old jersey and securing it at the wrist with twine.

They slept huddled together under the prickly juniper branches. Collun occasionally heard Fiain snort and stamp his feet to keep warm.

When they woke to the dim light of the winter sun, the snow was still falling lightly. The countryside around them was swathed in white, an undulating series of curves, broken only by the knob of an occasional tree.

With fingers made clumsy by the cold, they rekindled the fire and melted snow to drink. They carefully portioned out the last of their food, saving the rest of the dried fruit for Fiain. Collun gave the horse a vigorous rubdown, dusting the snow from his mane.

Soon they were under way. The snow, which had been falling only lightly when they awoke, began coming down more heavily as the afternoon progressed. The wind blew harder from the north, swirling snow into their faces. Fiain walked slowly, his head bowed low. The whirling whiteness became so thick that Collun could barely see beyond Fiain's ears.

There was no way to tell in which direction they were going. Despite the Ellyl horse's keen sense of direction, Collun did not think it possible that he would be able to hold to their course. It took all the animal's energy simply to keep moving through the blizzard.

"Collun." He could just hear Brie's voice over the whistling sound of the wind.

"Yes?"

"Try not to fall asleep. There is danger in sleep when you are cold."

They lapsed into silence. Collun shut his eyes and listened to the whishing of the wind and to the muffled sound of Fiain's hooves plodding through the deep drifts of snow. The fur of his hood was rimmed with tiny icicles that pricked his face. The large flakes of the day before had turned into small, fierce pellets of ice that hammered relentlessly at their bodies.

Collun began to lose all sense of time. There was only the stinging snow, the sound of the wind, and the movement of the horse beneath them. On and on they went through the blizzard.

Collun suddenly felt something clasp him around the waist. He looked down and saw Brie's hands with their makeshift mittens. She was squeezing him tightly. Then he realized with horror that he had fallen asleep.

"Collun?" Brie's voice was insistent and worried. "Collun, can you hear me?"

"Yes. I'm sorry. I was sleeping."

"I thought so." Brie sounded tired herself, but she was patient. "Please try to stay awake. They say freezing is an easy way to die, because it steals over you like sleep. But I do not think it is our time for dying. Not yet." She paused. The sound of the wind filled their ears. "What will you do, Collun, when this is over? Will you return with Nessa to Inkberrow?"

"No." Brie didn't seem to hear him at first, so he said it again, louder. "No. I will not return to Inkberrow."

"Why not?"

"There is no home for me there." Collun thought of Goban's dark face with its perpetual frown. He shivered.

Brie sensed his mood and quickly said, "Where, then?"

"I do not know."

There was silence. Then Brie said, "There will be a garden, wherever it is."

Collun smiled slightly. "I hope so."

"Tell me what you will plant in the garden."

Collun paused, thinking.

"Well?" she prodded him gently.

"It would depend on how much land there was." Talking was difficult, but it was better than the constant sound of the wind.

"Say there is much land, as much as you could ever want."

"Then it would depend on the soil. If it is heavy or light, too much clay or sand, which would depend on where the land was . . ."

"Put the land where you like."

"Very well. I will have it by the sea because the moisture in the air is good for growing. First, I will sow heliotrope seeds because the flowers are brightly colored. They are also sweet smelling and will attract bees. I would like a hive near my garden. Next to the heliotrope I will plant red valerian because the two grow well side by side. Then a small patch of paggle. It smells as good as it looks and makes a delicious pudding with cream, eggs, and rosewater."

Brie let out a muffled groan. "Please, no talk of food. What about a bit of wild hyacinth or harebell? The juice from the stalk makes a glue I use to attach feathers to my arrows."

"Then there shall certainly be harebell," said Collun. "And some blue clownrie; though it's an ugly, squat thing with nettles on its leaves, it is good for healing wounds and fever. And next to that perhaps some peppergrass for seasoning..." Collun's voice became increasingly animated as he warmed to his theme.

Though many of Collun's words were lost in the wind, Brie kept her head close to his and managed to follow most of what he said. She occasionally interjected a question, and Collun was surprised by her knowledge of gardening. They argued back and forth about the placement of the compost heap.

And so the hours went by. Just after Collun had described the vegetables adjoining the flower and herb gardens, they realized the wind had died down. They were very hungry. Brie reached back and knocked off the snow on top of the leather packs. With numb hands she clumsily fumbled in the packs for Mealladh's apple. Finally, she found it and passed it to Collun.

He took a bite. At first the fruit's cold flesh hurt his teeth. But the apple was delicious, bursting with sweetness. He took several more bites, then passed it back to Brie. He heard the crunch as she bit into it.

Then she passed it back. Collun waited a few moments before his next bite, running his tongue over his chilled front teeth. He brought the apple up to his mouth and let out a cry of surprise.

"What is it?" asked Brie anxiously.

"The apple is whole again." And indeed no matter how much of it they ate, the fruit restored itself; the skin healed and the apple remained whole.

"I have heard of such things, but I never thought to eat any," said Brie, shaking her head in wonder. It made a light meal, but it filled their stomachs, and they both felt their strength renewed.

By the time they replaced the apple in the pack, the

snow had stopped falling altogether. The going was still slow because of the large drifts, and they were both cold through. Their hands and feet might have been made of wood for all they could feel of them. But at least they could see what lay ahead.

Brie was the first to spy the river. The banks were high with snow, but they could see and hear the water rushing below. Collun took the map from his belt. Peering over his shoulder, Brie pointed at a river that cut Scath at a diagonal, flowing from south to north.

"The Omagh," said Brie. This was the river they were to follow to the top of Scath.

They could not tell where they were on the river. The blizzard could easily have pushed them off at an angle, either south or north, but at least they had found their course again. Even more welcome was the sight of a small dark hump, capped in white, which turned out to be a long-abandoned hut. Brie thought it must once have been inhabited by a ferryman who had provided passage across the wide, unfordable river, as there was the outline of a small boat propped up against the side of the hut. Holes gaped in the hut's roof, and snow lay in drifts inside, but there were dry patches. They entered while Fiain stayed outside, nosing about the banks of the river for food. There was a small pile of wood beside a stone-lined fireplace. Though it seemed to take a lifetime, they were finally able to kindle a fire.

At first the heat caused sharp pains to shoot through their fingers and toes, but as the warmth penetrated, it felt wonderful. They shared the apple again. As Collun took the fruit from Brie, he asked, "Do you think they have reached Temair by now?"

Brie nodded, her eyes on the fire.

"And do you believe Prince Gwynedd still lives?"

"I don't know," she answered. "He is young and strong."

Collun swallowed a bite of the apple. Then before he could stop himself he said, "It must have been difficult, saying good-bye to the prince."

Brie turned and looked at him. "He was in good hands," she said. "And I chose to journey with you."

They were both silent after that and fell asleep by the fire, their bodies huddled close together for warmth.

They woke up shivering. The fire had died to a few smoking embers, and while Brie rekindled it, Collun went outside to feed and rub down the Ellyl horse. Fiain ate of Mealladh's apple with obvious pleasure.

They left the shelter reluctantly. The wind was blowing, but not as hard as before. They mounted Fiain and began to follow the river northward. The sky stayed overcast, but no more snow fell. They made their way slowly across the frozen landscape.

Then sometime during the day they noticed the snow around them was glistening with beads of moisture. The air grew gradually warmer, though there was still no sign of the sun. At first the warmth puzzled them. It did not feel like sun heat; it reminded Collun more of the kind of heat generated by Goban's forge, with a faint metallic smell to it.

Then they realized what it was. The Wurme. Even at this distance its fire that burned without flame was powerful enough to melt snow. Patches of rocky land could be seen everywhere.

The river swelled as the snow melted. The terrain became increasingly craggy, and by the time they approached the northernmost coast of Scath it was almost all rock. Only the most tenacious vegetation grew between the shingles of stone, and the shrubs and trees that had managed to survive were misshapen and stunted.

As he breathed the acrid air, Collun felt a heavy dread settle on him. He tried to think about the garden he and Brie had planted during the blizzard, but all he could see were the contorted shapes of blackened trees and straggling bushes snaking over the cracked, stony land.

The metallic odor kept getting stronger. It began to take on a sickly, rotting quality. Collun was suddenly reminded of the smell of burning flesh the day Goban had dropped a red-hot ingot on his leg. Collun's stomach churned.

Soon the corrosive smell caught at the back of their throats, making them cough. The air grew so warm they shed both the fur-lined cloaks and the ones they had been wearing underneath.

Abruptly they came to the river's end.

Before them lay the Isle of Thule. Collun's heart started to pound. *Nessa*.

The island rose out of the water, a huge outcrop of jagged rock, as desolate and barren of any living thing as the land on which they stood. Covering nearly half the island was a glistening mound of dirty white. Part of the white mass shifted slightly, and Collun realized with a thrill of horror that it was the Firewurme.

TWENTY-FOUR

Firewurme

It was not possible to see where the monster began or where it ended. It seemed to be coiled in on itself. Forewarned as he had been by Crann, Collun was yet struck dumb by the creature's size. It was as high as the tallest pine he had ever seen, and it stretched at least as wide as the whole of the farmhold Aonarach.

Collun suddenly felt very small. He heard Brie exhale, and he turned and met her gaze. She managed a smile, but it did not reach her eyes.

The Isle of Thule was not far offshore. With the tide out, it even looked possible to wade to the island. The water was an opaque greenish color with a thin film of scum floating in patches on the surface.

The mound on the island shifted again, and Brie drew in her breath sharply. Collun saw it at the same time—the entrance to a cave, not a hundred yards from the nearest coil of the Firewurme's body. Collun looked again at the Firewurme. Its dirty white body had a wet sheen to it, as did the rocky surface surrounding it. This must be what Crann had spoken of, the sram that came off the monster's body and burned without flame. Collun wondered how quickly it would burn through their boots.

"The water doesn't look deep," said Collun.

Brie nodded.

"I'm going across," Collun added matter-of-factly, his eyes on the Wurme.

"Then so am I," answered Brie.

"No," Collun responded. "You gave your word."

Brie nodded reluctantly.

The waves broke around Collun's ankles as he waded onto the causeway. When he was halfway across, the water came up to his knees.

Suddenly he heard a loud squelching sound, like the sound a foot makes when pulled out of a puddle of sticky mud, only a thousand times louder. The mass of dirty white flesh lurched.

One coil separated itself from the others. It snaked across the stony ground until it was close to the edge of the island. Then it arched into the air.

Collun found himself looking directly up into the face of the Firewurme. He was separated from it only by the strip of causeway he had yet to cross. He stood frozen.

Naid's head was as large as a farmhouse. It was lumpy, like an enormous blob of dough, and the creature's eyes were a flat yellow. They were shaped like large almonds, with small black pupils in the center. Its wide, gaping mouth held no teeth. A thin black tongue lolled from one corner of the maw. Dripping from the tongue was a thick clear substance, part liquid and part solid. Sram. Whenever a drop of it hit the ground, it made a faint fizzing sound.

The flat yellow eyes stayed on Collun. The black tongue slid slowly to the other side of the Firewurme's toothless mouth.

Collun shuddered. He realized he was bathed in sweat. The heat that emanated from the Wurme was unlike anything Collun had ever known. It made his eyes water and lungs ache. It was a thousand times hotter than the forge at Aonarach at its hottest.

Collun's body tensed as he saw the Wurme's head dip, but it did not move toward him. It hovered above a large tree branch on the shore. The branch was thick and solid and as long as Collun's leg, but lying below the Fire-wurme's jaw it looked no bigger than a twig.

The creature's tongue slowly caressed the branch. Collun watched in horror as the wood began to disintegrate. He remained perfectly still, sweat dripping in large drops from his skin. The tongue lapped the shrinking branch again. Several minutes passed. The monster blinked its yellow eyes at him, then retracted its tongue with a hollow slapping sound. All that was left of the branch was a glistening yellow stain on the rocks.

The Wurme reminded Collun of a wolf he had once seen approaching a cluster of fat sheep in Inkberrow. And he thought he saw laughter in the Wurme's flat eyes.

The creature had thick, dirty white lids, which it kept half-shut. Then the sun came out. Though it barely penetrated the thick haze that hung over the island, Collun saw that the light—almost imperceptibly—made the Wurme's pupils dilate. At first he didn't take in the significance. Then he realized the Firewurme's pupils expanded when exposed to light instead of contracting.

Collun slowly inched his way backward across the causeway. The Firewurme's yellow eyes watched him go. Then the creature withdrew, recoiling its body. It kept its face forward.

Collun sank to the rocky surface, his throat raw from the corrosive air surrounding the island. Brie sat on one side of him, while Fiain stood on the other.

"Crann told me it cannot be injured," Collun said, clearing his throat. "And he thought it was like a garden worm; if it is cut, it regenerates itself."

"Has it a heart?"

"I do not think so."

"Does it have no weakness at all?" asked Brie.

"Crann thought not. Except perhaps its eyes. But the lids are thick." He paused. "Just now I noticed that the Wurme's pupils do not contract with light, but expand. I wonder..."

"Yes?" said Brie.

"If the creature were to be startled by a bright light of some kind..." Collun trailed off.

Brie was nodding. "The agaric. We could use it—"

Collun turned to her, his expression implacable. "Not we."

Brie looked down, her face set in a stubborn frown. Collun continued. "*I* will make a torch...and if I am lucky, perhaps the flash of light it makes will give me time to strike the Firewurme's eye with the dagger that was a trine."

"The dagger that bears the Cailceadon Lir," added Brie in a soft voice.

"If the Wurme's tongue finds me first, it will make little difference whether the stone is chalcedony or charcoal." Collun paused. "I ask one thing of you, Breo-Saight. When I face the Firewurme, go to the cave with Fiain. If my sister is there, and alive, take her away with you. Take her to Temair, if you can."

Brie opened her mouth to protest, but Collun silenced her. "If you are my friend, you will do what I ask and no more." Brie shut her mouth and nodded, her face pale.

Collun rose and set to work on his torch. He found a stunted tree growing nearby and broke off its longest branch. He took the remaining agaric and pounded it, adding small amounts of beeswax and water. Then he laid the mixture onto the end of the branch in layers, smoothing and pressing hard, so it adhered to the wood. When he was finished, he dusted it all over with agaric powder, then he set it carefully to dry. It resembled a very large lasan.

Collun crossed to Fiain and, as he fed him Mealladh's apple, told him what he planned to do. Collun could tell from the angry flaring of the animal's nostrils that he wanted to face the Wurme with Collun. The boy focused his thoughts, willing the animal to understand. *If I am to die, I wish to die knowing my sister is safe. She will be safe with you and Brie. Please do this for me, Fiain.* The Ellyl horse stood still, then bowed his head slightly.

Then Collun knelt and ran his fingers over the Ellyl horse's hooves. They were tough, he knew, much tougher than those of mortal horses, having no need for metal shoes. But he did not know how they would react to the Firewurme's sram. Fiain gave a nicker of disdain, and Collun felt reassured.

Collun spent the rest of the evening preparing to meet the Firewurme. He worked steadily, without fatigue. First he made mittens for his hands as they had done during the blizzard. Then, using the leather from one of the packs Mordu had given him, he constructed clumsy, makeshift overboots to wear on top of his own boots. Then he wrapped his body from head to toe in every spare bit of clothing they had with them.

Collun had seen the Wurme's sram turn the branch to a smear. It did not seem likely that even so many layers of padding would protect him for long, but the few extra moments they bought him could possibly make the difference between living and dying.

Brie watched silently as Collun made his preparations. She checked her own gear, plucking at the bow to ensure it was strung tight and feeling the tips of her arrows to test their sharpness.

Sometime after midnight and well before dawn, Collun called Fiain to him. He mounted first, with Brie climbing up behind. Earlier he had given Brie his wallet of herbs, tucking the shell Mealladh had given him inside.

The causeway was at low tide, and obeying Collun's gentle nudge, Fiain began to cross. Collun was sweating heavily underneath his layers of clothing. The torch he had made was clutched tightly in his damp, padded palm. In his other hand he carried a glowing fire stick with which he planned to light the torch.

The moon was not full and shone only faintly through the haze. In the eerie light they could just make out the outline of the Firewurme's body. When they had almost reached the shore of the island, they saw Naid's head rise. It watched them with its flat yellow eyes, the lids half-shut. The black tongue slid from one side of its wide mouth to the other.

As soon as Fiain's hooves hit the rocky surface of the island, Collun jumped off. He touched the Ellyl horse lightly on his hindquarters, sending him toward the cave.

Collun broke into a run, his layers of clothing making him clumsy and slow. As he ran toward the Firewurme, he tried to dodge the puddles of sram, but in some places they were too large. He landed flat in the middle of one. The ooze began melting through the bottom layer covering his feet. It made a soft hissing noise as it burned.

The Firewurme's head suddenly moved with a swiftness that took Collun by surprise. He looked up to see its face above him, the black tongue dangling not more than an arm's length from his shoulder. He heard a splat and a fizz as sram dripped onto the ground.

His heart pounding, Collun lifted the fire stick to light the torch, but Naid's tongue suddenly snapped and extended. Collun felt a line of fire along his right jaw.

He fell to the ground, clutching at his chin in agony. There was a hissing sound as sram ate into his top layer of clothing. He rolled desperately until the sound stopped.

He was lying on a dry patch of rock, his face on fire. He could hear the sound of water lapping nearby and realized he must have rolled near the edge of the island. He longed to crawl to the shoreline and sink his face into the cooling water. But he painfully raised himself on one elbow. The Firewurme was watching him. Then it swiveled its head toward the cave, its tongue flicking in and out of its mouth. Collun's heart pumped. He leaped to his feet.

"Brie!" he cried out.

He charged at the coil of flesh nearest him. Dropping the torch, he unsheathed his dagger. Collun fiercely swung the blade down, biting into the dirty white flesh.

It was like cutting open a ripe fruit. As the skin opened, a thin stream of yellowish juice trickled out. Collun cut deeper, ignoring the sram that was melting his mitten. But when he had made a valley in the flesh the length of his arm, he had to pull out. His mitten was gone and blisters were forming on his hand.

Then, in a matter of moments, the deep cut Collun had made knitted itself back together. Collun watched, unbelieving, as the flesh was regenerated. Where it had been riven there was now a large smooth hump.

The Wurme had turned its head back toward Collun, and again there was laughter in the flat eyes.

Collun sheathed his dagger. As he bent to retrieve the torch, a deep blank feeling of hopelessness washed over him. His face and hand were on fire. Sweat was pouring off him. What had he been thinking? That a cowardly farm boy would be able to defeat Naid, the deadly Firewurme from Cruachan's cave?

Naid's body abruptly shifted, and Collun had to dive to his left to avoid getting suffocated by the lurching flesh. The heel of his left hand skidded into a pool of sram. Collun let out a yell of pain, rolling onto his back. His nose was full of the stench of his corroded skin.

Naid had now positioned itself between the boy and the cave's entrance. Its blunt snout hung high in the air. Collun stared up at the enormous creature.

Using all his willpower, Collun pulled himself into a sitting position. He was down to one layer of leather on his feet, and his clothing was in tatters; in some places it was gone altogether. But in his burned left hand the small fire stick still glowed.

The Firewurme watched Collun as he rose to his feet and began to move forward.

When Collun had come within a hundred paces, the Wurme dropped its head. It began to undulate across the ground toward him.

The urge to turn and run was overwhelming, but he stopped and stood still, waiting. When the tongue was no more than twenty paces from him, Collun brought his two shaking hands together. The small speck of fire touched the agaric torch.

A blinding column of flame burst up from the torch. Naid's head arched up, tongue dangling. It hung motionless above Collun. The Wurme's black pupils widened until more black showed than yellow. Collun shifted the torch to his left hand and swiftly drew his dagger. He aimed the dagger directly at the center of the Firewurme's right pupil and catapulted himself forward.

Just as he was about to plunge the dagger into its mark, there was a flicker of movement beside him. The Firewurme's tongue.

Before Collun could react, the black thing had coiled itself around his arm, from shoulder to wrist. An indescribable pain coursed through his body. His vision clouded. Streaks of gray swam over his eyes. He heard someone screaming, and he realized it was himself. He began to lose consciousness.

Collun struggled against the grayness. Then, he saw something flying through the air. It was an arrow. One of Breo-Saight's arrows.

The arrow, looking no larger than a tiny dart, fell short of its mark. It disintegrated in a puddle of sram. Then came another arrow, and it, too, turned to a smear on the ground.

As if from a distance Collun felt his feet begin to sear. The soles of his boots were gone.

Suddenly he felt a sharp, choking hatred toward the monster that had turned his body to fire. His thoughts hardened, and his head came up.

Collun looked into the Firewurme's face. The creature's pupils had begun to contract. He didn't remember dropping it, but the torch lay useless nearby, extinguished by the sram. Amazingly, though, the dagger was still in his mangled right hand, as if it had been forged there with fire. Collun painfully shifted the blade to his left hand and grasped the handle tightly. Then, with a hoarse shout of rage and horror, he launched himself again at the shrinking black center of the yellow eye above him.

As he pierced the Firewurme's pupil, the yellow surface wrinkled. The blade met no resistance. Collun's arm followed until it was immersed in amber-colored jelly. Then a black, oily liquid pulsed forth, splashing Collun's face and chest.

A hard, sharp object slammed into his forehead, and he knew no more.

TWENTY-FIVE

Nessa

When Collun awoke he saw Brie's face. He felt a searing pain across his shoulder and arm. He screamed. Then he lost consciousness again.

He woke a second time, and he saw another face above him. It looked like Nessa. Or her ghost. Thin and stretched and dead white. Perhaps this was what dying was, he thought. Dark and scorching hot, with the dreamlike faces of the people you loved floating over you.

"Collun?"

Yes, it must be Nessa's ghost. Her voice was as hollow and thin as her white face.

Brie suddenly loomed up beside Nessa's ghost face.

"Collun? Can you hear me?"

He wanted to brush the sweat from his eyes. Maybe if he could see more clearly...But when he tried to move his arm, his vision went black, and he gasped for breath. He must have screamed again, for there was a high-pitched noise echoing in his ears. He thought to himself it wasn't fair that he still had to feel pain even after he was dead.

"He needs water."

"There is a spring. Freshwater."

Collun could hear the voices, but they sounded miles away. He could not see anything.

"Can you help me carry him?"

"I'll try."

There were hands at his armpits and feet, gentle and careful, but the fire on his skin was unbearable. He wanted to tell them to stop. He could not move his mouth.

When he woke again he was lying in something cool. Water, he thought. The burning was less with the cool water against his skin. For the first time it occurred to him that he might not be dead after all. A light flickered somewhere near. He tried to fix his wavering vision.

"Brie?" he croaked.

Her face appeared.

"Oh, Collun!" The ghost face of his sister came up beside Brie. Its eyes were brimming with tears.

It *was* Nessa. She was not a ghost after all. Nessa was alive. His heart beat faster with joy.

"Collun." It was Brie again. "Naid is dead. You killed it. You have been sorely injured, but you are alive. And Nessa is here, safe."

"Where . . . ?"

"We are in the cave. Where Nessa has been kept prisoner. There is a spring here. The water is helping you. But Collun"—her voice was urgent—"did you not tell me of a remedy for burns, an herb from the hag's garden? Please, try to think."

Collun tried to focus on Brie's words. His wallet of herbs. It had been almost empty, but he had filled it again at Mordu's garden. There was an herb he had found there. . . . Then he remembered the crone who sold him a cure for burns and insect bites. Was a Wurme an insect? he wondered, his thoughts becoming loose and unconnected. He willed himself to concentrate.

He had plucked the herb from Mordu's garden. Mallow. That was it. And Mordu had told him the recipe. But it would probably not work.

"Collun? Tell us."

"Mallow," he rasped out painfully. "Leaves are round with points, bright red flowers, dried. Boil them . . . with leek juice . . . gentian . . . goat's thorn leaves. Two parts mallow . . . one of the others . . . Make a paste. Mordu said . . ." He trailed off.

Brie disappeared.

Nessa stayed beside him. He looked up at his sister's face in wonder. Her skin was pale as curds, and the bones of her face stuck out sharply. There were purple-black shadows under her eyes, and her lips looked bloodless and thin.

"Nessa," he whispered.

"Collun." He could barely hear her voice.

"You are alive."

She nodded and covered his left hand with hers. Then he slept.

When he woke he was no longer in the water. Nessa and Brie were gently trying to peel away the layers of his clothing. In some places flesh and cloth stuck together, and during the agony of undressing, Collun lost consciousness several more times. Finally he lay shivering, both hot and cold, in a thin layer of sweat-soaked underclothing. He saw his sister holding something in her hands. He didn't recognize it at first, but then realized the sodden lump was the book she'd given him.

"Your . . . book," he quavered.

"I'll make you another," she whispered.

The mallow paste was ready, and Brie slowly began to rub it into a patch of fire that burned at Collun's wrist. He let out a high-pitched animal sound. From then on, they told him later, he was delirious. Nessa said it was Brie, her face pale and set, who rubbed the mallow salve into Collun's raw, mangled flesh, reapplying it several times.

When he finally came out of the delirium, Brie bathed Collun's flaming face in freshwater. She told him she thought the salve was already beginning to heal the oozing weals on his body.

They got him to drink an herbal broth that Brie had improvised, sweetened with bits of Mealladh's apple. Collun felt weak and wrung out, but his heartbeat was steady and the gray streaks only occasionally darkened his vision.

His jaw throbbed. It hurt to move it. In the wavering light of a candle nearby, Collun could see his arm. It had been burned in a spiral pattern where the Wurme's tongue had wrapped around it. Undamaged skin alternated with festering ribbons of red. His shoulder was a mass of blistered flesh, and his hand was swollen and seeped with red-and-yellow pus. He remembered what the Wurme's tongue had done to the thick branch on the shore and wondered why he had any arm left at all. Perhaps, he thought, the Cailceadon Lir had protected him.

The soles of his feet had been badly burned. He wondered how he was going to walk again. And yet he was alive, and the mallow salve was healing his body more quickly than he would have thought possible.

As Brie sat by him, bathing his face, Collun noticed that her hands were covered with blisters. She told him she had gotten them while pulling him away from the dead Firewurme and onto the Ellyl horse.

"Fiain," Collun said, suddenly afraid. "Where is he?"

"He is fine," answered Brie. "The cave is too cramped for him, I think. He prefers to wait outside. He gallops around the causeway at low tide."

Nessa joined them then with a new batch of herbal broth. Collun looked again at his sister's emaciated face, and his heart twisted in his chest.

"What did they do to you, Nessa?" Collun asked.

Nessa looked at her brother. For a moment her eyes were unfocused and strange, as if she did not know where she was or even who she was. Collun anxiously reached over and touched her hand. "Nessa?"

The girl's eyes suddenly refocused, and they filled with tears.

"Crann said you must have held out for a long time, because Urlacan set out late to find me," Collun said painfully.

Nessa nodded, covering her eyes with her hands. "For as long as I could. But in the end..." She dropped her hands, her mouth twisted in anguish.

Collun held her hand tightly. "It was Bricriu, wasn't it?"

"Yes. The night before my coming-of-age ceremony, there was a feast at his dun. Halfway through the evening, Lord Bricriu asked to speak to me privately in his library. I entered the room, and then everything went blank. I woke in the darkness in a dungeon below Bricriu's dun."

"The labyrinth," said Collun.

"Was it? I knew it only as darkness. Each day Lord Bricriu came, carrying a candle. He said I would be given nothing to eat or drink until I told him where the chalcedony was. I told him I didn't know what he was talking about, but he only laughed. Days went by, and I grew weaker and weaker. Every day Bricriu came. 'Where is the chalcedony?' he'd shout. 'Where is it?' Soon I became too weak to answer.

"I think he believed, finally, that I knew nothing of the stone. The next time he came he brought a piece of bread, some cheese, and a flagon of cold water. He said I could have them if I would tell him about my brother and my mother. I sensed that to speak might bring harm to you and Mother, though I did not know why. So I kept silent. Bricriu was very angry. After that he used needlelike pieces of metal, which he heated in a torch's flame." Nessa shuddered and bowed her head. After a while she spoke. "I don't remember much beyond that. Except that somehow I did not tell him what he wanted to know.

"There was a journey on horseback then. I was given a little to eat and drink, but it made me sick. Finally we came to a rocky land with air that hurt to breathe. By then I was able to eat again. It was night and we were camped by a large river. There were many Scathians around the fire, as well as a number of hooded creatures with yellow eyes that frightened me."

"Morgs," Collun interjected.

"There was suddenly a great commotion," Nessa continued. "Another large group of Scathians arrived, and at their head was a tall, fair woman. She wore a strange war helmet with two silver horns rising from the crown. It hung low on her forehead and over her nose, curving into the beak of a large bird of prey.

"I did not know at first who she was," said Nessa, "but then I heard one of the men call her queen, and I knew she must be Medb."

"You saw Medb herself?" asked Collun, his eyes wide.

Nessa nodded, her hands clenching and unclenching. Her face had gone white.

"What did she do to you, Nessa?" Collun cried out.

The tears came again. "I'm sorry, Collun," she whispered. "But her eyes..." Nessa faltered. "They were so pale, almost white, like her hair. And when she stared down at me I felt so cold, colder than I've ever felt before. I almost fainted, I think." She paused, then began again, her voice still a whisper. "I could bear Bricriu's needles better than those eyes..."

Brie poured Nessa a cup of chicory and handed it to the trembling girl.

"I was lying on my side, near the fire, my hands and feet bound. Medb stood looking down at me; she took off her war helmet, and her hair fell straight and white to her shoulders. She was beautiful, but in a cruel, frightening way.

"Then she leaned over and picked me up. Her arms

were like iron. She carried me as if I were a baby and walked to the edge of the causeway. She lowered me into the rancid water until I was completely submerged except for my head. Then she took hold of my hair with one hand, pulling it so tight I cried aloud.

"With the other hand she rummaged in the folds of her white cloak, then pulled out a stone. She held it up in front of my face. Something about the blue stone looked familiar to me, but I was too terrified and ill to remember what it was. 'Where is the stone like this one?' she demanded. I told her I didn't know. With the hand gripping my hair she pushed my head underwater and held it there. I was on the verge of losing consciousness when she roughly pulled me up again. I gasped for breath and she stared down at me, no expression at all on her face.

"'Where is the stone?' she said again. I told her I didn't know. Then she changed tack and began asking me the same things Bricriu had—where I was from, if I had a brother, if my mother was Emer. And on and on. She would ask, I wouldn't answer, then she'd put my head underwater just to the point when I thought I was dying. Then she'd pull me up and ask again. Finally, I broke. I told her about you and Emer and Aonarach. When I finished, all she said was, 'Does he have the stone?' And suddenly I remembered where I had seen a stone like the queen's: in the handle of your trine. I did not speak, but she abruptly let go of my hair. 'Yes,' she said. 'I thought so.'

"She lifted me back up in her arms and carried me across the causeway. I saw the Firewurme then. It was watching us. I think I was in a state of shock. I remember looking at the Firewurme's tongue and wondering what you and Mother were doing in Aonarach. Medb took me into this cave. She told me I would stay alive only if I remained inside. She pointed to a clear, wet-looking substance that lay on the ground, the Wurme'ssram; she said it would burn me.

"As she turned to leave, I finally found my voice and asked the queen why she was doing this to me. She smiled again, her eyes like ice. 'A little experiment,' she said, 'in brotherly devotion.' Then she was gone. I went to the cave's entrance and watched her cross the island. She walked directly up to the Firewurme. They seemed to be communicating in some way, then the Wurme opened its horrible maw and slid its tongue to one side. I'm not sure what I saw next. It was like a nightmare. But I could have sworn that the queen reached her arm into the Wurme's mouth, right up to her shoulder. She kept it there for only a moment and then turned and left the island.

"I saw her ride off with her men. When they were out of sight, I tried to leave the cave, in spite of what she had said about the sram." Nessa lifted her feet, showing them the burn scars on her soles and on her knees and the palms of her hands. "When my feet could no longer hold me, I crawled. But the Firewurme came with its yellow eyes and black tongue..." She faltered.

"How did you live?"

"There was food left for me at the back of the cave —salted meats and hard biscuits. And there was the spring with an occasional fish I caught with a spear I made out of driftwood. But the food ran out some time ago, and there haven't been many fish..." Her voice trailed off, then she fixed her eyes on Collun. "Why did she bring me here?"

Collun picked up the dagger. He told Nessa about the Cailceadon Lir. "Medb had you kidnapped believing you might have it, or at least would know where it was. When Bricriu told her you did not have the stone and would not tell him of your family and home, she had you brought to Scath. Then she sent the morg Urlacan after me, keeping you here as bait just in case Urlacan was to fail."

Nessa absorbed the information in silence.

"The wizard Crann also wondered if Medb thought to use us to flush out our father," Collun added.

"Our father? Why should she care about Goban?"

"Not Goban," Collun said softly, and then he told Nessa everything. He told her of their true father and of the chalcedony that had been passed down through Cuillean's family. Nessa listened quietly, shaking her head in wonder. She wept when she heard Emer had died, and for the first time since hearing of his mother's death, Collun was able to let his own unshed tears fall.

Then Nessa wanted to hear more of Collun's journey, but before he could begin, Brie interrupted. There was a note of suppressed excitement to her voice.

"I had forgotten all about it until now," she said, reaching into a pocket, "but I found this caught in a fold of your tunic after you killed the Wurme."

Collun took the object she handed him with an instinctive twitch of revulsion. It was a stone, covered with the oily black fluid that had gushed from the Fire-wurme's eye. Then he remembered the sharp object that had struck him on the forehead just before he lost consciousness. He rubbed the stone, and as the oily fluid came off he saw a glint of blue. His heartbeat quickened. Using the corner of his jersey, he began rubbing harder. When he was finished, a dull blue-gray stone lay in his palm. With trembling hand, Collun reached for his dagger. Though slightly larger and rougher, this stone was the mirror image of the one embedded in the handle.

Collun looked up at Brie. Her eyes were bright. "When I heard Nessa say the queen had put her hand into the Wurme's mouth, I wondered."

"Then," Collun said slowly, "the Firewurme was guardian not only of Nessa but of Queen Medb's shard of the Cailceadon Lir as well."

A silence filled the small cave as the realization of what they had found sunk in. If they could carry the stone out of Scath and to Temair, Medb would have lost both the Firewurme and the chalcedony. And perhaps then Eirren would be safe.

TWENTY-SIX

Wurme-killer

We must leave here," Collun said. "Now."

Brie shook her head. "You are not ready to travel. The burns—"

"It doesn't matter. She will come for us. She may even be on her way."

"Surely Medb could not yet know about the Fire-wurme."

"We can't be certain," Collun argued. "She has many spies. Or she may even have felt it when the Wurme died. She has great powers."

Nessa's eyes had grown wide and staring. She was again clenching and unclenching her hands. "Medb come here?" she said in a whisper. "We must escape.

We must get away!" The girl's voice was edged with hysteria.

Brie looked from brother to sister and shook her head. "We can try," she said finally.

They quickly prepared to depart. Collun placed the cailceadon shard in his wallet of herbs. Brie used up the last of the mallow making a large batch of the burn paste. Then she hastened to the entrance of the cave to call for Fiain. The Ellyl horse was already heading toward them.

But halfway there, Fiain slowed. He came to a stop and lifted his head into the air.

"Something is wrong," Brie said uneasily.

Then they all heard it. The familiar, unmistakable caw.

"What is it?" Nessa whispered in fear.

"A scald-crow. One of Medb's spies," answered Collun.

Brie crouched low, carefully peering out.

"There are three of them. They are circling the Wurme. Like vultures," she said.

The cries became louder.

"They have spotted Fiain," Brie told them. Collun let out a sound and tried to get to his feet. But he fell back, his face white with pain.

"One of the birds is splitting off, heading south."

"To Rathcroghan and its queen," said Collun grimly. "And Fiain?"

"Another is flying after him, but Fiain is too fast for it. He is heading south. I can barely see him now. I do not see the third bird anywhere." She scanned the sky for several moments, then crossed to Collun with a look of concern.

There was a sudden whirring of wings and a rush of cold air. In the dim light of the cave Collun could see only the bloodred eyes of the scald-crow as it bore down on him.

He grabbed his dagger with his unburnt hand and flattened himself against the wall of the cave. The bird rushed by within a fingernail of his scalp.

The scald-crow circled and dived again. Collun's blade made an arc in the air. The Cailceadon Lir glowed. There came a keening scream and then a thud as the bird hit the ground. A thin stream of blood spilled from the scald-crow's torn breast.

Collun let go of the dagger. He was trembling violently. Nessa cried without a sound, and a pale-faced Brie stared down at the fallen bird.

Then they heard hooves on rock, and Fiain appeared in the entrance to the cave. The Ellyl horse was breathing hard and frothing at the corners of his mouth. There was no sign of the scald-crow that had been following him.

Brie and Nessa quickly helped Collun onto Fiain, and with Nessa mounted behind her brother and Brie holding fast to her, they left the cave.

As they passed the head of the dead Firewurme, Collun stared with a sick fascination, unable to believe he had actually killed such a vast and evil creature.

A deep rumble of thunder echoed across the small island, and when Fiain's hooves splashed into the causeway, an ear-numbing crack split the darkening sky. Fiain broke into a gallop, sending up sheets of water that soaked them through.

By the time the Ellyl horse reached the mainland, the

darkness had thickened around them. Rattling cracks of thunder continued to follow close upon each other, but there was no lightning and no rain. Fiain sped along the banks of the River Omagh, and Brie had to cling tightly to Nessa's back to keep from falling off.

When the Isle of Thule was well behind them, Fiain slowed his pace. Collun sank onto the horse's neck, his mind numbed by pain. But when he felt Fiain's thoughts probing into his, he urged him to continue on.

The sky grew so dark it was difficult to tell exactly when night fell. They couldn't see the moon or a single star.

When they came to the abandoned hut by the river, where Collun and Brie had sheltered during the snowstorm, they finally halted. Collun was barely conscious.

"We will stop here," said Brie.

Collun let out a thin moan as they helped him to dismount. "Medb...," he muttered.

"We need rest," Brie responded.

Inside the hut they shared Mealladh's apple, then slept for an hour. Fiain kept watch outside.

Before they set out again, Brie touched Collun's forehead with her hand.

"You are burning."

Collun shook his head. "We must keep going."

They rode on. A gray, feeble dawn came, and over the course of the day the darkness did finally dissipate. That night they could see a few stars and the sliver of a new moon.

Collun remained conscious as they traveled on, but he did not seem to hear when they spoke to him. His body pulsed with pain, and it was difficult not to scream at every step Fiain took.

Not long after nightfall they came to one of the deserted Scathian villages Collun and Brie had passed through before.

Brie called out for Fiain to stop. She and Nessa again helped Collun to dismount. The only sign that he was conscious was his open eyes.

Brie and Nessa went around the empty village gathering kindling. Then Brie went off, bow in hand, and Nessa set about making a fire, with Collun slumped beside her. Fiain struck off on his own, in search of something to eat.

It was a relief to be still, Collun thought as he watched Nessa's clumsy attempts to kindle a flame. Moving carefully, Collun extracted one of the last of the lasan sticks from his jersey pocket. He rubbed it across the rough surface of a rock and handed it to Nessa, who took it gratefully.

In the brief flaring of light from the lasan, Collun thought he saw a movement in the shadows of the deserted buildings. He leaned forward, body tense, and tried to focus on the spot.

"What is it?" Nessa asked.

Collun didn't answer but continued to stare until his eyes felt hot and strained. He did not see it again.

Brother and sister waited by the fire. Collun dozed.

He came awake with a start. Nessa was asleep beside him. The fire had burned down to a handful of pale orange-gray embers. Collun moved stiffly, suppressing a moan. Where was Brie? And Fiain? The darkness pressed around them.

Suddenly he heard a hissing sound. It didn't come from the fire but from somewhere out in the darkness.

"Brie?" he called faintly. Nessa woke with a start.

Several moments passed. And then it came again. A distinct, sibilant noise. Nessa clutched Collun's arm.

"Morgs," Collun whispered in dread. Then the clouds covering the new moon moved away and they could see.

There were dozens of them. Shrouded in their cloaks, the morgs looked like ghosts standing among the shadowed, deserted buildings.

Nessa let out a cry. Brie was being led toward them, a morg on either side of her. There was blood on the side of her face. In her hand she carried the two halves of her broken bow.

There were morgs all around them now. Collun barely had time to pull himself to his feet before they were on him. His arms were wrenched behind his back, and he could not restrain a scream as rope bit into his mangled wrist and arm.

Collun, Brie, and Nessa were quickly and tightly bound. The morg that seemed to be the leader bent over Collun. His yellow eyes rested on the dagger sheathed at Collun's waist. The morg grabbed it and held up the blade triumphantly. A wave of horror washed over Collun.

The sky had lightened almost imperceptibly. Dawn was approaching. The morg quickly stowed the dagger in the folds of his cloak. Then he began searching through Collun's clothing.

"Hurry. The sun comes," hissed the morg beside him.

The first morg's hand came upon Collun's wallet of herbs, and eagerly he began to unfasten it.

Suddenly there came a noise in the near distance.

"What is that?" the morg said, whipping his hooded face around.

"Horses," said the second morg.

And as the sun blinked on the horizon, Fiain galloped into the deserted village. Behind him was a phalanx of Eirrenian soldiers on horseback.

The morg leader grabbed the wallet of herbs, breaking the cord around Collun's neck. He called out to the others, and the creatures scattered, fleeing in all directions. Collun watched in dismay as the morg carrying his dagger and wallet of herbs darted away, disappearing between the ruined buildings.

Fiain let out a whinny and went in pursuit. Collun heard the morg's voice cry out, but suddenly a morg with an arrow in its breast fell heavily on him, crushing his burnt arm. He let out a cry and almost lost consciousness. When his head cleared, he discovered his vision was blocked by the morg's cloak.

Collun heaved his torso, trying in vain to move the inert body off him, but the motion was agonizing. All he could do was lie still and listen to the sounds of battle all around him—screams and grunts, metal clashing against metal. It was impossible to tell at first which way the battle was leaning, but gradually he thought the Eirrenians' voices began to take on a note of triumph.

Abruptly he felt the morg's body being pulled off him, and he was looking into the flushed and smiling face of a young dark-haired man. The youth bore a faint resemblance to Prince Gwynedd, and when he spoke the voice was almost identical.

"Are you hurt?"

Collun flinched as the youth began freeing him from his bonds.

"Burns," explained Collun in a husky voice. He

slowly got to his feet. Nessa and Brie were approaching, accompanied by two Eirrenian soldiers.

"Nessa?!" said the young man who resembled Prince Gwynedd. "I cannot believe my eyes."

"Prince Kellean," Nessa responded in wonder. "Collun, Brie, this is Kellean, eldest of the king's sons."

But Kellean had shifted his gaze and was staring intently at Collun. "Is it possible? Are you...the son of Cuillean?"

Collun nodded.

"Well met," said the prince with a broad smile. "Rumors were flying at the battlefront that the hero Cuillean had a son who lived and who would appear at the eleventh hour and turn the tide of the war. I confess I thought it superstitious nonsense. Though as it turned out, we needed no—"

Just then Fiain appeared. The Ellyl horse whickered, and slowly Collun crossed to him. Fiain led Collun through the deserted village to the body of a fallen morg.

Collun leaned down and turned the body over. There, clutched in the morg's three fingers, was Collun's dagger and wallet of herbs.

"Thank you, Fiain," Collun said quietly. He retrieved the items, giving an involuntary shudder as he brushed the clammy gray skin. He returned to the others.

Kellean was still speaking. "...After the invasion collapsed and Medb's forces had scattered, my father sent a squad of us west along the border to be sure all was indeed secure. We came across an Ellyl horse. He seemed to want us to follow him, so we did."

"Medb's invasion...collapsed?" asked Collun in amazement.

"Yes. It happened when the darkness and the thunder came. We couldn't believe it at first."

Brie and Collun looked at each other.

The prince continued. "Medb's invasion was like an evil tide when it first began. There were thousands upon thousands of Scathians and morgs, all armed to the teeth and deadlier than any soldiers I have ever seen. They kept pushing southward. Our casualties were enormous. Even when reinforcements arrived, including a large army of Ellylon, it still looked hopeless.

"Then on the eve of the fourth day of fighting, the Scathian army faltered, becoming disorganized and uncertain. And when the thunder and the thick black clouds came, making night out of day, the Scathian army simply turned and fled. There was no explanation for their flight. It was not the retreat of a defeated army, for they had clearly held the upper hand until the darkness came. My father said it was as though someone was calling them home.

"We tried to get answers out of the few enemy soldiers we had captured and those too wounded to follow the rest. But the soldiers with weapons killed themselves before we could stop them, and the others refused to speak." The prince shook his head, his face clouded.

"The darkness came when we left Thule with Medb's chalcedony," said Collun.

"Chalcedony?"

"Yes. The Cailceadon Lir," Collun said. And with help from Brie and Nessa, he told the prince all that had befallen them, ending with the discovery of Medb's shard of the cailceadon.

When Collun had finished, the prince gave a low

whistle. "I see now. Once Medb learned she had lost both Cailceadon Lir and Wurme, she knew she no longer had the power to conquer Eirren. And so she summoned her army home." Prince Kellean put a hand on Collun's shoulder.

"It appears the rumors were true. As your father, Cuillean, saved our country fifteen years ago, so have you saved us, Collun, Wurme-killer."

TWENTY-SEVEN

Cuillean's Dun

It took them ten days to travel to Temair. When they entered the gates, Collun was astonished to see that the streets were lined with Eirrenians and that there were as many calling out for "Wurme-killer" and "son of Cuillean" as there were for Prince Kellean.

By the time they'd made their way to the royal dun, a large throng had gathered at the gates to greet them. Collun quickly spotted Talisen among the crowd, with Silien close behind him.

Collun winced as Talisen enfolded him in an enthusiastic bear hug. There was time only for quick greetings and introductions between Nessa and Silien before

Queen Aine whisked Collun, Brie, and Nessa off to the court healers.

The healers were gentle and thorough. They tended to Brie's burnt hands and Nessa's exhaustion and mal-nourishment, then sent both of them directly to bed. Collun had to stay for several days in the healers' hushed and darkened quarters. They had been impressed by the properties of the mallow salve and told Collun he was lucky not to have lost his arm altogether. They said he would bear faint scars for the rest of his life, but oth-erwise he could expect to be back to normal in a month or two.

Collun received visits from his friends, from Nessa, and from his aunt Fial, now recovered from her illness.

The afternoon the court healers released him, Collun received word that his presence was requested by the king and queen. Quince guided him to the king's quarters.

Collun was greeted warmly by Queen Aine and King Gwynn, who bade him join them at a table that was laden with food for the afternoon meal. Collun felt shy as he seated himself. The room was drenched in light, bringing out the vivid colors in the many tapestries and murals that decorated the walls.

Queen Aine filled Collun's plate with smoked capon, a mound of crisp runner beans, a creamy cheese tart, and a mouthwatering honey bun. Collun grasped his fork, his head swimming slightly. Since the blizzard he had eaten little. His stomach rumbled loudly and Collun flushed, certain the king and queen could hear it.

But Aine smiled at him, inquired after his health, and asked him to tell them all that had befallen him. "We have heard bits and pieces," she said, "but we would like to hear it in your own words. If you are up to it," she added kindly.

At first Collun's speech faltered, but gradually he relaxed, and between mouthfuls of the delicious food, he told them everything. He apologized to Aine for keeping from her the truth about Emer. She told him she understood, although it had been a shock to her when Silien had told her of Collun's true identity.

"Where is the Cailceadon Lir now? The shard you brought from Thule, that is," asked the king, his eyes serious.

Collun drew the stone from his wallet of herbs. "Please, take it," Collun said. "It belongs in your hands, not mine." He felt a weight lift off his shoulders as King Gwynn took the stone. Then, more reluctantly, Collun reached for his dagger. "And you should have this, too. Then the three shards can be together, as they were meant to be." He placed the dagger that had been a trine on the table.

The king laid the two stones side by side and gazed at them solemnly. Then he looked up at Collun.

"Son of Cuillean, this would be a sacrifice for you, to give up the stone you have carried since childhood. And it is a sacrifice that I do not believe is necessary. The shard has been in your family's possession perhaps longer than it was part of the one stone. Furthermore, Aine and I believe the three shards of the Cailceadon Lir should never be reunited. It would be far too dangerous. No one, not even those of us who consider ourselves incorruptible"—he gave a ghost of a smile—"should have access to such power. I think the wizard Crann would agree with me.

"However, I will accept your gift of Medb's shard of the Cailceadon Lir, and Aine and I will endeavor to find a hiding place as safe as we believe that of the first shard to be."

King Gwynn then handed Collun's dagger back to him. As Collun took it, Aine spoke, a frown creasing her forehead. "We realize that by asking you to continue to carry this stone, we place you in danger. Although Medb has been defeated and her power severely weakened, it would be naive to believe that we have nothing more to fear from her. There may come a time when she will seek you and your stone again. Have you given thought to the future, Collun?"

Collun gazed up at one of the murals on the wall, the dagger clenched in his hand. During the past few days, as he'd lain in the quiet rooms of the court healers, he had thought about little else. He knew he could not return to the farmhold Aonarach; except for his garden, there was nothing to draw him there. Several days earlier, Nessa had told him she wished to remain in Temair with Fial. She had already written Goban, telling him that she was safe but would not be returning to Inkberrow.

Life in Temair suited Nessa well, Collun knew. The fine food and clothing, the many books, the music, the feasts; she thrived on these things. But Collun was uncomfortable there. The clothing they had given him made him feel awkward. He was a gardener and a farmer, and he sorely missed the fresh air in his lungs and on his face. He missed watching the sunrise, pink and gold, over a field of newly mown hay. He missed the sound of a bird calling through a dusky twilight evening and the stars just beginning to come out, one by one.

"Cuillean's dun . . . ," Collun began hesitantly. "I have heard it lies by the sea."

"Yes," replied Queen Aine, "and it is empty. In the absence of your father, it is yours by right."

"But you are welcome to make your home with us, here in the royal dun," said King Gwynn. "There are quarters next to your aunt Fial's that you and your sister could share."

"Thank you, King," Collun answered slowly, "but I will go to Cuillean's dun. My place is where there is a plot of land to till. And I have always wished for one by the sea." He thought again of the garden he and Brie had created during the blizzard.

"If that is your wish," said the king. "But first I will send some of my soldiers ahead. The dun has lain empty for some time. And I would ask that you permit a small guard to stay on with you, indefinitely. The son of Cuillean and the Cailceadon Lir he bears must be protected from the Queen of Ghosts and those who serve her."

Collun began to protest, but he stopped when he saw the look in the king's eyes. "It is settled, then," King Gwynn said.

Soon after, Collun rose to leave, thanking the king and queen for the delicious meal. He paused and then asked, "Prince Gwynedd, how does he?"

The queen did not answer for a moment. Finally she spoke with measured words. "The wounds to his body are healing well." The king reached over and took Aine's hand. Collun thought he saw the glimmer of tears in her eyes.

Later Talisen told Collun he had not seen Gwynedd since delivering him safely to Temair. He had heard the prince shunned all visitors, and the few people who had encountered him on his rare, solitary walks through the dun courtyard reported that his face was badly scarred and that he walked with the aid of a cane.

Collun tried to see Gwynedd himself but was turned away by a servingman. A day later Collun spotted him in the early hours of dawn, walking through the courtyard. He quickened his pace to catch up with the prince, but when Gwynedd turned and saw Collun behind him, he walked away as fast as his crippled leg would take him.

Collun saw that the right side of the prince's face was disfigured by a jagged white scar. But it was the expression of bitterness on the once open, handsome features that filled Collun with sorrow. Brie told Collun that Gwynedd had refused to see her as well.

The evening after Collun's meeting with the king and queen there was a feast. It continued through the night and on into the next day and the day after that, showing no signs of abating. Collun was embarrassed by all the attention paid him, but Talisen delighted in telling anyone who would listen about his own heroic role as bard on the son of Cuillean's victorious quest. Nessa, too, enjoyed the attention. She quickly regained her strength, and with her face thinner and more thoughtful after her ordeal, Collun believed that she was even more beautiful than before. Silien was enchanted with her. He was teaching her the Ellyl way to make paper. Nessa told Collun she was already at work on a new book for him.

One evening, as the festivities wound to a close, Collun found himself at a table with Brie, Nessa, Talisen, and Silien. His head felt woolly from too much bayberry wine. As the talk swirled around him, he thought back to the previous morning. He had been standing by his window, looking out at the still barren winter landscape, when he heard the song of a cuckoo. Back in Inkberrow, the cuckoo song was always the first harbinger of spring. It would soon be time for planting. He'd been told that the land at Cuillean's dun had lain untended for a year or more. There would be much to do to prepare it.

A loud laugh from Talisen brought Collun out of his reverie. Silien had just recited an impromptu poem, inviting Nessa to Tir a Ceol the moment she gave the word. Brie was leaning back in her chair, amusement in her dark eyes.

"I leave tomorrow," Collun broke in, surprising even himself with his words. They all turned toward him.

"Oh, Collun," said Nessa.

"What do you mean? You can't leave," protested Talisen. "I am to debut my song about you and Naid and all our adventures at the feast three days hence."

"Where do you go?" asked Brie.

"Cuillean's dun. The king and queen said it was mine by right until my fath—until Cuillean returns." He turned to Nessa. "I know that you wish to remain in Temair. The queen has told me it is not such a long journey between here and the sea. We will visit each other often."

"I knew you would be leaving," Nessa said softly. "It is almost time for spring planting, is it not?" Collun nodded, his throat catching.

"I would like to journey with you, Collun," said Brie, "if you wish the company."

Collun's eyes brightened. "Of course," he said.

"You will need help with the planting," Brie went on. "I have unfinished work of my own, but it will keep."

"I want to come, too," objected Talisen. "Why can't you wait just three days?"

Collun shook his head, and Talisen knew his mind was made up. "You are welcome anytime," Collun said. "What are your plans, Silien?" he asked the Ellyl.

Silien shrugged. "I will return to Tir a Ceol soon."

"Not until you have heard my song," said Talisen. Silien smiled.

"Why can't we hear your song now?" said Collun suddenly. "Since Brie and I will not be here for the official debut..."

"Yes. A dress rehearsal!" Nessa clapped her hands in pleasure.

Talisen hesitated, but the lure of an audience proved too tempting. "If you insist," he said magnanimously. His fingers began thrumming the strings of his harp.

Collun sat back in his chair and let the melody wash over him. Now that he had made the decision to leave, he felt better than he had in days.

When Talisen had finished, they applauded loudly and said it was his best creation yet.

Early the next morning, after leaving a long note for the king and queen telling them of his departure and thanking them for their kindness and hospitality, Collun met Brie at the stables. Fiain greeted them with a happy whicker, and they were soon on their way, Brie once more astride her Ellyl horse. The streets were quiet except for an occasional merchant setting up his stalls for the day's market.

Once they had passed through the last of the villages surrounding Temair, the horses simultaneously broke into a gallop. The air was cool, but the morning sun was bright, and the deep blue sky was filled with puffs of white clouds. Collun smelled spring in the gentle breeze.

When the horses finally slowed to a gentle trot, Collun took out Crann's travel-worn leather map and showed Brie the course he had charted to Cuillean's dun.

They had not been traveling long when they heard the sound of horses coming from behind. They turned and spotted two riders who were apparently racing each other to see who could catch up with Collun and Brie first.

Silien won the race, but Talisen was only a length behind him.

"Thought you'd seen the last of us for a while, eh?" Talisen said breathlessly.

"But what about your debut?" asked Collun, smiling his welcome.

"Oh, I realized the audience that truly mattered gave their ovation last night. Besides, I've gotten a better offer."

"What's that?"

"The Eisteddfod," Talisen responded. "I know, you don't think I'll last a week at that school with its list of rules and regulations as long as Farmer Whicklow's nose. But the king and queen selected me."

"Congratulations, Talisen," Collun said.

"So, I cannot stay with you long at Cuillean's dun. I have to be at the Eisteddfod by the beginning of Fearn."

"And Silien, do you also journey with us?"

Silien shook his head. "I must return to Tir a Ceol. But I wanted to bid you farewell on the road, where we first met."

And so the four traveled on, falling easily into their old patterns. Brie found the trail and used her bow, which had been repaired in Temair, to bring down fowl or game for roasting. Collun made each meal a feast with his herbs. Silien, with his keen ears, always found freshwater, and Talisen amused them with his music and his gift for making laughter.

As he slept on the ground during the second night, Collun dreamed a woman with pale eyes and pale hair came to him carrying a red ribbon entwined in her fingers. She slowly reached up and tied it around her own neck, her pale eyes holding him against his will. And then he blinked, and her eyes were dark and they were Brie's . . . no, they were Nessa's, and the red was not a ribbon but blood, and there was a scald-crow at her neck, pecking and pecking. And then the crow was gone and the ribbon turned black. It wound itself tighter and tighter around her neck and it dripped with a clear thick fluid. . . .

He woke with a soundless scream. He was bathed in sweat. The scars from his burns were stretched and aching. He remembered seeing a small stream that ran through a nearby thicket of young trees, and he shakily got to his feet. The moon was bright as Collun crossed to the trees, weaving his way through the slender trunks and listening to the soothing rustle of the cool night wind stirring the leaves. He found the brook and, kneeling beside it, removed his shirt. He splashed cold water on his arm and chest.

Collun sat quietly for a moment, shivering. He wasn't sure what made him think of it, but reaching into his pocket, he drew out the seashell Crann had given Mealladh. Collun thought about the wizard with his white beard and long fingers and green cloak. Tears blurred his vision for a moment. He missed Crann sorely.

He heard the muffled sound of footsteps in the bracken and looked up to see Brie coming toward him. He tucked the seashell back in his pocket as she crouched down beside him. "I had a nightmare," he said.

Brie clenched her hands. "I'm often troubled by bad dreams."

They were silent for a moment.

"I have been thinking of Crann," Collun said.

Brie nodded. "I think of him, too." They were silent for a few moments.

"I wonder what it will be like to live in Cuillean's dun," Collun said, beginning to shiver again. He quickly dried himself with his jersey and slipped it over his head. "It is still difficult to think of him as my father," Collun went on, his face thoughtful. "He is one of Eirren's greatest heroes."

"You are a far greater hero than your father ever was," Brie burst out, her tone fierce.

Collun looked at her in surprise, then laughed. "That is indeed generous of you, Brie, but—"

"It is the truth." There was an intensity to her manner that puzzled Collun.

"Why do you speak so?" he asked.

Brie bowed her head. Then she lifted her eyes to his. "Perhaps it is time I told you the truth," she said.

Collun watched her, uncomprehending.

"You remember when I told you about my father's death?" Collun nodded. "I did not tell you everything. I purposely withheld something—something I thought might hurt you. The news of your true father was still so fresh." She fell silent again.

"What is it, Brie? Tell me."

"He was there."

Brie's voice was so soft, he could barely hear the words.

"What?"

"Your father was there. I saw him. While my father was being tortured and murdered, Cuillean was there, sitting on his horse, watching, not moving. He just sat and watched, and then he rode away with the Scathians." Brie's face had turned pale as snow.

Collun stared at her. "Cuillean . . . Are you sure?"

Brie nodded. "That is the true reason I hated you when I first realized you were the son of Cuillean. It is also the reason I continued to travel with you. I thought you might somehow lead me to Cuillean. And to my father's murderers."

Collun did not answer. He gazed at a small silver fish darting through the clear water of the brook. He knew he ought to feel horrified by what Brie had told him, but all he felt was a deep weariness. Brie spoke of a man he had never met. There were many stories of Cuillean, but for him they were only stories. The man who had defeated Medb's armies, had wed Emer, had fathered Collun and Nessa, and had betrayed his blood brother, this man was a stranger to him.

"It is hard to believe. But perhaps there was a reason," Collun said.

"Perhaps, though I have spent much of the past year trying to discover it."

Collun looked down again at the silver fish. It was trying to find a way through an obstruction of leaves and wood. He reached his hand into the cold water and pushed aside a submerged log. The fish sped through the opening.

"Cuillean was once brave and honorable," Collun said slowly. "During the Eamh War he helped to save Eirren from the Queen of Ghosts."

"That is so," Brie responded.

"Emer loved him," Collun went on, "and he is my father."

Brie was silent. "I know. And I understand your choice to live in his dun. But for myself, I will never forgive him. Never."

Collun nodded his understanding. The breeze stiffened, and he shivered in his damp jersey. "You're cold," Brie said. She stood, offering him a hand up, and they made their way back to the campsite.

Silien left them the next day. They exchanged sad farewells with pledges to meet again. The Ellyl told them they were welcome in Tir a Ceol at any time, promising them a warmer greeting than the last time. He also vowed to be in Temair when Talisen completed his schooling and was named a bard.

The remaining three arrived at Cuillean's dun before twilight on the same day. The king's men were there to greet them.

Collun gazed at the small fortress with its battlements facing the sea. As he and Fiain walked through the gates, he felt a heaviness in his heart. This had been his father's home. But who was his father? Hero, traitor, grieving widower—and father? He pictured Cuillean standing on the battlements, staring out at the water, mourning the wife he loved and believed to be dead. Now, perhaps, they were both dead.

The soldiers told Collun they had searched the dun from top to bottom and, aside from several thriving colonies of mice, it was completely deserted.

Collun made his way through the dusty, chilled rooms. His melancholy deepened. He began to believe Cuillean truly was dead. There was an air of complete emptiness about the dun—no feeling of anticipation that he who had lived here would ever return.

But when Collun came out onto the land that stretched between the dun and the sea, his spirit lightened. He sank to his knees and crumbled the soil between his fingers.

Talisen was inside the dun, dangling his legs out an open window. Collun could hear the notes of a harp song beginning to take form. He smiled and brought a fistful of the earth up to his nose. He breathed in deeply. Brie silently came up beside him.

"Is the soil good?"

"It is good."

"The herbs will go there?" she asked, pointing.

"Yes," Collun nodded, "and roses for Nessa there. She loves roses."

"And the flower garden?"

"On that slope there, I think. First the heliotrope and next to it—"

"Valerian." Brie broke in with a smile.

"Because they grow well side by side," Collun replied,

smiling back at her. "Then a small patch of paggle—
we shall have paggle pudding every night—and harebell. And then blue clownrie and peppergrass..." Collun
reached into his wallet of herbs and drew out a handful
of seeds.

Brie knelt down beside him, her eyes alight. "But
what of the drainage, and where will the compost pile
go, and what do you think of myrtle there...?"

The last rays of the early spring sun warmed their
faces as they bent over the ground, shoulders touching.
A sea wind blew gently over the bluff, and it carried the
sound of their voices up into the ramparts of the empty
dun.

Available now—

the thrilling second volume of
the Songs of Eirren

Fire Arrow

Turn the page for the first chapter of
Breo-Saight's story....

ONE

The Wyll

"What think you of revenge?" Collun asked the soldier Kled, though his eyes were on Brie. She smiled to herself.

"Revenge? Why there's nothing I like better than a good tale of revenge, dripping with blood and avenged honor and all." Kled handed Collun his cup of chicory for refilling. "Have you one to tell?" he asked.

Collun shook his head, impatient. "No, I am speaking of true revenge, outside of books and stories."

Kled looked puzzled. "Well, I have had no experience with it myself, but certainly if one has been sorely wronged, then revenge is a just and honorable—"

Brie let out a laugh. "Wrong answer, Kled."

"Why wrong?"

"Collun wanted you to say that revenge is a contemptible thing, fit only for cowards and scalawags."

"Why?"

"Because of me."

"You?" Kled's face was a study in bewilderment.

Brie's smile died. "Because I am sworn to revenge myself on the men who killed my father."

"In truth? How many men?" Kled asked, his eyes kindling with interest.

"There were twenty or more, all Scathians, but I would be content with the lives of three."

Collun let out a sound of disgust and threw the dregs of the chicory on the fire, making it hiss.

Brie ignored him. "Two who delivered the death-blows. And a third, whose orders they followed. When the killing was done it was he who came down off his horse to ensure they had done it well." Brie's voice was steady.

"By Amergin," Collun interrupted, "can neither of you see the folly? Ending the lives of these men will change nothing. The only one changed will be you, Brie. Remember the tale of Casiope, the archer? Revenge is as an arrow; it will surely return one day and pierce the one who shoots it."

Brie glared at Collun. She started to say something but bit it back. There was an awkward silence.

Kled cleared his throat. "Perhaps I should brew another pan of chicory, or have we all had enough?" But neither Collun nor Brie responded.

Abruptly Brie's mouth curved into a smile. "An arrow. That was clever."

Kled looked at Brie, then at Collun, uncomprehending.

"I thought you'd like it," Collun replied with an answering smile.

"Very clever."

"Does that mean you agree with him now, Brie?" asked Kled.

"No, not exactly."

Kled gave a shrug and drank the last of his chicory.

Brie gazed into her own cup, preoccupied. A moment ago, as Collun spoke of Casiope, the archer, Brie had caught something in his eyes; it was beneath the anger, a look of such deep-reaching kindness it had made her heart skid in her chest. No one before had shown her such a look, no one—not her father nor Masha, the nurse who cared for Brie after her mother died. She could not meet Collun's gaze again, and soon after made an excuse and left them.

The next morning Brie rose early, leaving Collun asleep by the campfire. Ever since they had come to the dun of Collun's father they had chosen to make camp outside. The dun had lain empty for almost two years, ever since Collun's father, the hero Cuillean, had disappeared, and the rooms were musty and ill-kept. On the few occasions it had rained heavily, they had sought shelter in the stables.

Brie found the Ellyl horse Ciaran grazing in the forecourt of the dun. The horse ambled over, searching her hand for a sweet. Though they had been companions for many months, Brie was still in awe of Ciaran. The horse came from the land of Tir a Ceol, where the folk called Ellylon lived, out of sight of human eyes. Ellyl horses were smaller than Eirrenian horses, as well as leaner, but they were more graceful. Ciaran was the color of foam capping a sea wave, with gray stockings, a patch of gray at her forehead and another on her cheek. She was a beauty and knew it, but had a gentleness of spirit that made her vanity easier to bear. It was astounding to Brie that Ciaran continued to stay with her. She had expected the horse to disappear back to Tir a Ceol long ago.

Brie swung herself onto Ciaran's bare back, and they made their way west, to the sea and a sandy bay they had discovered a fortnight ago. It was the perfect place for a gallop.

Dismounting, Brie let Ciaran frisk at the edge of the water. Brie dug her toes into the sand and squinted at the horizon of sea and air.

There was an old Eirrenian story—part of the coulin that explained the beginnings of Eirren and included tales of all its great heroes and gods—about the god Nuadha, who had wielded a magic arrow, or teka. He had stood at the rim of the new world and, to chart a course through the wilderness, had repeatedly shot his teka from a bow and then run to catch up to it. Along the route he followed did appear the first ash tree, the first goshawk, the first flint, and the first hyacinth plant. The ash tree was to make the shaft of an arrow, the goshawk for its fletching, the flint for the arrowhead, and hyacinth for glue to bind the feathers to the shaft. Of course, unlike Brie, Nuadha was a god and had no trouble traveling over the sea with a magic arrow that would not sink beneath the waves. Certainly it was not a journey one could undertake in real life, but . . .

Impulsively Brie pulled her bow off her back and nocked an imaginary arrow to the string. Ciaran cocked an ear in Brie's direction.

With a grin Brie pulled back and let the imagined arrow fly. With her eyes she traced its invented arc over the waves and pictured it cleaving silently into the water, startling a passing school of fish as it sank slowly to the bottom.

Perhaps if she were an Ellyl, with the Ellyl's fishlike swimming ability, she could chart such a journey. Brie laughed softly to herself and lowered her bow to her knees. It was absurd of course. Such journeys were only for gods and heroes.

As Brie watched the Ellyl horse gallop along the sickle curve of the shoreline and thought back over her time at Cuillean's dun, she felt unaccountably peaceful. It was a new feeling. Indeed, it was the first time within her memory that the hard knot within her—of loneliness and the need to be best in all she did—had loosened. She had never had a brother or sister, but she imagined that this bond between herself and Collun was similar to what a brother and sister might share, and she savored the closeness.

There were moments, however, when she looked at him and a breathless, foreign feeling came over her, unexpected and fierce. Like yesterday when her heart had felt like it was flipping about in her chest. The feeling made her uncomfortable and somehow did not seem quite sisterly. The few times she had felt it, she had fled, going off with Ciaran to gallop in the countryside or on the beach of the Bay of Corran. Collun never asked where she went or why.

Brie gave a long whistle, and Ciaran wheeled around,

sending sprays of seawater up around her gray stockings. Soon Brie was astride the Ellyl horse, and they were pounding along the sand.

The night of Midsummer, Collun and Brie climbed the highest tower of Cuillean's dun to view the bonfires that blanketed the hills.

As they gazed out at the blazing fires, Brie was reminded of a night from her childhood when her father had carried her up to the ramparts of their dun and showed her the Midsummer bonfires for the first time. His strong arms held her as she stood barefoot on the cold stone of the parapet. She had been awed by the sight of all those glowing, leaping flowers of flame, stretching as far as her eye could see. The brightest one blazed at the foot of the hill that bore the White Stag of Herge, illuminating the enormous figure. The Stag had been etched into the hillside long ago by people who cut away turf to expose the white chalk of the cliff.

Brie had told her father she wanted to dance around the bonfire and feel the fire's heat on her face and arms. He had said she was too young. But even when she grew older, Brie didn't dance. She would gaze enviously at the abandoned twirling forms of the dancers, but her body felt hemmed in, awkward. And there was the unspoken word that it was somehow unseemly for the daugher of the hero Conall to join the bonfire dances.

"Brie?" Collun broke into her thoughts. "Where have you been?" he asked with a smile.

"At the bonfire dances, long ago," she said musingly. She shivered slightly. Brie did not often think of Dun

Slieve. Her uncle and aunt lived there now. She had left the day after her father's burial—to seek his murderers—and had never returned.

"Perhaps we should go inside?" Collun asked, trying to read Brie's face in the darkness.

"Not yet. I was thinking of the last time I saw the dun where I grew up." She paused. "And the pledge I made when I left there."

Brie felt Collun's eyes on her. "It has been two years, or more, since then..." She trailed off.

Then she turned to Collun with a ghost of a smile. "I have been wondering of late if I oughtn't leave my father's murderers to their own fates."

Collun let out a breath, smiling broadly. "I'm glad," he said simply.

As they made their way down the inside stairway, a loud crack of thunder echoed in the tower. "If we wish to remain dry, we'd best stay inside tonight," Collun said.

They had to rummage about to find bedding, and it took some time to sort out where to sleep in the long-deserted dun. But finally Brie lay on a pallet, Collun in the room next to hers. It felt strange to be separated by walls. She listened to the rain, glad it had held off until after the bonfires. She dozed, thinking again of her childhood in Dun Slieve.

Brie was in the Ramhar Forest, crouching beside her father's body, her heels skidding in the blood-slick grass. Hatred raged inside her, roaring in her ears. The three men stood before her, like ghosts: one with wide shoulders and thick pale arms; another tall, with yellowish eyes; and the last, the most evil, with his arrogant, coarse face and black eye-patch.

As she stood to face them, they disappeared. Then there was darkness. A throbbing, quiet stillness. And suddenly out of the silence plunged a blazing yellow bird of prey. Its talons were extended and it dived at Brie. She raised her hands to fend it off.

There was a pale face hovering over her and the faint sound of a voice speaking. But the features of the face were blurred, black smudges where the eyes should have been, and she could not recognize it. Panic filled Brie, as if she were falling backward into darkness, nothingness. Her hands flailed; she didn't know if she should be trying to catch hold of something or to push it away.

"Brie?" Collun caught one of her fluttering, cold hands in his. She tried to snatch her hand away, hating the feel of his warm skin. But he held fast, keeping his voice low, soothing.

Her racing heart began to slow. She was able to focus on Collun's face, on the comfort in his voice. But for some reason, she still wanted her hand back.

"Let go," she croaked, pulling away, and suddenly her hand snapped loose of Collun's grasp. She cradled it against her chest. Collun drew away slightly.

"A bad dream?" he asked, his voice neutral.

"Yes. My father," Brie replied indistinctly. And a bird, she thought. She didn't understand about the bird. It had been familiar, yet not like any live bird she had seen. Its yellow feathers were overvivid, unnatural. Perhaps she had dreamed it before.

"Can I bring you something? Water or . . . ?"

Brie forced her lips into a smile and shook her head. "I'm better now. It was probably all the peach mead we drank." Collun's face relaxed. They had discovered an overgrown orchard of peach trees and for the past week had eaten little else but peaches: peach pie, poached peaches on toast, guinea hen flavored with peach juice. It was Kled's idea to make several barrels of peach mead for Midsummer.

"It was rich," Collun agreed. He paused. "This is the first of those nightmares you've had in a long time."

Brie nodded. "The first since coming here." They were silent for a moment. "No more peach mead for me," Brie added with a thin smile.

Soon Collun left the room, and Brie rose, crossing to the heavy tapestry that covered the window. She pulled it aside. It had turned into a wild night. Through lashings of rain she could just glimpse the sea.

The next day as she and Collun labored to rebuild a stone wall separating pasture from crop-producing land, Brie felt edgy, her eyes prickly from lack of sleep. She worked hard, hoping to sweat out her unease. Collun tried several times to start a conversation, but Brie's responses were perfunctory. At midday, Kled came by to share their meal. He offered Brie a cup of peach mead, which she refused with a frown. Kled raised his eyebrows, then turned to Collun.

"You'll never guess what Renin came across this morning," he said, munching on a peach tart.

"What?" asked Collun, trying to coax some damp kindling into a fire for brewing chicory.

"A wyll."

"A what?"

"A wyll. A kind of witch-woman or fortune-teller. Haven't you heard of them? You find them mostly in the north, closer to Dungal. That's where they come from. Dungal."

Dungal was a small kingdom north of Eirren, separated from it by the Blue Stack Mountains, a formidable, almost impassable mountain range that began practically at the Western Sea then swept inland, curving northward until it crossed over into Scath and became the Mountains of Marwol. The mountain range provided a natural boundary between Dungal and Scath as well.

To the people of Eirren, Dungal was a place shrouded in myth. Dungalans were said to have more than a little Ellyl blood running in their veins, and it was not unusual to find at least one person in a village with the ability to perform magic of one kind or another, be it the curing of ills or weather-working. They spoke their own language and worshiped their own gods. Traditionally they were ruled by a queen, but in recent years a prince named Durwydd ruled the small kingdom.

"She's a tiny thing, the wyll; Renin thought her a child when he first came upon her. He found her sheltering in that broken-down dovecote," continued Kled. "She knows all sorts of things you can't figure out how she would. The others are all worked up. Renin has already given her his favorite torque because she told him he was going to marry the girl he fancies back in his birth town. The wyll knew the girl's name and everything. You two ought to come, have your fortunes told."

Brie was skeptical and her head ached with fatigue, but Collun was curious, so they accompanied Kled to the soldiers' quarters in what had once been the dairy barn.

When Brie and Collun entered, the soldiers were listening raptly as the wyll told a story.

She was indeed small and had long coppery gold hair. It was woven into dozens of braids that fell past her waist. Her forehead was broad, unusually broad for such a small face, which—coupled with her large amber eyes—kept her from being beautiful. She wore colorful clothing that seemed to consist of many layers, and bright earrings sparkled at her ears. The wyll took note of the new arrivals but did not pause in her storytelling. She spoke with a lyrical, accented voice, and Kled whispered that her name was Aelwyn.

Despite her sore head, Brie found herself getting caught up in the story. She wished she had been there from the beginning. Then the wyll fell silent, her story finished. She turned toward Brie. A smile curved her small mouth, and she suddenly spoke in a tongue Brie did not know. At Brie's puzzled look, Aelwyn shifted back to Eirrenian. "Are you not from Dungal?"

Brie shook her head.

"I'm sorry. You have a look about you of home."

"They want their fortunes told, Aelwyn," Kled said. Brie started to demur, but Collun stepped forward. Aelwyn motioned for Collun to sit before her, and she took hold of both his hands, shutting her amber eyes. She was silent for several moments, her wide forehead ridged with concentration.

"I see a long journey. A monstrous creature. Burning pain. But then relief and peace." She paused, then opened her eyes. "You have learned something ill of a blood kin, yet where there was honor before, there will be honor again."

Collun stared at the wyll, his mouth open slightly.

"Didn't I tell you she was a marvel, Collun?" said Kled, breaking the silence.

Brie wondered just how much the soldiers had told the wyll of Collun's history, but she said nothing.

"It's your turn, Brie," said Kled.

"I really don't...," Brie began.

"Come," said Aelwyn with a smile. Reluctantly Brie sat before the wyll, who gathered up her hands. Aelwyn started to close her eyes then seemed to change her mind, opening them. She gazed straight at Brie. The wyll's amber eyes were glittery, like faceted gemstones.

Suddenly a shudder went through Aelwyn, and she tightened her grip on Brie's hands. Her eyes seemed almost to spin, and she began speaking in a rasp, unlike the voice that she'd used with Collun. But she spoke in the language of Dungal.

Brie felt cold, as if an icy hand had clamped on to the nape of her neck. She wanted to withdraw her hands but was mesmerized by the wyll's eyes. The wyll continued to speak, the strange words flowing out of her mouth, almost like a melody.

Finally Aelwyn fell silent. Brie heard one of the soldiers nervously clear his throat.

Aelwyn gently released Brie's hands. She blinked several times, then smiled at the assembled group as if nothing untoward had happened.

There was an awkward silence. Kled muttered to Collun, "Haven't seen her do *that* before."

Then the soldier Renin said, "So, did you see anything?"

"I did."

"By Amergin, are you going to tell us or not?"

Aelwyn turned her now-still eyes on Brie. "Do you wish to hear what I saw?"

Brie wanted to say no, but it seemed cowardly. Besides, it was all foolishness anyway. She nodded.

"I saw a brave man hewed down in a forest while a girl"—the wyll looked at Brie—"watched."

She could have learned that from the soldiers, Brie thought.

Aelwyn continued. "There were many, but two struck the most, the deepest. A man with broad pale arms, and another, tall with eyes like saffron, part morg. And last, one who led them, with a dark covering over one eye. Evil." The wyll shivered slightly. She stopped speaking.

Brie drew a deep breath. She had told no one what the killers looked like except Collun, and she knew he would never speak of it. "That was in the past," she said, her voice high and stretched thin. "What of the future?"

The wyll's amber eyes widened. "That which you seek lies in Dungal," she said.

Brie's pulse quickened, and the invisible cold hand at the back of her neck tightened its grip. "My father's murderers?" she asked, locking eyes with Aelwyn.

"If that is what you seek."

The wyll adjusted the torque on her arm. "It has been long since a seeing took such hold of me. Do you yourself have draoicht?" Aelwyn asked, curious.

"You mean magic?" Brie gave a short laugh. "Of course not."

Collun spoke up, his hand on his trine. "I carry a stone...?"

Aelwyn shook her head briskly, uninterested in the cailceadon. "No, it is from her." She turned back to Brie. "What is your name?"

"Breo-Saight. Or Brie."

" 'Fire arrow..,' " the wyll said thoughtfully. "Listen, there is more." She drew Brie closer and spoke softly into her ear. "Shifting water and earth. Sacred standing stones covered with seabirds. A crippled man. And a man of power. Treachery. I saw hatred, the lust to kill. I saw death." Her breath tickled Brie's ear. "And...an arrowhead pointed at your own heart."

Abruptly she resumed her normal voice. "There. That is all." She reached up and smoothed a coppery braid. "Now, does someone have a bauble for Aelwyn?" she asked, flashing a catlike smile.

Brie was too dazed to respond. Kled nudged Collun, who had been watching Brie with a worried frown.

Aelwyn crossed to Collun and said in a teasing voice, "Didn't you say something about a stone?"

"Uh, no...I mean..." He stumbled over his words, reluctantly tearing his gaze from Brie. "That stone is, uh, too precious..." He trailed off.

"Not the cailceadon," laughed the wyll. "I have no interest in so potent a stone. I mean the one in your other pocket."

Puzzled, Collun felt in his pocket and drew out a chunk of rock he had found while plowing several days ago. It had several large saphir gems embedded in it, and he had thought to dig them out and make a bracelet or hair clasp for Brie.

Kled gave him another nudge, and Collun offered the rock to Aelwyn.

She took the chunk of rock with a look of pleasure, holding it up to the light coming through the dairy door.

Brie had been sitting very still, unaware of the conversation around her. Abruptly she rose, a flash of blue from a saphir banding her cheek as she began to move across the barn.

"Will you go to Dungal?" Aelwyn called after Brie.

Brie paused. "Perhaps," she said, her voice sounding muffled.

Startled, Collun gave Brie a sharp look.

"Be warned, Breo-Saight," said Aelwyn, rummaging in her colorful layers of clothing for a soft leather pouch. As she slid the rock into the pouch she continued, "Once you go to Dungal, it is not easy to leave."

"You left."

"Because I like pretty, shiny things, and your people will pay well for the skills I have. But the hiraeth, the heartsickness from being away, it is with me all the time, like a knife in the heart. Farewell, Breo-Saight."

"Farewell, Aelwyn," Brie said, and left the barn.

There was a roaring in her ears and her breath came short as she moved away from the barn. Her father's killers. In Dungal. She would have her revenge.

Let your imagination fly with the best in fantasy

MAGIC CARPET

BOOKS

The Kingdom of Kevin Malone (0-15-201191-9) $6.00
BY SUZY MCKEE CHARNAS
Amy finds a magical world in Central Park where bully Kevin Malone is a hero.
Worse still, he needs Amy to save his kingdom and himself. Will she help this
punk she doesn't even like?

Knight's Wyrd (0-15-201520-5) $6.00
BY DEBRA DOYLE AND JAMES D. MACDONALD
Will Oddosson is told his wyrd—his fate—on the eve of his knighting: He will
meet Death before a year has passed. Soon he is beset by one evil beast after
another. Which will be his wyrd?

DIANE DUANE's thrilling wizardry series

So You Want to Be a Wizard (0-15-201239-7) $6.50
Fleeing a bully, Nita discovers a manual on wizardry in her library. But magic
doesn't solve her problems—in fact, they've only just begun!

Deep Wizardry (0-15-201240-0) $6.00
The novice wizards join a group of dolphins, whales, and one giant shark in an
ancient magical ritual—a ritual that must end with a bloody sacrifice.

High Wizardry (0-15-201241-9) $6.00
Nita and Kit face their most terrifying challenge yet: Nita's bratty little sister,
Dairine—the newest wizard in the neighborhood!

The Weirdstone of Brisingamen (0-15-201766-6) $6.00
BY ALAN GARNER
All of Evil's minions are working to stop Colin and Susan from returning the
Weirdstone to its rightful owner, the wizard Cadellin, but the earth's fate
depends on them.

Magic Carpet Books is a registered trademark of Harcourt Brace & Company.

Two fantasy classics by MOLLIE HUNTER

The Smartest Man in Ireland (0-15-200993-0) $5.00
To prove his boast of being the smartest man in the land, Patrick Kentigern Keenan tries to outwit the fairies. But wit is not much against an opponent who has magic. . . .

The Walking Stones (0-15-200995-7) $5.00
A wise old man gives Donald the knowledge—and the power—to prevent developers from destroying an ancient mystical circle of stones.

A Dark Horn Blowing (0-15-201201-X) $6.00
BY DAHLOV IPCAR
Nora is stolen away one night and taken to Erland. There she must tend sickly Prince Elver and avoid the eye of his father, the wicked Erl King, who would have Nora for a wife.

The Forgotten Beasts of Eld (0-15-200869-1) $6.00
BY PATRICIA A. McKILLIP
Sybel's only family is the group of animals that live on Eld Mountain. She cares nothing for humans until she is given a child to raise, changing her life utterly.

Tomorrow's Wizard (0-15-201276-1) $6.00
BY PATRICIA MacLACHLAN
What's wrong with Tomorrow's apprentice? Can he not hear the High Wizard's warnings? Or is it that the apprentice would rather be a human instead of a wizard?

Are All the Giants Dead? (0-15-201523-X) $7.00
BY MARY NORTON
To stop Dulcibel from marrying a toad, James must get Jack-of-the-Beanstalk and Jack-the-Giant-Killer to leave retirement and to kill the last of the giants.

The first book in EDITH PATTOU's epic *Songs of Eirren*

Hero's Song (0-15-201636-8) $6.00
The trail of his sister's kidnappers leads Collun to a giant white wurme whose slime is acid to the touch, a wurme that Collun must kill if he is to rescue his sister and save his world.

Volume I of MEREDITH ANN PIERCE's classic *Darkangel Trilogy*

The Darkangel (0-15-201768-2) $6.00
Aeriel must kill the wicked Darkangel before he finds his fourteenth bride—even though within him is a spark of goodness that could redeem even *his* evil.

Let your imagination fly

. . . by joining the Magic Carpet Book Club!

Buy any three Magic Carpet books, and get a free fantasy novel!

Getting your free fantasy novel is easy. Just buy three Magic Carpet books and clip the proof of purchase tab from the corner of each book club page. (If the Magic Carpet books you buy do not have a book club page, send in your register receipts listing each title purchased as proof of purchase.) Then fill out the order form below and send it, along with proof of all three purchases, to:

Magic Carpet Book Club
Harcourt Brace & Company
525 B Street, Suite 1900
San Diego, CA 92101

And we'll send you a free book!

- -

(please print)

Name: _____ Age: _____

Street Address: _____

City: _____ State: _____ Zip: _____

Favorite Book: _____

Send to: MAGIC CARPET BOOK CLUB
           Harcourt Brace & Company
           525 B Street, Suite 1900
           San Diego, CA 92101

Reproductions or copies of proof of purchase tabs (or receipts) will not be accepted and will receive no response. Harcourt Brace will choose which titles will be sent as premiums, depending on availability. Premiums will be shipped within 4–8 weeks of receipt of order form. Harcourt Brace is not responsible for lost or incomplete orders and may discontinue the book club at any time. Offer expires two years after date on proof of purchase.

Magic Carpet Books is a registered trademark of Harcourt Brace & Company.

5/98

Hero's Song
0-15-201636-8

PROOF OF PURCHASE